Acclaim for Jane Turner Rylands and

ACROSS THE BRIDGE OF SIGHS

"Rylands writes with playful elegance and a crisp layer of understated wit."   —*Los Angeles Times*

"A dazzling storyteller at the top of her game. . . . [She] conjures up an incredible array of eccentric characters, bizarre situations, and plot twists."   —*Tucson Citizen*

"Read these vignettes by a fire, and you will get all the melancholic chill of Italy's most romantic city with none of the sticker shock."   —*Milwaukee Journal Sentinel*

"Rylands's stories are like a teaspoon of grated Parmesan washed down with a swallow of hearty red wine. They're a discreet indulgence."   —*Salon*

"Witty . . . shimmeringly wistful. . . . Each of the tales Rylands spins proves entertaining, and the interwoven stories borrow from each other's casts with ease."   —*Publishers Weekly*

"Beautiful. . . . Rylands writes from the perspective of someone experiencing the world in translation."   —*San Francisco Weekly*

Jane Turner Rylands

ACROSS
THE BRIDGE
OF SIGHS

Jane Turner Rylands is the author of the collection *Venetian Stories* and has lived in Venice for more than three decades. She is married to Philip Rylands, the director of the Peggy Guggenheim Collection in Venice.

ALSO BY JANE TURNER RYLANDS

Venetian Stories

ACROSS THE BRIDGE OF SIGHS

ACROSS THE BRIDGE OF SIGHS

More Venetian Stories

JANE TURNER RYLANDS

Anchor Books
A Division of Random House, Inc.
New York

FIRST ANCHOR BOOKS EDITION, DECEMBER 2006

Copyright © 2005 by Jane Turner Rylands

Grateful acknowledgment is made to **Warner Bros. Publications U.S. Inc.** for permission to reprint an excerpt from the song lyric "Let's Misbehave" by Cole Porter. Copyright © 1927 (Renewed) WB Music Corp. (ASCAP). All rights reserved. Reprinted by permission of Warner Bros. Publications U.S. Inc., Miami, FL 33014.

The Library of Congress has cataloged the Pantheon edition as follows:
Rylands, Jane Turner, [date]
Across the bridge of sighs : more Venetian stories / Jane Turner Rylands.
p. cm.
Contents: Restoration — Youth — Probability — Mobility — Fortune — Integration — Art — Design — Enterprise — Service — Vocation — Finish.
1. Venice (Italy)—Fiction. I. Title.
PS3618.Y38A65 2005
813'.6—dc22
2005047674

Anchor ISBN-10: 1-4000-7951-9
Anchor ISBN-13: 978-1-4000-7951-3

Book design by Virginia Tan

www.anchorbooks.com

Printed in the United States of America
10 9 8 7 6 5 4 3 2 1

For Shelley Wanger

and

for Michael Kahn

CONTENTS

RESTORATION   3

YOUTH   35

PROBABILITY   59

MOBILITY   95

FORTUNE   125

INTEGRATION   165

ART   197

DESIGN   227

ENTERPRISE   249

SERVICE   267

VOCATION   289

FINISH   323

ACROSS
THE BRIDGE
OF SIGHS

RESTORATION

Winter settles down in Venice like it means to make friends and stay forever, feeding the sea with rain, gusting attention on listless canals, and wrapping all wetness in a companionable mist. Even in April when everyone is wishing it would take its leave Winter lingers on like a gloomy guest with nowhere to go until all of a sudden brash, insouciant Spring blows in and sends it packing, leaving a trail of puddles in its wake. The campos still shine under scattered pools, when the first harbingers of renewal ring out over rooftops and echo down the canals—*tock-tock! bam-bam! pink-pink!* and the piercing *fffffwwwwinnng* of a saw cutting through marble. These are the sounds of Spring in Venice, when workmen swarm over palace after palace weaving scaffolds like webs, up and up, until it seems that half of Venice is lost behind dust sheets and the only things left to look at are signboards describing building permits.

*

Architetto Fallon stood in the campo behind Palazzo Patristi watching one of his men in a hard hat swing onto the scaffolding. He could hear him climbing behind the dust sheets. A signboard slipped out through a gap and wiggled into position. The man looked out from beside it.

"How's this, Architetto?" The workman held the sign in place.

"I think it's a little too far up, Beppe; I can hardly read it. Let's try it down one level where it's easier to see."

The sign retreated into the dust sheeting and appeared a minute later ten feet below. Beppe peeked out beside it. "Okay?"

"That's perfect, Beppe. As soon as you get it secured, come down. I want to take everyone over to the bar to celebrate their fast work on the scaffolding."

As he waited in the campo, Vittorio Fallon looked at the signboard. He had decided against putting up the standard sheet of ready-printed enameled tin with the blanks filled in by hand with a felt-tipped pen. Instead, he had gone to some expense to make it match in elegance the amplitude of the project as well as the dignity and symbolic significance that Venetians attributed to the building. This house and its family were so woven into the history and pride of Venice that the restoration had even been reported in the newspapers and mooted as the largest private restoration in the city for many years. The works, the signboard announced, had been commissioned by the owner, Dottore Barone Edmondo Patristi, whom all Venetians knew as the scion of one of the founding families of Venice and whose house was unique in being still owned and occupied by direct descendents of the family who built it. The sign also said that the works were being directed by Architetto Vittorio Fallon, the most sought after of the up-and-coming Venetian architects. For the man or woman in the street, this sign was a nice document of modern Venice: the old and the new working in harmony for the betterment of the city. For the man or woman about town, however, it touched on something far more interesting: the Baronessa Patristi, the heiress who with her husband the Barone had launched the project four years earlier, and the new Signora Fallon, who with her husband the architect was overseeing the project, were one and the same person.

Venetian society had gradually come round to viewing this development in the Patristi story with a single mind and two points of view. Everyone agreed that Scandal and Rumor should let this woman pass unscathed, while at the same time maintaining that Edmondo, with all his faults, was a charming instance of his class. She was in the right, but he was in a category of his own. Of course even Venetians had to admit that Edmondo's inveterate philandering gave ample cause for a wife to decamp, and they were impatient with Sofi because she had let him go on with his adventures for so long—long after everyone had concluded that she should have put her foot down, if not the first time, at least the second or third. In the end, she filed for divorce but agreed to continue to pay for the restoration of the family palace, with the proviso that it would be entailed to their fifteen-year-old son, Matteo, just as the Patristi Villa in the country, which she had a few years before bought back into the family, would be entailed to their seven-year-old daughter, Esmeralda. The long-term agreement was that she would in due course go back to the restored Palazzo Patristi and live there with the Patristi children until Matteo married. Edmondo would maintain as his primary residence the Patristi Villa near the Euganean Hills. Edmondo was not very happy about the outcome. On the other hand he could see that it achieved more or less what he had hoped to gain from his fortunate marriage.

As a young woman, Sofi had been looking forward to a stint as an Italian career girl, but she hadn't had time to decide what she wanted to do before she found herself making the Venetian marriage of the century. Now that the marriage was over, she found herself rather happily taking up a role in an interesting project. It was what she needed. She threw herself heart and soul into the restoration of Palazzo Patristi and discovered that some of her ideas were not so bad. She was keeping pace with the architect, marching through the project point by point by point, when they both noticed that they were perfectly in step. Before they realized where they were going they had turned the corner and started finishing each other's sentences and ringing each other to share idle thoughts and funny instances. Meanwhile, Sofi and Edmondo's son, Matteo, who by this time was in his last years of *liceo,* became so interested in the restoration that he did a project on the house and decided to become an architect himself. His sister Esmeralda, who was eight, followed his example and designed her own room in art class, then submitted the sketch as a point of reference to hang in the office of the architectural firm. The two children, their mother, and the architect were all so happy in each other's company that it wasn't long before Sofi and Vittorio saw no point in trying to hide the fact that they were madly in love, so they shared their secret with the world and married. The whole of Venetian society claimed to have seen it coming a mile away and indulged in a pleasant flurry of self-congratulation—which in Venice was as close to an outright cheer of approval as such an unusual match could ever hope to merit.

Before the divorce, Edmondo and Sofi had summoned Vittorio many times to lay out the plans for the restoration. During their first tour of the house Edmondo told Vittorio the story of the infamous broken arch over the landward entrance.

The front door of Palazzo Patristi from the campo was tall and handsome like the family it served, and its ceremonial presence stemmed not from its bulk but from its elegance. Of white Istrian marble, the doorposts were decorated with slender rope pilasters supporting a lintel with a central medallion bearing the Patristi arms. The lintel was overarched with a tall ogee, like a crown. The soffit had always been bricked in and had once probably been decorated with polychrome marble, long since disappeared. Instead, in the soffit's upper right quadrant, there was a small square window that looked as though it had been thrust with such force against the curve of the arch, just below the point, that the marble had given way like meringue and let the corner cut the curve in two. Most people found the window disconcerting. It was almost like an eyeball rolled toward the heavens in dread.

Edmondo wanted to share with the architect the privilege of knowing the story as he had heard it himself from his grandmother, Moceniga Dan. The whole business stemmed from her sympatico habit of passing the mornings, in the manner of those days, making lace with her old mother-in-law in the long mezzanine room overlooking the campo, a strange corridor-like space that ran the whole width of the palace. The room had two small square Gothic windows at each end, but only one had good light. The other was blocked by a stately magnolia that was hundreds of years old and the subject of a local pride that had grown up over the generations right along with it. Moceniga was a woman of decision. If she couldn't cut down the tree, she could at least do something to improve the situation. She called the handyman to the lace room and told him to get his tools; she wanted a window directly in the center to match the two at either end. She pulled her worktable away from her mother-in-law's at the far window and positioned it in the center. "There," she said, pointing at the wall above it. "Put the window there."

In those days the owner of a house could do virtually what he liked with it, short of tearing it down. So old Antonio the handyman measured the two existing windows and traced the outline on the wall above Moceniga Dan's worktable. By that afternoon, he had the stone pieces cut to measure for the sill and frame and had already made a small hole opening out into the campo. When Moceniga Dan went down to see how the work was coming, she found the room transformed and congratulated herself. The light was going to be wonderful. As she watched, Old Antonio took out brick after brick. The wall was four bricks deep. She went away and came back several hours later to find the hole almost finished and a pile of white stones on the floor beside the bricks.

"What on earth is that?" she asked.

"It's marble," said old Antonio. "I had a terrible time breaking through it. But I've done it now. I'll go and fetch the window from the carpenter." When he came back that evening with the window, Moceniga Dan was in a state.

"Antonio! Didn't you see as you came in? The window

cuts through the arch above the great portal just underneath the point!"

When she had positioned her worktable in the center of
the room, she failed to take into account that the front
door of the palace was not quite centered in the façade, or
that the rooms on one side of the *androne,* the entrance
hall, were a little larger than those on the other.

She said the arch had to be put right at once, but the
handyman said it was already late so he would install the
window for the night and then come back as soon as he
could to put it right and move the window to the center of
the arch.

Edmondo's grandmother gathered up the pieces and
stowed them safely away in the great press where the
Patristi women stored the precious fruits of their labors,
the wedding veils and trains, the christening robes and
banqueting cloths. Fate decreed that Antonio had an ur-
gent roofing job, so he asked if he could come a bit later.
This reminded Edmondo's grandfather that there was
something to be done on their roof, too. While Antonio
was working on the roof he noticed that the *altana,* the
roof deck, was a bit shaky so that took precedence, and in
the meantime Edmondo's grandmother moved her table
under the new window and worked there until he could
get back to correct it. Winter came and they decided to
wait until summer. Then his grandmother was working on
a lace tablecloth that she wanted to finish before moving

away from the window. Winter came again. Then Antonio got too old.

Over the years, various stone pieces were pressed into service as doorstops, paperweights, and spools for winding thread—one piece even found its way into a goldfish tank as an underwater ruin. The smallest chips were harbored in a pin box in his grandmother's worktable. Not a single piece had been lost because the work to correct this ridiculous mistake was always imminent. Rocco Zennaro, Vittorio's old stonemason, had with Edmondo's help tracked the pieces down to the smallest chip within a matter of days. Edmondo laughed that after so many years it had fallen to him and Sofi to put it right. Vittorio had to warn him that in today's Italy an architectural mistake, no matter how horrendous, once it was established had as much moral right to stay put as an illegal immigrant who's landed a job. The prospects were not improved by the fact that there was hardly a soul in Venice who didn't think that the ravaged arch should be repaired: civil servants, on principle, do not support their political bosses by attending to public opinion, unless somehow encouraged.

Sofi hated the broken arch. The first time she had walked under it on Edmondo's arm, she had been unnerved by a flash that made her start and look up straight at the ruined stone. Perhaps the maid had opened or closed the window so it winked in the rays of the setting sun. Whatever the cause, the flaming light triggered her memory.

When she was a child, the captain of her father's yacht had sent up a flare because a man had fallen overboard and they couldn't find him.

All through the dinner with Edmondo's parents, Sofi's heart was heavy. It was their first time together *in famiglia,* before they were officially engaged. She apologized to Edmondo afterwards for being so dull. She told him that somehow the broken arch had made her sad, but she couldn't explain why. He said he didn't think a broken arch was bad. A broken column, for example, could stand for fortitude. Anyhow, the arch didn't harm the building's stability. On the other hand, tearing out the walls in the room behind the arch to make an indoor bocce court in the eighteenth century probably did. And of course it was the absence of those walls that led his grandmother into the mistake about the placement of the window. He thought it might be a good idea one day to put the walls back again. Sofi wasn't interested. It was the arch that had flagged her like a warning. Edmondo made a joke: Instead of the curse on the *Casata di Atreo,* the House of Atreus, his family had a curse on the *atrio della casa*—the atrium of the house. Sofi stopped talking about the arch, but after they were married she came to believe that it had to do with the ever-mounting Patristi pride leading up to some crushing blow that she would have to be very lucky to escape.

She never mentioned the matter again until she met Architetto Fallon almost fourteen years later at the Decardis' cocktail party. The architect had done some work for the Decardis, and Carlo Decardi was recommending him to everyone. When Carlo excused himself to welcome some arriving guests, he left the two of them standing together in front of the fireplace. The first thing she heard herself say was, "I have to repair the arch of the great portal" and he said, "It's disturbing, isn't it. An arch is one of those things that should never be broken, like a mirror." From the first words he ever addressed to her, he struck the right note. Looking back, she thought that maybe she'd begun to fall in love with him then and there. She could see now that he had helped her to survive the divorce when she didn't even realize she needed help. It was probably, subconsciously, because of him that she had decided to take on the restoration of Palazzo Patristi in spite of the divorce. It kept him near her.

Donata Manina Fallon, Vittorio's widowed mother, had known long before anyone else that Sofi Fierazzo Patristi was the woman destined for her son, but when the courtship was seriously under way and everyone else began to see how things were going with them, Donata Fallon began to lose interest in the match. True, Sofi had been a little patronizing when she met her future mother-in-law. The problem was that for many years Donata been the mainstay of the family's upscale soft furnishings business, Morello & Figli, and had come to the Fierazzo house to take orders for curtains from Sofi's mother. Sofi had no way of knowing in what high regard her future mother-in-law held her nor any idea of how long Donata Fallon had been observing her from a distance. Vittorio had tried to convince her that his mother was more important to their relationship than he could explain, but Sofi regarded his sentiments as filial loyalty: charming but irrational.

Vittorio was both surprised and a little disappointed that his mother accepted Sofi's coolness with such uncharacteristic resignation. He had resolved to bring Sofi gradually around to a better understanding and was completely unprepared for his mother's next step. True, he had been trying for years to convince her to give up her noisy apartment above a vaporetto stop, but he was hurt and suspicious when she rang him and told him that she had made arrangements to move and dumbfounded when she told him where she was going to live. He went immediately to see her.

"Look here," she said, when he came in the door. "This apartment will be a perfect studio for you, now that Sofi's little sister has joined your firm. You and Natasha can each have your own office. In fact, it will work much better as a studio than it did as an apartment. You always said it didn't make sense to have the bathrooms down by the front door. Maybe it was meant to be a studio with the bathrooms opposite the waiting room."

"But Mamma, I never meant for you to go into a retirement home. We could sell this and you could buy something more convenient."

"No. I've decided. I want to retire, really retire. I don't want to have any more responsibilities; I don't want to be your responsibility. I've already booked the place. I'm going to the *Ca' di Dio*."

Vittorio's jaw dropped. "The *Ca' di Dio*?"

"Don't be dramatic, Vittorio. I'm not talking about the one in the sky. It's the one down on the Riva, looking out towards San Giorgio."

"Nevertheless," said Vittorio. "It's a dead end. You can't be without a house. You're not sick."

In some ways, Donata Manina had once again done Vittorio a good turn. The apartment made a perfect studio, and its position overlooking the vaporetto stop was no longer a noisy nuisance but a real advantage. It troubled him that he found himself in effect dealing with her estate while she was still alive, but that was how she had planned it. She told him to get rid of anything he and Sofi didn't want, but he couldn't bring himself to do it. In the end he got rid of nothing except a couple of circulars he found in a wastepaper basket. He hired a warehouse on the mainland and put everything there. He couldn't face doing otherwise; he felt like he was burying his mother alive. For her part, she refused ever to leave her lodgings and in so doing relieved him of the need to include her in gatherings where she might have been snubbed and thereby given him cause for distress. He was aware of the social difficulties, but he would never have considered giving in to them.

He made a point of visiting her every Friday morning and took pleasure in refusing Friday morning business appointments as evidence of his devotion. But it didn't put his conscience at rest. In fact, he was building up to a confrontation with her to try to convince her to reconsider when he was detoured by a family tragedy of the kind he couldn't bring himself even to read about on Monday mornings in the *Gazzettino*. It altered his life. Even his practice changed direction after the decision that Palazzo Patristi had to be sold.

In suddenness and brutality that decision matched the accident that fostered it, and Edmondo had practically no say in the matter. The works were to be cut back and hurried through so the palace could be sold out of the main line of the Patristi family forever. That was the objective. It didn't mean that some other Patristi might not one day buy it back, but for Edmondo, unless he married another fortune and produced another male heir, it would never in his lifetime pertain again to the heirs of Patristi doges and admirals. For Edmondo, the shock of divesting himself of his property was worse than the tragedy itself. The Venetian maxim rankled in his mind. *Chi vende sende*—he who sells goes down in the world.

In effect, Edmondo's family seat had gone up for sale the night Sofi Fierazzo Fallon lay dreaming that she was on a dark road where a bell was tolling, only to start awake in time to hear both the telephone beside Vittorio and her cell phone ringing simultaneously. Vittorio had picked up the phone and was saying, "Yes, she's here, but she's answering her cell phone. I'm his stepfather."

Sofi was already in tears as she dug the cell phone out of her handbag. She knew this was the moment she had prayed would never come. Matteo was her first child, but the joy she felt when she held him for the first time was tainted by a sadness that marked him like a stain and never went away. She felt it was the selfsame dread that had assailed her when the flash of the window made her look at the broken arch. One night, lying in the great canopied bed where Matteo had been conceived, Sofi had tried to share her fears with his father. But all Edmondo could say was, "My sweet Thetis of the shining breasts."

By the time Sofi found her phone it had stopped ringing. It was Giulia Panfili. Matteo had gone to a birthday party in the Veneto, invited by Giulia's son, Bobino, who was also the younger brother of Marco Panfili, the husband of Sofi's sister Natasha. Bobino was older than Matteo, nearly thirty to Matteo's seventeen, and he was driving. There was another missed call, this one from Matteo. She put the telephone to her ear and waited as her heart sank down, and down again, like an old elevator that couldn't bear its load. She listened: "Ciao, Mamma. Sorry we're so late. I've been trying to leave for hours, but that Segusio girl made Bobino let her come back with us so we had to wait. I told Bobino I'm not sitting with her in the back. I guess you're in bed already. I wish I hadn't come out here. Goodbye."

Vittorio came over to her side of the bed where she was standing and put his arms around her. "We have to get dressed," he said sadly. "We have to go to Treviso."

"I know. I've had a message from Matteo." She couldn't catch her breath. "They were getting ready to leave. He said goodbye." She put her hands over her face. "Not good night, Vittorio. He said goodbye." She sobbed for five minutes before she could even speak. "I have to ring Giulia back."

Giulia answered on the first ring. Her voice was hoarse. "Sofi? I guess you've talked to the police. Bobo and I are on the way to Piazzale Roma. Marco is coming to pick us up in his car. We talked to Edmondo; he'll get there first since he's in the country. Are you leaving now? Sofi, I'm so afraid for them."

Sofi listened and murmured "Yes, yes," from time to time, so Giulia knew she was still there. She could hear their footsteps sounding in the empty calles as they hurried through the dark passages. Behind shuttered windows people were asleep, untouched by the misery that was drawing them all to the mainland.

"The police wouldn't tell us anything except that we should go to the hospital," said Giulia.

"They said the same to us," said Sofi, but she knew with a certainty to confute any pretense of urgency that their children were already dead.

Sofi and Vittorio drove through the dark countryside in silence. They were the last kin to arrive at the hospital.

They found Edmondo waiting outside the emergency room beside a policeman and a doctor, who asked them to follow him to another part of the hospital. They found Giulia and Bobo Panfili in a small waiting room talking to another policeman. The policemen and the doctor asked Edmondo and Bobo to leave their wives and come away to settle a preliminary matter. The doctor apologized, as he led them into the morgue, for obliging them to look at the remains of their sons. The car had skidded on a curve and rolled over twice in a field; it was going fast. The boys must have been knocked unconscious before the car caught fire. Their seat belts were still fastened.

Sofi and Giulia sat together in the waiting room with their heads bowed. They covered their eyes with one hand

and held their rosaries in the other, but neither was praying. They were trying to make contact in the ether around them with the lingering spirits of their dead sons. They wanted to apologize to them, to tell them they were sorry for their disappointed lives, that they loved them—and that they were dying too.

When Edmondo came back to the waiting room and saw Sofi and Giulia so distracted with grief, he began to feel uneasy. He sensed even then that he had lost more than a son. Far from sharing a bond of grief with Sofi, he felt afraid and alienated. He feared, before it had even occurred to her, that he was on the way to losing his palace. Instinctively he walked across the room to stand with his architect, Vittorio, who was looking through the Venetian blinds at the hospital car park. But when Edmondo came up beside Vittorio, he was surprised to see that his lips and eyes were ringed with red as if he had been crying. Edmondo jumped to the conclusion that Vittorio, being an architect, must have realized, even before he had, that the works in Palazzo Patristi might be cut short so it could be sold. Vittorio was the first to speak.

"I can't say how sorry I am, Edmondo. Matteo was a wonderful boy. I loved him like he was my own." Vittorio's voice had started to tremble so uncontrollably that he had to whisper the rest. "Sofi and I were so looking forward to giving him a younger brother. You must be devastated."

Edmondo was so unaccustomed to pity that tears sprang to his eyes, and before he could snatch his handkerchief from his pocket they had coursed down his cheeks. When Vittorio, so soon to be a father himself, saw the tears of the man to whom he had attributed so little capacity for human emotion, he too had to retrieve his handkerchief. They stood united in grief: Vittorio wondering if there were something he could do to ease the suffering of this man who had thrown away his precious wife and now had lost his only son, and Edmondo trying to remember an historical precedent, in his own family as it were, when Priam wept with the man who had done him the greatest injury. Edmondo lowered his head as he struggled to compose his memory: *Piagea questi il perduto Ettore ai piè dell'uccisore, e quegli / Or il padre, or l'amico*—At the feet of Achilles, Priam wept for Hector while Achilles wept for his own father and for Patroclus. Edmondo couldn't help but be heartened by the recollection; he hadn't looked at that passage since he was in *liceo,* the same age as poor Matteo.

The police approached Edmondo and Vittorio to mention that in another part of the hospital there was a young woman who had also been in the car. Edmondo recognized the name as that of the younger sister of his former mistress, Marda, but didn't let on. The girl had been thrown clear before the car caught fire and was being treated for multiple fractures. Her father and mother did not come down to offer their condolences to the parents of the boys who had not survived. Her mother's brother was an infamously aggressive lawyer. Vittorio wondered if their behavior might be hostile, and asked Bobo and Edmondo whether they felt inclined to go up and offer the parents their best wishes for their daughter's recovery. Bobo and Edmondo didn't see the case for it. People from another part of society going their own way seemed natural enough to them. It was a difficult argument for Vittorio to counter. He let the matter drop.

Matteo's funeral in the chapel at Villa Patristi, followed by his burial in the family vault, changed Sofi's life. As she explained to Vittorio when they were driving back to Venice, she realized as she was sitting in the chapel, weighed down with all that regret and bitterness, that she had no choice but to force the sale of Palazzo Patristi. She knew that Edmondo would marry again and probably father another son. That didn't bother her. After all, she was having another son herself. What bothered her was that she had no idea how many women had been shadowing her from the margins of her marriage to Edmondo, and the thought that one of them and her offspring could benefit from

Matteo's death by inheriting the house she had restored for him was insupportable. She begged Vittorio to wrap up the building works and arrange the sale of Palazzo Patristi as quickly as possible.

This decision presented the question of where she and Vittorio, Esmeralda, and the new baby would live. Neither she nor Vittorio had been looking forward to living in Edmondo's palace. They were going there for Matteo and Esmeralda. They didn't want to stay on in the Fierazzo Palace either. Sofi's mother kept suggesting that they might like to move down to the mezzanine because its low ceilings would make it warmer for the baby. The truth was that Loredana Fierazzo liked to keep the *piano nobile* available for her own use even though she rarely came to Venice.

In no time the word was out that Vittorio and Sofi were thinking of changing residence, and the telephone at the studio began to ring incessantly. As architects, Vittorio and Natasha were prodigiously favored with inside information from fellow architects, from real estate agencies, unlicensed private agents, and even from friends alerting them to rumors of circumstances, personal or financial, that might eventually put a certain property on the market. But Vittorio and Sofi were hard to please. Neither wanted to reside in the architectural mediocrity of a top floor, nor did they want other owners above or below them, nor did they want to take on the restoration of another whole palazzo in

Venice. Anyhow, most of the palaces on the market were destined to become hotels. It was all part of the trend to encourage tourism at the expense of residence—a market force that was shifting even the architecture practice of Vittorio and Natasha away from restoration towards hotel conversion.

When Sofi gave birth to her new baby a little more than three months after Matteo died, she had no power to do other than put aside her mourning and take up happiness. She and Vittorio had long before decided that the ideal name was Secondo, which had been Vittorio's father's name, because it had the additional advantage of giving precedence to his older brother. Instead the name became a subtle memorial to Matteo and somehow redoubled the joy Secondo brought them. He was the epitome of the bouncing baby boy—happy to be here, happy to eat, happy to sleep, happy to dirty his diapers, happy to be cleaned up. Vittorio and Sofi thought he was the most personable infant ever to come into the world. For Sofi, the fact that he had none of the melancholy aura that had clouded her happiness with Matteo confirmed her growing resignation that her first child had been born to a bad fate. Secondo seemed determined to fill their lives with love and contentment. Sometimes it even seemed to her that Secondo was trying to tell her that he had been entrusted to bring her a link with Matteo. The very thought that they had made friends in heaven made her spirits soar. She called him Secondo-my-little-mondo and embraced him almost as a religion.

Vittorio brought Secondo to his mother at the first opportunity. He didn't wait for his usual Friday morning appointment, but dropped in at *Ca' di Dio* one afternoon when he and Sofi had the use of the firm's motorboat. They had to pick up Esmeralda at school and park briefly at the Riva while Vittorio ran inside to show Secondo to his mother, and then they had to go back up the Grand Canal to the office to pick up Natasha and take her to Piazzale Roma, where she kept her car. While Vittorio took Secondo into the *Ca' di Dio,* Sofi stayed with Esmeralda in the boat trying to get her to start her homework so she didn't have so much to do when she got home.

When Vittorio's mother came into the *Salotto,* the lounge area, she looked around as if she weren't sure she recognized anyone. She hardly seemed to notice that her son was beaming with pride as he held up his new baby boy. "Meet Secondo the second!" He grinned. His mother seemed to understand, but she remained enigmatic. "Well, look at you," she nodded, not quite smiling, at the baby. "When my son was born," she said, looking straight at Vittorio, "he was scrawny. I thought he looked like a frog. I remember thinking at the time—that boy is going to need a princess." She said it without a hint of playfulness. "I should give him something," she said, looking almost tenderly at the bright little face. She turned and went back upstairs. Vittorio had never seen her room; he didn't even know on which floor it was. He still hadn't come to terms with the fact that she lived here.

While Vittorio waited, he fell to thinking about his own living arrangements. He and Sofi weren't finding what they wanted; they seemed to know only what they didn't want. Secondo lay watching Vittorio for a few minutes, slowly blinking, blinking, then drifted off to sleep. The sound of the front door slamming and someone shuffling past the door of the *salotto* brought Vittorio's thoughts back to where he was. Sofi would be wondering what was taking so long. He got up with the sleeping baby in his arms and tiptoed over to the office.

"I'm sorry to bother you," he said, in a half whisper, "but I was talking to my mother here in the *salotto* when she said she wanted to get something for her new grandchild and disappeared upstairs. She hasn't come back. Should I go up to find her?"

Miss Nonino got up from her desk and came out into the lobby. "Don't worry. I'll go up." Two minutes later she was back downstairs. "If I'd been thinking," she laughed, "I could have saved myself the stairs. Your mother has this curious trait: She *never* deviates from her schedule. At first I thought she was fighting memory loss, but now I think she's just filling up her time."

"She doesn't really seem the same."

"That's interesting. Has there been some sort of breach between you?"

"Nothing serious. I suppose there might have been some undercurrent with my wife. What does my mother do all day?"

"I'm ashamed to tell you how she occupies herself, because it's my fault. I sensed that she was bored, so I asked her if I could come up from time to time and watch my favorite soap operas on her TV. She got interested, and now she keeps me up to date because I told her I didn't have time to watch them anymore."

"So she seems fine to you?"

"If you want the truth, I don't think she should be in an institution like this, and I'm a little sorry we gave her the place. She seemed so keen to have it and we had an unexpected vacancy, but there are others who need us far more than she. I'm not saying we don't like her. We'd take her back in an instant if she needed to be here."

"So you'd like me to take her away?"

"If she would go. Has she got over whatever it was between you?"

"Apparently not, if she's not coming back down."

"Of course she's not going to do that. She's watching *La Mia Seconda Madre—My Second Mother*. She wouldn't miss it if the house was on fire. In fact it's worth making a note: Don't come again at this time for at least two months."

*

Natasha's baby arrived only two weeks after Secondo. He was named Umberto—Bumbi for short—after their late father, and also Matteo Roberto after the two young godfathers-to-be who didn't live to see him. As soon as Natasha came home, Sofi took Secondo and the nanny out to the country to stay with her, while Esmeralda, who had to go to school, went to stay with her *papà* in the apartment he had rented in Venice so he could supervise the closing down of the works at his palace and its eventual sale. After school on Saturday morning, Vittorio collected Esmeralda from Edmondo to take her with him to the country.

While Natasha and the maid were putting lunch on the table, Sofi took Vittorio aside and showed him a review in the *Gazzettino* about a drawings exhibition. The illustration was a most oddly evocative sketch of the broken arch of Palazzo Patristi.

"Good heavens!" exclaimed Vittorio. "What a thing to commemorate. But he's made it strangely interesting."

"I bought it," said Sofi. "I rang up the minute I saw it and said I wanted to reserve it, but the woman was hesitant so I told her that I'm a new collector and I buy paintings. I said I wanted this for a friend's collection, and she could keep it until I decided how to present it."

"Do you really want it?"

"No. I only want to be the one who decides where it ends up. Anyhow, you have to go on Monday and pay for it."

After lunch, Natasha took Vittorio on a tour of the farmhouse. Vittorio hadn't seen it since Natasha and Marco bought it a year ago. Natasha had made the most of the wonderful large rooms with huge fireplaces and stone floors, but the pièce de résistance was the beautiful carved staircase she'd found at an architectural salvage center. She was explaining her theory about what villa it might have come from when she was called away to the telephone.

"Guess what," said Natasha a few minutes later coming through the French doors. "That was the Carras who own the villa behind us—the ones who sold us this farm. It all used to be one estate; we share the first part of the drive. They've decided to sell their villa, and she wondered whether we'd like to buy it or whether, being an architect, I might know someone in the market for a major piece of real estate. Do I?" She looked at Vittorio.

Vittorio looked at Sofi. "Does she?"

"Yes you do," she said, smiling. "This is fate. I love the idea of living in the country. The babies can grow up like brothers; Esmeralda can have a pony like we did. Do you agree, Vittorio? Can we move out here near Natasha and Marco? It would make a new beginning for us."

"It's a great idea." He laughed. "I've never lived in the country. No place is less convenient than Venice now that everything is geared to tourism. What do you think?" he said, leaning toward Esmeralda. "Would you mind changing schools?"

"Where is the school?" asked Esmeralda. "I want to look at it."

"We'll go and look today," said Sofi. "You'd have to go in a car, or maybe in a bus. If you didn't like it, you could stay in Venice with Papà and come back on weekends, but we'd rather have you here."

"You might even go and look at the villa while you're on the way to see the school—I mean if you're thinking of buying it," laughed Marco. "Actually, it's very nice. We would have bought it ourselves if it had been for sale when we bought this. But now that we've fixed this up the way we like it, we are not moving again, believe me."

Vittorio and Sofi followed Marco's car down the lane from the farm. Marco was taking Esmeralda to look at the school while they looked at the villa. When Marco got to the main drive he waved and turned left towards the gate, while Vittorio turned right and followed the avenue of cypresses and limes. The house was a classic example of the Palladian type, with a square central building and two wings. It was pink brick with white marble and had a porch with columns. The drive traced a circle in front of it; in the center of the circle was a fountain surrounded by gravel with dandelions and clover. The Carras came out to greet them.

Inside, the house followed the standard layout of a Venetian palace. The rooms were tall and stately with frescoes in the main reception rooms. Sofi and Vittorio were quick about it.

When they finished the tour Vittorio asked about the little gatehouse down by the entrance. It was a curious folly built right into the park wall with a tower on one corner and an oriel window above the wall looking down onto the beginning of the village's main street. Was that included? The Carras said they were thinking of selling it separately. "That's okay," said Vittorio. "I can buy it separately."

In the car on the way back to Natasha's, Vittorio said to Sofi, "It's not in bad condition. Do you like it?"

"I love it. I think we'll be really happy there. You and Natasha can commute together. The boys can grow up together. Why were you thinking of buying the gatehouse separately?"

"I was thinking of putting my mother there. I can't bear the thought of leaving her in that rest home."

"Why don't we buy it together? I'd love to have her with us in the country. My mother is not much of a grandmother. Your mother could take on Esmeralda as a granddaughter as well. I've decided that I want these children to

31

have a traditional Italian childhood. What did you think of
the park?"

"Needs some work."

"I think so too," said Sofi.

"But it has capabilities," said Vittorio, turning onto the
Panfili drive.

"That's the great thing about the whole setup," replied
Sofi, lost in her own thoughts.

Donata Manina finally agreed to come live in the gatehouse, but only on the condition that Vittorio buy it with
the money he was earning from his share of the Fallon soft-
furnishings business, Morello & Figli. Miss Nonino had
warned him to take it easy and not push her or she might
rebel. He invited her to come to the warehouse to look
over the furnishings he had put in storage. She said no, she
didn't need to do that. She asked for a set of plans for the
gatehouse instead. On his next visit she gave him a list of
what she wanted delivered. He took Sofi to the warehouse
instead.

"You know what," said Sofi as the movers started unloading the storage containers so she could see what was
there, "tell them not to bother to unpack it. Let's just send
it all to the villa. We have that huge, empty attic and children love full attics. Anyhow, we know now that your

mother is capable of changing her mind. So she might decide she wants to have some of these things after all."

The weekend before Donata Manina was scheduled to move in, Vittorio was down by the street near the gatehouse with Rocco Zennaro and one of his apprentices. He was beginning to worry that his mother might be bored living on her own. He had built a terrace for her behind the house with a bird feeder. He'd installed satellite television. Now he'd had another idea. As he was talking to the workmen, Sofi's car turned into the drive. She rolled down the window.

"What are you doing, darling?"

"I thought I'd have a bench built, with a little roof, a kind of shelter for the bus stop here."

"But we never use the bus. Of course the gardeners and the cleaners take the bus; it would be nice for them."

"It's for everybody, really."

"Isn't it rather close to the gatehouse?"

"Well, I thought that way we could keep an eye on it."

"As a public service?" Sofi seemed dubious.

"Actually, I thought it might be nice for my mother, when people she knows come and go."

"For her visitors! How sweet! What a lovely son you are."

Vittorio's face brightened. "I thought it might remind her of the vaporetto stop where she used to live."

But Sofi had already rolled up the window and driven on.

He turned back to Rocco Zennaro, who was measuring and making a sketch for a stone bench to fit neatly between the tree and the drive.

"If we put a roof over it, Rocco, it will block her view. Do you think maybe I should hook up a little closed-circuit surveillance camera inside so my mother can see what's going on? I mean so she feels safe, of course."

YOUTH

In all his seventeen years Gilmo Polo had never come up against anything more excruciating than the sight of his red cell phone sinking through the green water while his mother was still talking. Watching from the bridge, he could almost hear her laying down the law all the way to the bottom of the canal where at last his beloved *telefonino,* already invisible, sent up a goodbye puff as it interred itself, forever, in the slime.

"Madonna!" Gilmo raised his eyes from the water and heaved his book bag to his shoulder. He stepped down the bridge and headed for Campo San Stefano. This was going to be as bad as the time he flunked Latin; it could even be worse than the time he stayed out all night. He winced at the memory of tiptoeing in his stockings to his bedroom, shoes in hand, trying not to make a sound and glancing down the corridor, only to see his mother and father sitting in the *salone* in their dressing gowns waiting for him at six o'clock in the morning. But some good came out of it; they

35

gave him a cell phone. Out of this crime, however, he couldn't imagine any boon arising. For one thing, he had loved his red telephone and it probably couldn't be replaced.

Gilmo was homing almost by instinct towards Bar Paolin for refuge until he could work out a plausible explanation for losing his beautiful birthday present. He looked at his watch and noted in passing that he still had his Christmas present; his mother would already be making his lunch. So he would be late as well as the bearer of bad news. "Why didn't you ring to tell me you were going to be late?" That would be the first thing she said when he walked in the door. It was a matter of some pride to Gilmo that he had one of the busiest cell phones in his crowd, even discounting that half his calls came from his mother. She was famous among his friends for her uncanny knack for ringing his phone, bang on cue, like a guilty conscience.

Ah ha ha HA ha . . . Ah ha ha HA ha. . . . Woody Woodpecker's tune sang out from Gilmo's cell phone the instant he turned it on walking out the school door onto the *fondamenta.*

"*La Mammma! La Mammmma! La Mammma!*" Alvise, Marco, and Matteo took up the chorus in trio. "It's *la Mamma* calling *il Bambino!*" Even Giulia and Loretta joined in. Only Elena went her way without looking at him. Why did she always ignore him like that? He ran onto the bridge before he answered, leaving them to go on their way, laughing and talking, without him.

"Ciao Mamma."

"How did you do on your exam? Did you get it back?" She was good about helping him to study. His problem was that he couldn't stop daydreaming when he studied alone, and she made him focus. Her problem was that she was too focused. His father said she was like a terrier; once she picked up a scent she stayed on it all the way down the rabbit hole.

"No, Mamma. He didn't hand it back. He said he hadn't finished them yet." He thought for a second, then added, "He said that none of them were very good."

It was true that the teacher hadn't returned the exams; he always took weeks to mark them. Gilmo sensed that his mother was as eager to assess the teacher's performance as to know his grade. She had a mission regarding the teachers. They had established a norm of giving oral examinations instead of written ones so they wouldn't have to take any work home. But a group of mothers, led by Gilmo's own, felt that their children were not being properly prepared if they took only oral exams. The mothers— Gilmo's mother always to the fore—had put pressure on the principal, an old school friend, who agreed to make the teachers introduce an occasional written exam. The teachers, many of whom traveled long distances to work and resented the extra time, rebelled and took care to be very leisurely about marking and returning these exams. For Gilmo—remembering the girls around him scribbling whole paragraphs in the time it took him to write his name, while he struggled to think of something to fill up the page—the delay was an act of mercy. Ten years earlier, when Gilmo's sister went to the same schools, the teachers were ambitious for Venetian children and pulled them along. But there was more to it: Orseola loved school and never wasted her time on fantasies.

"Well, that isn't good enough," snapped his mother. "It's pure laziness." She knew that they were retaliating. "They don't like to do the marking, and that is why you students aren't prepared for the *Maturità*. I have half a mind to come down there . . ."

Those were the last words Gilmo heard before he saw his *telefonino* flying towards the canal.

Sitting in front of Bar Paolin looking out over Campo San Stefano Gilmo felt as naked and familiar as he did sitting half dressed in his bedroom. There was hardly anything this place didn't know about him. He had played here as a child. Here he had assimilated the rudiments of Venetian social politics; he had howled over a cut knee until he turned purple and a doctor came running from the Ristorante San Stefano; he had once wet his pants so copiously that a little river coursed among the playing children all the way to the drain, causing outrage among the mothers and the nannies; he had ventured fearful and uncertain over its broad expanse to his first school; had crossed it in another direction, this time assured of inevitable tedium, to his next school; he had played football at the far end and outsmarted the *vigili;* he habitually wasted his time and squandered his whole week's pocket money in a single evening idling with friends in this very bar, and he had eaten no one knew how many *Gianduiotti* sundaes and drunk more *cappuccini* than he could count. It was a film set of his life where flashes of silly, hopeless, poignant, funny memories rushed in an endless stream to the ultimate zoom on a red telephone fading through green water. His was the despair of a drowning man.

By the time Gilmo was born, Venice had already succumbed to its suburban fate. In appearance, with its noble palaces and shady *pensieroso* calles opening into sunny *allegro* campos, it remained much as it had for centuries. Gilmo grew up in the happy awareness that his birthplace was like no other place in the world. Nevertheless the siege was on, and he gradually distanced himself from his mother's view that it was the best place in the world. He was happy to grant that it *had been* the best of all possible worlds when she was growing up; after all, that had been a long time ago and the history of Venice was the envy of the world. But for the present, he quietly espoused the heresy common to Venetian youth that modern Venice was no place to make a mark in the world. There were of course among his contemporaries girls, even some boys, more spurred by sentiment than ambition, but he was not among them. His friends never even talked about Venice. It was a dead issue. The only interesting question was how to escape and where to go.

"Ecco Bel Giovanotto"—The waiter swooped a cappuccino from his tray with the daring grace of a *Frecchia Azzurra* and slid it toward the pensive youth staring at the campo—"and good luck with your studies."

Gilmo blinked. *"O grazie, Gianni, grazie."* He conceded the joke with a smile. Gianni had the jester's privilege: he had been a waiter at Paolin's for as long as Gilmo could remember. Moreover, he sometimes worked as an extra waiter when Gilmo's mother had big dinner parties; he'd been around the house ever since Gilmo used to have his supper in the kitchen with his pretty English nanny while the waiters rushed in and out chatting to him and flirting with her. When he was little he loved the festive preparations for dinner parties. The maid would be having fun sticking bouquets everywhere and shoving the furniture around to make space. The waiters would be making jokes setting up the tables and floating white tablecloths down onto them. Once they floated one down onto Gilmo and made him, for a minute, into a terrifying ghost. They laid out places with cards and fancy napkin steeples. His mother didn't like rolled-up napkins, but she let the waiters do them anyway because they made a game with Gilmo to put them around—"Hey there, Giant! We need some more mountains over here."

In this amiable world Gilmo eased into the effortless good nature of a storybook prince. Being one of the fair-haired Venetians with blue eyes and classic, intelligent features, he actually looked the part. Even so, he was not a prince; no one knew that better than he. He wouldn't have minded being a prince, but in fact Gilmo Polo was nothing more—his mother would have said "nothing less"—than the happy convergence of numerous Venetian bloodlines channeled into the island state from as far afield as Treviso, from grand to not-so-grand, from rich to not-so-rich, but above all Venetian. His intrinsic mission, the privilege that his heritage rested on his shoulders like a chain-mail domino, was to flourish and rejoice in the modern semblance of the storied lives of his ancestors.

For fiction Gilmo preferred films. Last summer, swinging through the back calles on the way to have pizza with some friends at Tre Oche before going to the outdoor cinema in

San Polo, he had turned to cut through Campo San Cassiano and found the bridge blocked by a solid mass of people. He had squeezed and wheedled his way through the crowd to the top of the steps and discovered that they were blocked by a film company getting ready to shoot. He stood on the bridge looking at the actors being fussed over and the extras leaning against the church smoking. Over on one side near the bar was a buffet of coffee and sandwiches where a crowd of extras and technicians were picking over the snacks. He had worked as an extra once, but his mother made him stop because they wanted him to take time off from school. There were always film companies in Venice, and he could see that nothing was likely to happen here for hours, so he worked his way down the steps to the campo and asked the young man with a clipboard if he would mind if he just ran across to the next bridge because he was late.

The young man said, "Sure. Okay. But come over here a minute." He walked with him towards the snack table and stopped near it. "Are you Venetian?"

"*Sì, sì.*" Gilmo nodded.

"I help with a lot of films in Venice, and I could use a person with your looks: you're the type directors like. Would you be interested in working occasionally?"

"*Sì, sì.*" Gilmo kept a tight grip on himself; it was important to stay cool. "I'd love to do that. Do you need me in this film?"

"No, we're virtually done here. Tomorrow we go back to Rome to finish at Cinecittà. But I'm here every now and then. In fact, I think I've seen you in a campo somewhere when I've been here before. Look, here's what you need to do: Get a portfolio of photographs made by a professional." He reached in the back pocket of his jeans and pulled out a small stack of cards. He gave one to Gilmo. "This guy is a very good photographer. Very professional. He knows exactly what I need. Tell him it's for me." He pulled another stack of cards from his shirt. "Here's *my* card. As soon as you get the photographs send them to me with all your contact information, and I'll get back to you." He waved and went back to the other bridge where people were growing impatient and shouting at the girls who were trying to hold them back.

As Gilmo walked away holding the two cards in his hand he could hardly think where he was going for sheer joy. He took the steps of the next bridge in three leaps. And as soon as he was out of sight he stopped, looked up the graying sky, put his hands over his face and whispered, *"O Dio mio!"* He looked at the cards. Luca Caravalli was a project coordinator with a company called Cinema Service in Rome. And the photographer—*"Cazzo!"*—the photographer was in Padua. To get there he would have to skip school for a day. Common sense issued a sharp reminder: His billowing spirits sagged, and sank to earth. His mother would never sanction anything that might in any way jeopardize his getting a proper university degree. His father's assumption that he would take over his law firm loomed before him. But it hadn't escaped Gilmo that now that his father had moved his offices to Mestre on the mainland, his mother was slightly less committed to the succession. In the purest sense, the firm was no longer Venetian. She said so herself. So a deviation from the original plan might, with skill or luck, find its way into the strategy. He hated to deceive his mother, but he had no logical arguments to promote his case, no cards of his own to play. The situation called for either skill or plain dumb luck, neither of which he had. His father said luck followed hard work, which proved he didn't even know what it was.

Gilmo had to keep foremost in his mind the conviction that the ends would justify the means, that once he was successful, he would have the authority and respect they wanted him to have and they would be satisfied. In fact it was what he wanted, too. He wasn't after the glamour or the starlets. Elena was perfect for him. After he was fa-mous, he would come back to win her and maybe even live here if that was what would please her; he'd never had the chance to ask her about it. He imagined that he would come riding back and sweep her away to a life of big lawns and limousines, but of course the choice would be hers. His vindication was all laid out in *Crime and Punishment:* You could break the rules, but you had to be sure to suc-ceed, in which case you would no longer be subject to the rules. It was quite similar to the Venetian saying—"Steal a little, go to jail; steal a lot, make a career"—but his teacher, when Gilmo suggested it in class, refused to see the parallel. The teacher said it was wrong to bring great literature down to the level of ordinary life. Gilmo dropped out of the discussion and turned his thoughts to how in a film he could open out Raskolnikov's idea to show its validity.

Sometimes when he saw people with camcorders panning over him in a crowd he used to daydream that the film might be destined for a talent scout or a casting agency. They would pick him out of the crowd and come around to Paolin's with a snapshot asking whether anyone knew this young man. Gianni would tell them where he lived. And then? His mother would tell them to go away.

Five or six tables over, at the far corner, Gilmo could see other people sitting at the table where Bobino Panfili used to sit for hours on end with his chums. Gilmo remembered him from all the times he came to the house to study with Orseola when they were at *liceo* together. It was strange how Bobino had completed his university degree in Rome and started a job there, then, for no apparent reason, had come back to live in Venice when his brother Marco came back to get married. His return had kindled a general interest because although everyone thought it was tragic when young people moved away, when someone came back everyone thought there must be something wrong. To Gilmo it flew in the face of common sense; Venice was a trap and there was Bobino letting it close around him a second time. Whenever he saw him he wanted to take him aside and say to him, Look out, man. You are tempting fate: you will never escape again.

The last time Gilmo saw him before he was killed in a car crash, Bobino was sitting at his usual table behind the kiosks, where there was no view, with a boy called Bici, who had a bad reputation. People whispered that Bici peddled stuff. His father owned restaurants on the mainland and had plenty of money. People thought Bici did it for mischief and for the power it gave him over his friends. He was generally regarded as bad news.

In fact one evening last summer when Gilmo was passing the time with some friends here in Paolin's, Gilmo caught sight of three *vigili* sidling up behind Bici and told the others to look. Little by little awareness crept from table to table through the crowd. The scene was taking shape like the climax of a TV crime serial. Bici's wickedness had been in the rumor mill for so long that no one had a grain of doubt about what was happening. Conversations stopped. Suspense was stretching tighter and tighter when—*whap!*—one of the *vigili* grabbed Bici by the shoulders. At the touch Bici leaped up and spun around so fast that the *vigile* let go and jumped back in surprise. An audible gasp burst from the crowd. But when Bici saw who it was, he threw back his head and chortled. He feigned a double slap at the *vigile* who had grabbed him; then they all laughed and gave each other the high five, *slap, slap, slap.* A grumble like distant thunder passed among the tables.

Today it flickered through Gilmo's consciousness that it was as well his mother hadn't witnessed the affair. She might have tried to perform a citizen's arrest—of the *vigili,* for dereliction of duty. Gilmo's mother was blessed with certainty on many issues. One day at lunch some weeks later, when they were having a good time together, he had treated her to a recital of the incident. She understood immediately the dynamics of the whole business and appended the incident to her mounting case against that supine Mayor Grandi. Gilmo suspected that in her heart she knew Venice nowadays was too idle a place to be salubrious for the young, but he never elaborated the point and hoped she wouldn't take up the issue until he was safely out of the way.

Gilmo had started out in begging mode to convince the photographer to do his photographs on a Saturday afternoon so he wouldn't have to play hookey, but when he heard that the fee was going to be 220 euros, he realized that the photographer wasn't doing him a favor. To get the money Gilmo sold all his signed CDs of Vasco Rossi and Francesco de Gregori. On the whole, he wasn't sorry he'd done it. He felt that he had taken a small step in the right direction and that he had learned something. The photographs were stylish. The photographer was clever with poses and suggested expressions to make him look like different people, but after almost a year, he felt like he hardly resembled any of them anymore. He had never heard from Cinema Service.

A few weeks after he sent the portfolio he had telephoned the number on Luca Caravalli's card. They told him that Luca was working in California but would be back in a month. When Gilmo rang after a month they told him that Luca had got a job in America, but they were in touch with him and would tell him that Gilmo Polo was looking for him. One day when the moment was right he meant to ask his mother whether she had ever taken a call from Luca Caravalli about working in films. He hadn't found the courage yet because the thought of hearing that she had sent him away as a bad influence for her son's future upset him so much that he didn't trust himself not to scream the house down. In a few years he would go to the University of Rome. That was the lifeline he was swimming for. He had almost convinced his mother that it would do him good to try studying in a new environment. Once there, he would put in for some kind of work at Cinecittà, and unlike Bobino, once he got as far as Rome, he would not come back to sit around in Paolin's every day.

A surly seagull scowling down from the newsstand

turned towards him; it unfurled its great wings as if it meant to strike but turned away laughing like a hag. It sailed up onto the high roofs opposite, where it frightened a crowd of pigeons down into the campo. Gilmo waved to Gianni for the bill. He had to get moving.

A ball bounced against his chair. A young nanny rushed up and retrieved it, apologizing. Children weren't supposed to play ball in the campo, but they always did. He shrugged and smiled at her. "It's nothing," he said. She retreated, blushing. Gilmo looked over the campo and saw a little boy on a red plastic tricycle without pedals, just like the one that was still hanging up in their attic because he wouldn't let his mother throw it away. The boy reminded him of himself, sitting there oblivious, putting down invisible roots in Campo San Stefano. He was only a toddler sucking on a pacifier, a *ciuccio,* and staring into space with large brown eyes. He was sleepy. The *ciuccio* had a string running down to the handlebar, where it was tied to keep it from getting dirty if he dropped it. With one hand he was playing with the knot on the handlebar.

Gilmo had a weakness for the familiar atmosphere of this campo. The action drew him in. He identified with the children and liked animals, except for rats and maybe pigeons. His father had always wanted him to have a dog, but it was too much bother in Venice. You had to keep it on a leash, muzzle it on the vaporetto, take it for walks, and clean up after it in the streets. Some people let their dogs run free so they didn't have to do any of these things, and they hardly ever got caught. His mother always said that Venetians gossip about each other but they don't tattle to the authorities no matter how much they condemn the *maleducati,* the badly behaved. She said the prevailing rule was: Let he who is without sin among you stick his neck out first. He could see that the mothers and nannies were talking about a stray dog that had trotted up to where the children were playing. It was a little brindle and white terrier with bright eyes and a nervous prance, like a soccer player on the sidelines waiting for his turn to play. The nannies tried to shoo him away. He took it in fun and stayed nearby, looking for a chance to join the game.

That morning the German professor had read from *Faust* about the devil dog whose feet made sparks when he ran. Gilmo cast him with a mischievous face like this one. The thought of school made his heart sink; his red cell phone was gone. Everyone had been so jealous when he showed up with it on his birthday. He missed having it on the table. It had all his phone numbers. If only his mother had found a way to hook it to a cord like she used to do with his mittens—like that little boy's *ciuccio.*

Somehow the little boy had managed to untie the string and was standing astride the tricycle waving the loose end for his mother to see. She ran towards him, scolding, and reached for the string. But the little boy was in no mood for scolding; he was tired and irritable. He grabbed the *ciuccio* from his mouth and threw it as hard as he could away from her. It went a surprisingly long way. The terrier watched its flight and tried to catch it. Gilmo sat up with interest. The mother was cross and ran to pick it up, but the terrier got there first. He grabbed it from the ground and ran away, then turned and bounced this way and that, begging to be chased.

He ran towards the baby, who waved excitedly. Then he ran toward the mother, chewing the rubber in his laughing mouth and teasing her to chase him. Gilmo could see that the mother was determined not to let the dog get away with it. She made a move towards the dog. He waited and tilted his head as if to offer the *ciuccio* for the taking. She put out her hand, but he skittered backwards and waited for her to try again.

She was so concentrated in her effort that she didn't notice that the excitement had caught the attention of the whole campo. Everyone in Paolin's was watching. The tourists lunching under the awning at Ristorante San Stefano were rising from their tables and gathering at the opening in the privet border with their video cameras. They spilled into the campo, filming.

One of the workmen sitting on the monument jumped up to help the mother. He tried to chase the dog towards her. Some of his companions joined him and together they tried to trap the dog.

Gilmo could hear Gianni laughing in the background. Gianni slapped his legs with delight. This was the Venice he loved, the life of the campo. He was on everyone's side at once. His heart went out to the terrier, to the good-natured construction workers, even the tourists getting up to take videos. The mother looked horrified as she realized that the drama was being filmed; she didn't want her boy appearing as a joke on one of those amateur TV video programs.

The dog started to play with the workmen and forgot about her. He came near her and stopped, his eyes on the workmen. She leaned over and snatched the string. The terrier jumped away, alarmed, and started to pull. The mother jerked. The dog clenched his teeth to hold on and the *ciuccio* broke. The baby screamed, first with excitement and then distress, as hunger and fatigue overtook him. He rolled off his tricycle and lay on the stones wailing. The cameras zoomed in on him. Some of the tourists walked in for a close-up. "So cute," they were saying. The mother ran with the broken *ciuccio* bouncing on its string to save her baby from the infamy of the video cameras. She grabbed him up in one arm, hooked the tricycle in the other, and fled down the Calle delle Botteghe.

Gianni put his tray on the empty table beside Gilmo and cleared away the glasses. He turned to Gilmo as he started back to the bar. "The joys of Venetian life, eh?"

Gilmo's heart went out to the cross mother. He could see she was trying to protect the boy. He'd been an idiot to throw his telephone in the canal outside school. There was no point in telling his mother that someone had pushed him or thrown it in the canal because she would ring the other mothers to complain. He couldn't say it was stolen because she would ring the principal and the police. He would have to pretend that he'd been careless and balanced it on the railing of the bridge while he shouldered his backpack.

Gilmo put 5 euros under his cup and stood up; he waved to Gianni and left. Leaving a big tip raised his self-esteem. Some waiters refused to take a big tip from him because he was so young, but Gianni was a friend and let Gilmo behave like a man. Gilmo had every intention of rewarding him for accepting his tips one day.

As he crossed the bridge into Sant'Angelo, remorse caught him again. From here he usually rang home to tell his mother that he was near, that she could throw in the pasta. *Sono in campo, Mamma, puoi buttare la pasta.* His father used to do the same, but since he'd moved his firm to Mestre and no longer came home for lunch, his mother made lunch for just the two of them. *Uffa!* How he dreaded breaking the news about his telephone. He would tell her the lie about knocking it off accidentally. That would get him through lunch at least. Eventually she would get the truth out of him. She always did. As he walked along Calle degli Avvocati he thought he smelled *peperonata*. He hoped it would fade away, but as he neared the house the smell was unmistakable floating down from the kitchen window: *peperonata* to add to his misery. She would have prepared his favorite lunch: *cotoletta Milanese* and *peperonata,* either to celebrate a success in his exam or to cheer him up in case of failure. It was typical: She was his sharpest critic, with X-ray vision, and his brutal defender: so ruthless to his adversaries that he forgave them at once. His father teased her about being the *dogaressa* of Italian mammas, and so did his sister. His friends claimed that their mothers were exactly the same, but he doubted it.

He rang the doorbell.

Chi e? Who's there? It was only Rita, the maid.

Sono io. It's me.

Sei in ritardo. Tua madre ti sta aspettando da parecchio. You're very late. Your mother's been waiting for you for a long time.

The door clicked.

He pushed the great door open and walked into the *androne.* So far, so good. He wasn't in a hurry to climb the stairs. He stood among the marble pilasters and crumbling bricks, letting the atmosphere of home drift over him. It always felt the same no matter how delinquent he might be. He wondered if it had seen so much in its five hundred years that it had lost all sense of right and wrong. The house had known his father all his life, and his grandfather, who had once been the Mayor.

He stopped again at the foot of the staircase. A few years ago he had come in from playing football in the campo and found his father standing there. It was the day he finally decided to move his offices to Mestre. He had been saying for years that all his important clients were on the mainland and he needed to be nearer. He had waited for Orseola to go to university and he had tried to hold on for Gilmo, but he had put off the decision until it was almost too late to save his practice. His father knew that the change would snap to flitters the weak old tapestry of their Venetian life, and that it would never be mended. He could foresee that eventually the whole fabric would be cast away like the moth-eaten counterpane of old Venetian lace Gilmo once found in the attic that no one alive even knew was there. The worst thing about the move was that it betrayed the vision of the future that he and his bride had embraced together so many years ago.

"Well, Gilmo," said his father, "we have to change with the times." He was clearly glad to have Gilmo there beside him, shouldering the bad news side by side, up and up. For Gilmo, actually, it wasn't such a burden. He hadn't been around when they made their plans and didn't feel betrayed at all, but he didn't let on. In fact Gilmo already had an inkling that his father's move had holed the wall for his own escape.

Now Gilmo waited at the stairs. Up there behind that door reigned soaring expectation, while here below, resolute as a boulder, sat grim reality. He started up the steps; no kind son would come to help *him*. And it was hard work every day pushing that weight of shortcomings, that gathering mass of laziness, extravagance, carelessness, and ingratitude—wanting both to escape and then show them up by exceeding their wildest expectations. But that would be a long time coming. Today his lost telephone seemed to outweigh everything. Gilmo cheered himself on. . . . Steady does it, *coraggio,* almost there. The nearer he came to the top, the greater the effort to put one foot above the other, up and up and up and up. It was the only way, steady, steady, *coraggio,* Gilmo.

He neared the door. It opened. The maid stood in the doorway shaking her head as if to say, You are not worthy of this house.

"Hello, darling." His mother called from the kitchen. "What happened to your telephone? I've been trying to ring you for an hour." She appeared at the pantry door.

"Oh," said Gilmo. "It's a long story."

"A man rang for you this morning," she went on. "He said your cell phone was turned off. He said he had photographs of you. How did he get them? You'll have to tell me about that. He said you were good-looking in a special way. I told him I completely agreed with him. He was very civil. I promised to get you to ring him. He's in Rome and

56

will be back in his office at three o'clock, so we should hurry up and have lunch. I think it has something to do with a film, darling. Aren't you excited?"

"Very," said Gilmo, looking around, bewildered. The air was flushed with promise, rosy with forgiveness. Only Rita was immune to the atmosphere, plumping the sofa cushions in the drawing room with real resentment, furious with his wishy-washy mother who spoiled him rotten. Rita had warned her time and again that she had spoiled her own son and he had very nearly gone to the bad, but no one ever listened to her. Gilmo's mother said that Rita did her best work when she was annoyed, but that was not why she didn't listen to her. She simply didn't believe that Rita's son could be anything like Gilmo.

In his heart, Gilmo sympathized with Rita's attitude towards him, but he was grateful anyhow that his mother didn't share it. In this atmosphere, he felt he might as well confess over lunch. He could see that his mother was going to forgive him like she always did, no matter how little he deserved it. So what did it matter adding a bit more guilt to that vast hoard? He could almost hear it rolling back down the stairs to greet him on the morrow. Gilmo was worn out from the hard work of getting himself home after the crime on the bridge, but he was beginning to perceive that under it all he was happy, and lucky too, just like his father said. This burden was his own, and it wasn't only his faults; it was partly weighed down with all the optimism and generosity and forgiveness that his family endlessly piled onto him, that he couldn't do without. Gilmo was beginning to realize that when the time came he was going to be sad leaving Venice and lonely striking out on his own.

But for now, he was wondering how long he'd be without a cell phone.

PROBABILITY

Something strange was happening. Giovanni del Banco recognized the feeling. It was like the time he'd seen a ghost at his grandmother's house. *"Porca miseria!"* he had cried to himself. *"I* am seeing a *ghost!"* Only this time he was saying to himself, *"Santo cielo! I* am seeing a *flying saucer."*

He was trotting fast, up, up, up the Rialto Bridge from the market side, with his newly repaired pocket watch still cool in his hand, picking his way through the crowd of mothers herding children, men taking the steps with a purposeful rhythm, and shoppers drifting from window to window in a haze. He instead was reflecting on something pressing and real: He was thinking about Medina, the jeweler he had just paid, who had thrown him a shrewd look as he pocketed the five folded 20-euro banknotes— 200,000 old lire! No receipt!—and then dispatched him with the word *Shalom.*

As Giovanni gained the top of the bridge he was looking straight ahead into the winter sky, still wondering what difference it made that the jeweler recognized him as a Jew, when out of the blue, a silver disk glowing like a sparkler sailed saucy as you please straight across his vision and disappeared behind the foreground of buildings. In size it seemed far, far away, but in speed and brilliance it seemed as near as the rooftops in front of him. It was glorious!

He stopped to look around, elated, only to discover that of all the people on the bridge, he alone had seen it. *He alone.* No one else had looked up. How could it be? At first he was disappointed, then annoyed. And then he resigned himself—going down, down, down the steps—to yet one more proof that he was not the same as other people. It was this kind of occurrence, happening with increasing frequency nowadays, that brought him back repeatedly to the idea that being a Jew, even a baptized Jew, might be what made him different.

"Hello. Yes?" Giovanni wedged the telephone between his shoulder and his ear so he could type while he talked, or while—as was usually the case—he waited on the line. For many hours each day he sat like this with his head tilted to one side, like an organ grinder's monkey listening for the tune, trying to wheedle interviews for his newspaper articles. Waiting made him nervous. He hunched over his laptop chewing his pencil and tapped with one hand randomly over the keyboard as he waited. Sometimes he tapped

the keys as though practicing a scale on a piano; sometimes
he capered with two fingers like a Mick Jagger strut.

qwertyuiopdrw Of man's aoig9Zxc,gl;bs,.04[e;/*/
first llkkkkj; disobedienceom2skdmf mjhbk and-
ikoihjn/ thebflnd fruit5a';l.lmi of.,mo;q/ thatzxcndi,
forbidden..;kn4 tree{[whose ppoioilkjilnl mortal-
xncmvu2e tastecmkldky broughtaiondi\ death-
poiu;lkjsaf intomuuttytge vxeeeeee the dknfligni
world.,kom/ andmkoy783h9 all3kn.,k ourknd9owm
woe!!!!!!!!@#$% &+*456
Scroll: delete

To save money, Giovanni tried to make all his professional phone calls from the little "press office" that the
security guard Luigi—or Gigi, as Mayor Grandi had nick-
named him in a postprandial flush of bonhomie—let Giovanni use in exchange for a very reasonable monthly tip.
The room was at the back of the old municipal office
building and seemed to have been forgotten by the City of
Venice, which nevertheless in its benign ignorance went on
supplying electricity, paying the telephone bill, and pro-
viding the gray metal table and chair.

With a journalist's nose for anomaly, Giovanni would
have loved to expose the absurdity of his office—had he
not needed it so badly. Instead, he found himself justifying
it in his own mind as recompense for the way the Mayor,

and all the other politicians following the Mayor's ex-ample, took advantage of him. Ever since the newspapers had restructured and forced so many writers into freelance status, journalists had been obliged to ingratiate them-selves wherever they could to get work. The more enter-prising ones joined forces to overrun the newsstands with hack-vehicle magazines and cut-and-paste potboilers. Even Giovanni, loner though he was, gamed the system in self-defense: His office was a perquisite of the barter system and hard proof that opportunism makes the world go round.

Gigi Esposito was the perfect exponent of both. He had worked for the post office in Venice for fifteen years, just long enough to qualify for the "baby pension," and then retired. Baby pensions were more often taken by women than men because they were too meager for a breadwinner but made a nice little annuity for a housewife. There was also the catch that once a person took a pension, he could never work again, except *in nero,* on the black market; oth-erwise he would lose a large part of the pension. Women could do housework or other casual jobs that were unregu-latable. Gigi, however, had to have a full-time job. He played his cards with finesse. The security firms in Venice had so many museums and banks to look after that they could never find enough people to work as guards, so sometimes, to fulfill their contracts, they had to take illegal personnel. One such was Gigi. For some months the security company kept Gigi on call to cover staff shortages, but they once made the mistake of sending him to the *Municipio* of Venice to fill in for a guard on vacation. By the end of his two-week stint, Gigi had ingratiated himself with everyone from the cleaners right up to the Mayor. He had hardly started his first week when he struck a deal with the agent who serviced the coffee machine. In exchange for Gigi's keeping the machine clean and topped up, and taking care of little problems like straightening out the cups when they got jammed so the company didn't get complaints, the agent gave Gigi permission to use his key to help himself to a cup of coffee now and then. Gigi made a lot of friends through the coffee concession.

Gigi had befriended Giovanni when he used to write up his notes with his laptop perched on any ledge or wastepaper basket he could find in the *Municipio*. As Giovanni was the first to admit, he typed like a chimpanzee at the best of times. When he had to struggle to keep his laptop balanced on a narrow windowsill, he could hardly type at all. And when he had to take a call on his cell phone and had to run outside to find a signal, he risked losing his laptop altogether if he left it behind. Gigi understood his problems. He would offer a steadying hand while Giovanni typed, and when Giovanni had to run outside to talk on his cell phone, Gigi walked around with the laptop under his arm. Sometimes, if Gigi happened to read what Giovanni was writing, he would offer tidbits of information from papers he'd happened to see while checking offices after hours. To thank him, Giovanni brought him wine from his father's cooperative near Portogruaro, and when he went abroad he shared his ration of duty-free cigarettes.

Before many months passed, the security firm put Gigi on a legal footing. They couldn't risk giving the *Municipio* a black eye if anyone found out they were supporting illegal employment. The firm had to pay top dollar for him because they had to cover the loss of his pension income as well as give him the standard salary. Gigi didn't mind losing the pension. This way he would get a bigger pension when he turned sixty-five.

One day Giovanni was walking around the lobby of the *Municipio* looking for a place to balance his laptop when Gigi motioned to him. Through back corridors, Giovanni followed Gigi's lumbering walk around and around until they arrived at an inconspicuous door that had the appearance of leading to a cloakroom or a broom closet. Gigi licked his fingers and wet an area near the top of the door, then invited Giovanni to lean over and look at the space in a raking light. PRESS he was able to make out before the spittle dried and the letters disappeared into the dark varnish. Gigi gave him a triumphant grin and unlocked the door. Giovanni followed him into a wedge-shaped cubicle with a high window, which Gigi said let in light from a big storeroom that gave onto a corridor on the other side of the building. The cubicle offered a table and a chair where he could work in peace. Giovanni was delighted. "Could I work here sometimes?"

"Of course." Gigi was impatient. "But this is what's important." Gigi had picked up the telephone and was shaking it in front of him.

Gigi made him listen to the story of how he had discovered the room when he was taking the night duty for a guard on vacation. He thought it strange that there was a door that no key on the guard's key ring could open, so he had his friend at the locksmith come over the next night with a box of keys to unlock it. Gigi had spotted the telephone jack the first time he looked inside even though the floor was stacked with old mimeograph stencils and useless forms. Once Gigi got his hands on a spare telephone, he was able to confirm that the jack was connected to a private line, independent of the switchboard and apparently completely forgotten. The trick had been to find the telephone number, but he had a friend, a *vigile,* who had helped him get subsidized housing on the mainland when his house in Venice burned down. Gigi had returned the favor by telling the *vigile* about a piece of land that was going cheap, and now they were building houses next door to each other and were best friends. This *vigile* had a friend who worked on the Crime Squad. One day he rang the Crime Squad from this telephone and got his friend to trace the call. Naturally, the *vigile* was one of the select group who had a key and the right to use the telephone, but they needed a proper registered journalist to give the use of the room legitimacy. For Giovanni the room was a godsend. He asked Gigi if he could always have it in the mornings, and Gigi promised to keep it free for him. Giovanni gave him 50 euros a month—in addition to the occasional crate of wine and carton of cigarettes.

Giovanni's wife, Irene, had taken over the office at home. She was another who had a baby pension. After fifteen years of traveling by train and bus through the featureless Veneto plain into towns with scrubby trees and somber houses to teach German and French in village schools, she gave up. To get a teaching job in the historic center of Venice a person had either to know someone in a key position or have incredible luck. And once people got these jobs they stayed in them until they were sixty-five. There was a long waiting list for every position. She took early retirement and started working from home renting holiday apartments. She took her commissions under the table, *in nero,* which was easy with foreign clients. She used the spare bedroom that their parents, when they bought the apartment for them, had intended for their grandchildren, but which Irene and Giovanni had immediately identified as a home office.

Waiting with the telephone tucked against his shoulder, Giovanni was trying to speak to the Assessor of Culture

about why the Fortuny Museum, which had been willed to
the city decades ago, had never been properly restored and
set up in accordance with the donation. Giovanni felt
called upon to do something for Venice; he wanted to be a
whistleblower, an opinion maker; he wanted to be a
prophet. Venice had lost its place in the world. Giovanni
wanted to point the new way. The assessor's secretary came
back on the line.

"I'm sorry, Giovanni. I think he knows you're after him
and is hiding. I've looked everywhere. Do you want to
send over some questions so I can try to get him to answer
them?"

"No. You know what that's like." Politicians were prima
donnas with local journalists. They always wanted to route
questions through their PR specialists, who changed them
and added questions of their own—like, What has been
your most important achievement on behalf of the people
of Venice?—which they answered with long documented
replies that the newspapers always cut. Then when you
rang again they would say, "You cut my last interview
without my permission."

"Wait a minute!" said the secretary. "Someone just told
me he's in the Mayor's office. I'll transfer you over there."

"Del Banco?" A man's voice came on the line. Giovanni
had a sinking feeling.

"Yes."

"This is Grandi speaking."

"Mr. Mayor, I was trying to reach the Assessor of Culture."

"I know. But I want to talk to you. Where is that article I asked you to do about the history of guidebooks on Venice? It's supposed to go in the first issue of the new magazine. You know, del Banco, this isn't such a big deal. My daughter's going to do the same thing for a school project. I could pay her to do it if she weren't my daughter. If she can get hers done in the next two weeks and she's only seventeen, you should be able to do it in one week. I'll expect it next week."

"Okay. I think I can manage that. Is Assessor Delmuro with you?"

"Another thing, del Banco: Don't forget the article about the future of Venice. I want you to come and see me about that. I have some points I want included. Make an appointment for week after next. That's for the second issue, but we should get moving. I want the second issue out before the European Parliament elections. Here's Delmuro."

"Del Banco, I know you want to talk about Palazzo Fortuny, but I can't do anything for you for another month at least. I have pressing issues on the environment for the European Parliament and won't be back for ten days."

"The problem"—Giovanni was struggling not to whine—"is that my paper wants this article, and I don't get paid if I don't write it. If it's all right with you I can do a two-part article: I'll do the negative part first and let you set the record straight in the second part. Would you go along with that?"

"No, I don't like that. Come over and see me tomorrow at one o'clock. I have a lunch at one-thirty in Mestre."

Giovanni put down the phone then picked it up again. He rang the Assessor's secretary. "Liliana? Thank you for finding Delmuro for me. He gave me an appointment tomorrow at one o'clock."

"One o'clock? He has to leave for Mestre."

"I know. I'll come early and hope for the best. I wanted to ask you about the Mayor's magazine. Would you know whether there's a budget to pay for the articles?"

"Oh yes, Giovanni, but they like to save it to pay for big names to do the lead articles, and fill up the rest of the magazine with free articles. I'm afraid yours will be one of the free ones. You know how it is."

Now that Irene worked from home, she made lunch for Giovanni. He liked having lunch at home and was glad to save the money, but he missed the gossip he picked up lunching in the bars around San Luca and the Rialto. In his work he had to keep talking to people; otherwise he ran out of material. As he passed through Campo Manin he noticed that the builders' shed that had taken over a large part of the campo with an ominous aura of permanence was little by little yielding ground to the statue of the hero Daniele Manin. Giovanni had a soft spot for old Manin, another Venetian with Jewish origins. He stopped by the newspaper kiosk in Sant'Angelo and picked up some newspapers to look at after lunch; he might have some articles coming out. Giovanni also had under his arm a new free newspaper that Gigi had picked up at the vaporetto stop. Gigi had talked to the van driver who was dropping them off in Piazzale Roma about getting some articles for Giovanni to write. Gigi would try anything; sometimes he had amazing success with the oddest connections. As Giovanni paid the newsagent at his temporary kiosk, he pointed at the old one beside it which had a fence around it wrapped in tattered plastic.

"Any news about their plans to restore these old kiosks?"

"Nope. You probably know more than I do."

"Hm. Do you think it will ever happen?"

"Nope."

In Campo San Stefano he passed another fenced and derelict kiosk with a temporary new one beside it.

"Excuse me." He addressed the girl reading a magazine inside the new kiosk. "Do you have any idea whether you'll ever get your old kiosk back again?"

"Nope. Anyhow, this one's better."

As he climbed up the Accademia Bridge he was thinking

about an article on the temporary builders' sheds that were springing up in all the campos; he might link them up with the business of the derelict newsstands. The bridge itself was a ridiculous example of the weak-kneed policy of *com'era, dov'era,* which politicians fell back on as an easy option. The phrase dated from the beginning of the twentieth century when the Campanile of St. Mark's fell down. The government of the day determined on the instant to rebuild it *com'era, dov'era*—as it was, where it was—which made sense for an important landmark that perfectly served its purpose. There was another reason, too: It reassured the voting public. But to rebuild a bridge that had been thrown up in the thirties in forty days as a temporary measure until a suitable design could be chosen, *com'era, dov'era* was nothing more than a cowardly dodge. Not only that, but the wood was inferior to that of the earlier temporary version and had already deteriorated to the point where Irene wouldn't walk on it in high heels because the heels got trapped and pulled loose in the cracks. Then there was the Fenice. That too would be a monument which for motives of political reassurance would have to be *com'era, dov'era,* but many architects objected. There was plenty to say about the opportunity to save some of the Venetian artisans from extinction following that policy. He could ask Carlo Carain who had a firm of restorers and artisans about his view on that issue. There could be several points of view. The idea would be to get a little controversy going that stayed alive for a while. As the ideas began to come he quickened his pace stepping up, up, up on the disintegrating boards.

At the top of the bridge he was struck with joy at the sight of a familiar silhouette leaning on the railing looking out towards the Dogana, the customs house. What a piece of luck! He loved to talk to Professor Faleiro. He knew more about Venice than anyone else in the world and never stopped picking up new threads. They used to have lunch together sometimes, and their conversation would keep Giovanni full of articles for a month.

"*Ciao, Professore!*" Giovanni walked up beside him and put out his hand.

Faleiro turned. "*Ciao, Giovanni!* Well met!" He shook Giovanni's hand and patted him on the shoulder. "You know what I was thinking about?" He gestured towards the Salute. "Around the bend is Palazzo Treves, the home of Giuseppe Treves dei Bonfili. He was the first Venetian Jew to be raised to the nobility."

"But not by the Venetians," said Giovanni. "He was Napoleon's banker."

"Well done. I wonder if the schools bother with all that nowadays. Do you think many teenagers know that the Ghetto lasted through the eighteenth century? I'll bet they think it's medieval. My assistant told me that the first reach of the Grand Canal has a large representation of families with Jewish antecedents. He thinks it might be the same the whole length of the Canal, but it isn't his field. He just happened to notice while he was researching early palaces. By the way, I've been reading some splendid articles about Shakespeare's Venetian mistress."

The professor started walking down the bridge towards San Stefano as he talked. Giovanni followed him back the way he had just come. "That's the sort of thing Irene loves to know about so she can tell her tourists. Would you like to come home with me for lunch?"

"I can't today, but thank you. I have to get over to the library. I've got a stack of books waiting for me. But when I'm working at the Marciana, I go to that new restaurant Il Bacaro for lunch, where the Cinema San Marco used to be. I go almost every day. Come and have lunch with me one day. I'll give you some interesting things to read." He stopped to address Giovanni. "Are you Catholic?"

"Nominally."

"And your wife?"

"Yes. But that's a different story." Faleiro continued walking down the bridge as Giovanni talked. "Her family were Waldensian, but they hadn't been practicing for generations, so when we decided to get married and her family wanted to have a big church wedding, the obvious thing was for her to become Catholic. So she converted— for *me*." Giovanni laughed.

Faleiro stopped and laughed too. They were in front of San Vidal. "Now that's a nice variation."

"My father liked it. He wanted us to get married in the church of San Moise—St. Moses," said Giovanni as they continued into Campo San Stefano, "but in the end we chose San Samuele. Funnily enough the priest who married us had an important Jewish surname. I don't even remember it anymore, but my father pointed it out." *Brekekekex, ko-ax, ko-ax, Brekekekex, ko-ax.* His cell phone rang like a frog in his pocket.

"Yes, yes. I'm just coming." He put his phone back in his pocket. "That was Irene. I'm late for lunch. I'd better go. I'm sorry you can't join us."

"Are you going my way?" The Professor gestured towards San Marco.

"No," said Giovanni, sheepishly. "I go back over the Accademia Bridge. I'll come and look for you in Il Bacaro in the next few days. I have to do some research in the Marciana myself, about guidebooks."

"Look at that," said the Professor as they parted, indicating the confetti still blowing over the pavement from Carnival. "Somebody has to tell the Mayor we're not in Brazil. Will you do it?" He smiled and waved.

Giovanni had never known anyone who shared his thoughts like Professor Faleiro. Even that last little comment was true. There were two Venices with two different personalities, the Mayor's street-vendor Venice and Faleiro's venerable state: one the grotesque old reveler from *Death in Venice* and the other—he thought for a minute—who *was* the Solomon of Venice? Maybe the more important question was: Who will be the David? In a way he was glad he had been named Giovanni and not David—if names meant anything.

On Sunday mornings Giovanni liked to sit in the dining room in his dressing gown, drinking coffee and collecting information from the Internet for the articles he had to write in the coming week. Nowadays, Irene tended to be out on Sundays taking care of her tourists. This morning she had gone early to meet someone at the airport and left instructions for him to start cooking the roast for their lunch.

At eleven o'clock he went to turn on the oven. As he was going back to the dining room, the doorbell rang. Irene was always forgetting her keys and chasing him around town to borrow his. Whenever his phone rang in a lecture or a press conference he could be pretty sure it would be Irene saying, "Hello, Baby, where are you? I'm locked out." He clicked the downstairs door open and opened the hall door as he passed on the way back to the dining room. As he sat down at the dining table, he congratulated himself for remembering to turn on the oven before she got home. Then he heard voices in the hall. Good God! he thought, Irene has brought her clients back without warning me, and here I am in my dressing gown. As he got up to close the dining room door, two strangers, a man and a woman, peeked around it.

"*Buon giorno?* Oh, there you are. Thank you for opening the door," said the woman. She was middle-aged and dressed with evident care in a gray tweed coat with a gray flowered scarf covering her neck. The man beside her was younger but equally well-dressed. He bowed slightly and stepped forward. "We are *Testimoni di Geova,* Jehovah's Witnesses. We've come to talk to you about our faith."

Giovanni pulled his dressing gown closer and tightened the belt. His mother, who never liked to offend anyone, had once got rid of some Sunday morning missionaries, who were waiting at the door hoping she would open it, by leaning out the window, shrugging her shoulders helplessly and saying, "I'm sorry, but I'm Jewish." In fact she wasn't, except by marriage, but the missionaries couldn't know that so they bowed politely and left her in peace.

"I'm sorry," said Giovanni, with an apologetic shrug, "but I'm Jewish."

"Ah," they said, stepping forward in unison. "We have much to share. We can tell you so much that you need to know."

Giovanni's eyes opened wide; what had changed? He

felt as if he'd tipped the wrong way in a rocking boat. He wondered hurriedly whether inclining the other way would help. "Well, actually I'm not really Jewish," he said, putting out his hands to stop argument.

"Are you Catholic?"

"Well, yes and no." He shook his head impatiently. He still wasn't out of danger. How did he get into this fix?

"Then you are on the way." The young man reached for a chair, glancing from Giovanni to his companion as though asking permission to invite her to sit down, while easing into a chatty manner. "Has anyone ever talked to you about the conversion of the Jews and the end of the world?"

"Were you," asked the woman earnestly, "converted in preparation for the second coming? Were you told of how Christ will come again? You know that He will come again, and soon. He *will* come again. You must be saved in time."

Giovanni panicked. Away! But he was in his dressing gown. Wait: This was his own house. What were they talking about? The New Jerusalem! What about floods in San Marco and Noah's Ark? "Santa Cielo!" he shouted. "My bath! The neighbors will crucify me. Let me go! I thought you were my wife without her keys." He rushed them out the door.

Giovanni went back to the dining room and called up his draft for an article on how to save Venice and the proposed MOSE floodgates. He had started the article: *Every-*

one knows that a flood like 1966 will come again. Venice must *be saved in time.*

Irene thought it was pretty funny. "Did they really talk about Noah's Ark?"

"No. I just thought of that because they were coming up with all these Bible stories about God and the heavenly city and the Second Coming. To tell the truth they were very polite and I think I upset them. I'm kind of sorry about it. It's your fault because you always forget your keys."

They had just finished watching one of the classic Sunday-night films of Don Camillo, played by Fernandel, in which the priest in his tireless efforts to outsmart the Communist Mayor receives counsel from the life-size crucifix that hangs above the altar of the church.

"I'd like to go to that town, Brescello, where the church is, where they made the film. Do you think that crucifix is really there, or is it a just a prop? I'd love to do an interview."

"Don't be silly, you infidel. It's not the crucifix that talks. It's Jesus. You know that because in the episode where he goes to Russia, another crucifix he finds in the church that's being used as a barn talks to him there. It's God talking. You have to have a special relationship with Him to have a conversation. That's the whole point."

"Maybe I do. Sometimes I think I do."

"Well, for one thing you're not ordained. You're hardly a good Catholic, even. Anyhow, you're a journalist. Of course the man who wrote the script was a journalist too. So maybe there's some hope for you."

"That crucifix talks about politics," insisted Giovanni. "He talks about the real world."

"You mean physical world. I wonder if that's heresy. In the Inquisition you'd be in trouble. And with a name like yours?"

"Well, what about the Waldensians? Given a choice, the Pope would probably choose the Jews."

"If we had had children," Giovanni continued seriously, "would we have had them baptized? We never go to Mass."

"Of course. Wouldn't we? It doesn't do any harm. They'd want to be like everybody else."

Giovanni thought about it. She was right, really. Nowadays the Catholic Church was not oppressive; it was like an elderly parent, disapproving perhaps, but no longer in a position to discipline.

What a struggle. Giovanni stared at the wall. He was sitting in his press office trying to plan an article on the future of Venice. He was supposed to draw together all the attractions of Venice that could be stimulated into prosperity. The Mayor would add the inspirational passages about the golden glow that would encompass Venice shortly after his next reelection.

Giovanni called up his template: WHAT, WHERE, WHEN, HOW, WHY, WHO, and started to make notes on Churches, Museums, Music, the Ghetto, the Biennales, the Film Festival; local festivals: Regata, Voga Longa, Redentore, Salute, Carnival; Commerce: masks, lace, glass, baubles-bangles-beads, art dealers, antiques, jewelry, fashion. This was a bore. *Roba da matti!* What madness! He'd forgotten tourism. *Magari!* Would that he could! But that was the part that really interested politicians—revenue without a vote attached.

Brekekekex, ko-ax, ko-ax, Brekekekex, ko-ax. Giovanni answered. "Irene?"

"Hello Baby. I'm just walking into San Luca on my way home to make lunch. Do you want to come down and have a coffee? And could you bring your keys?"

Giovanni was glad for the break. As he walked through the lobby, Gigi hailed him. He had just come on duty. He brought over an envelope.

"Here's a copy of an article I found on the Mayor's desk the other day. It's a secret report from England on MOSE, the movable floodgates. They just got it back from the translator."

"Great, Gigi, thanks. I'll let you know what I learn from it."

Giovanni found Irene at the bar in Rosa Salva. He put

the article on the counter. "Look what Gigi just gave me." Irene picked it up and looked inside.

"Oh, I forgot to tell you. I was telling my Americans on Sunday about MOSE and why it had that acronym because of Moses separating the waters. They told me a joke about Cecil B. DeMille filming the Red Sea bit in *The Ten Commandments*. He had three cameras set up just to be sure he got it on film, since it was costing a fortune."

"Like MOSE?" offered Giovanni.

"*Sì,*" said Irene. "So DeMille gives the signal: Action! Cameras! They roll back the sea: *whoooooom!* The Israelites cross, everyone gets onto the shore, they let the waters roll back, *boom-de-booom-boooom,* and it's all over. DeMille radios the first cameraman: How did it go?

"'*Madonna!*' says the first cameraman. 'The lens steamed over.'

"'*Mio Dio!*' says DeMille. He radios the second cameraman. 'How was it?'

"'*Disastro!*' says the cameraman. 'The cable got wet.'

"'*Dannazione!*' says DeMille. He rings the last cameraman. 'Is everything okay?'

"'*Sì, sì.* Ready when you are, CB!'"

"*Dio mio,*" said Giovanni laughing. "I wonder if MOSE will work like that—uh-oh, too late. Okay, Dolly. I have to get ready to see the Mayor this afternoon on the Future of Venice article. Here's my keys. I'll be home pretty soon; I have to be back here at three."

*

The next day Giovanni spent the morning reviewing his notes from the meeting with the Mayor about the future of Venice. Grandi had acted as though Venice were his personal property and treated Giovanni like an employee. Giovanni wanted to get rid of both articles as quickly as he could. It was clear that he was not going to be allowed to write about Venice's future in the context of its past. Mayor Grandi was only interested in recreating Venice as a quasi-modern, quasi-convenient suburb of Mestre with mass tourism as its main business.

Giovanni had been seething when he got back to the office. He had written:

Erstwhile Empress

When Venice married for the second time, jilting the romantic but ne'er-do-well partner of her best years, The Sea, in favor of noisy, smoking, Mainland, she was caught on the rebound. She had suffered a series of sad affairs—the worst with a French general who made off with her riches and tried to hurt her name. But for Mainland the match was a chance in a million. After all, he was growing stronger and richer by the day; what he needed now was a little touch of class. She flattered his image. He encouraged her frivolity. He prospered. And

82

she? . . . And she, the erstwhile Empress of the Sea, became his Little Wife, *la mogliettina*—a trophy on the arm of Mainland, living on her looks.

He doubted that he would ever find a way to use this, but he saved it anyway.

Giovanni was relieved when half past twelve rolled around. He left the *Municipio* for the day and set out for the Marciana Library. As he walked toward the Frezzeria, he telephoned Irene. Her cell phone blared:

> *Tarara-BOOM-tiay,*
> *Did you get yours today? . . .*

When the message service came on, he rang off and dialed again. He always had to ring twice to give her time to find her phone.

"Hello. Are you on your way home? Don't forget I won't be back for lunch; I'm going to the library. I'll get something at Il Bacaro. I have to write that guidebooks article for the Mayor."

As soon as he walked into the restaurant he spotted Professor Faleiro, sitting alone reading a journal. As Giovanni neared his table, Faleiro looked up.

"Giovanni!" The Professor stood up and gestured

towards the chair opposite. "Sit down and have lunch with me. I was hoping you'd show up one of these days."

Giovanni put his coat on a neighboring chair and sat down. "I came here to find you. I'm on my way to the Marciana to do that article on guidebooks."

"No problem: Most of the books are right there in the reading room. You can start with Sanudo and Sansovino. There are some foreign ones upstairs, and I'll order some books for you from the stacks so you can make it a bit recherché and maybe teach the Mayor some respect."

"It only has to be acceptable. I don't think I'll get paid, so I don't want to waste too much time on it. What are you working on?"

"I'm supposed to be writing a lecture on Venetian Literature for some American millionaires who are coming in June. They want something light with Casanova and Goldoni. Here's that article about Shakespeare's Venetian mistress." He pulled a reprint from his briefcase on the chair beside him. "Ever heard of her? She was descended from the musical family Bassano who worked for the Doge in St. Mark's and then went to London to work for Henry VIII and stayed on. This article says that the family was almost certainly Jewish and that she was almost certainly the famous Dark Lady of Shakespeare's sonnets."

"It's hard to remember," said Giovanni, looking at the article, "that this frivolous backwater once counted in the world. Sorry. Writing for the Mayor is putting me in a bad mood."

"I can imagine," nodded the Professor.

"My problem is that I want so much to think well of Venice and hold out hope for the future. I'm always looking for its divine essence, the quiddity that makes it so wonderful, something that will save it."

"Aren't we all," smiled the Professor, "searching for its soul so we can save it?"

"I'll tell you something strange that happened to me a few days ago," said Giovanni. "I saw something amazing in the sky. I haven't mentioned it to anyone, not even Irene. No one else saw it."

"Not so fast. I'll bet *I* did. I was sitting at my desk talking to my assistant, who's leaving to take a research grant. While he was working out his termination benefits, I felt a sudden urge to stand up and look out the window. And there it was—something silvery flying by very fast. I guess it must have been a flying saucer. Is that what you saw?"

Giovanni nodded.

"It *was* amazing, wasn't it," the Professor continued. "So beautiful, so . . . so ethereal. So fleeting." He put his hand over his eyes and took a deep breath. "It made me think of my son." He looked up. "Anything that touches me makes me think of my son. It's like a default key. I can't help it."

"I didn't know you had a son," said Giovanni. "What happened to him?"

"One of those Saturday-night accidents out in the Veneto, the ones you read about in the *Gazzettino* on Monday mornings: kids driving around after a party. It happened eight years ago. It might as well have been yesterday." He folded his hands under his chin. "Thank God for our daughter. Without her I don't think we could have lived through it."

"I had no idea," said Giovanni. "I'm so sorry. I can see why you were moved. I was too. It seemed like a vision."

"I suppose," said Professor Faleiro, "we look to the sky for signs from God, like the rainbow. I never thought about it before, but I always try to share the sighting of a rainbow."

"I do too. I suppose that's why I was so disappointed that no one around me saw it: I had no one to share it with. My father saw Halley's Comet twice and talked about it like he was among the elect."

"Oh." Faleiro nodded. "Halley's Comet links the ages. It's the star in Giotto's Nativity."

"That was one of the things my father loved about it— having something in common with Giotto. He always hoped they would someday prove that the Bethlehem star was Halley's Comet."

"Anyway," continued Faleiro, "I was going to telephone you if I didn't see you this week. My assistant is leaving.

He's received a grant to finish his book on early palaces in Venice. He's made some important discoveries and wants to get it published. Did I tell you he found out that the palace we now call Palazzo Gritti-Pandin, which was supposed to have been built by the Capellos, is actually the earliest Patristi palace on record. It's owned by that English lord, or maybe his wife."

"Oh, I know which one," said Giovanni. "Irene is helping Lady Nolesworthy set up the mezzanine for holiday apartments."

"I was wondering whether you would like to have the job. You'd be my last assistant before I retire so it would only last a few years, unless I got some grants to go on with certain projects. But it would put you in a position to get something else if you wanted to continue doing research. I'd enjoy working with you. Talk it over with Irene. You could still do some journalism, but you wouldn't have much free time."

"Can I say yes right now?"

"I'd be delighted. As soon as you've cleared away these articles, come over to the office and we'll get the paperwork started. And then you and Irene should come for dinner. I'll invite my daughter and her husband."

They walked towards the Marciana under the arches of the Procuratie Nuove, both of them vaguely aware, as they passed under those arches, of those who had walked there before them, like the Bassano family, musicians to the Doge, on their way to work. Giovanni was troubled.

"When I saw the Mayor yesterday, he told me that the article on the future of Venice had to include the new hotels. I even have to go and look at hotels in Mestre and out by the airport."

"The sooner you're out of that game the better. Just look at those crowds lined up to be herded through the Basilica," said Professor Faleiro standing in the arch at the end of the Procuratie. "Look at how many people there are in the world. And they all travel. Only a few years ago you could wander in the Basilica just as you liked. Do you want to go in?"

"Not with that line."

"No, come over to the side. The guard knows me. I go in with the worshipers." They went into the side chapel and stood for a moment. Professor Faleiro went over to a shrine, put in a coin, and lit a candle. He came back. "I can never resist."

"Do you believe in it?"

"Believe in it? To do what? I never ask for anything. It's one of those religious things that I don't *not* believe in. We all live in hope."

Giovanni looked around. "I wonder what the Jewish Bassanos felt like working here. Like hypocrites?"

"Maybe not. It might have been pure expedience: Render unto the Doge that which is the Doge's—the right to call his employees Christian. You can be sure there was no better music job in Venice. An offer from the Doge would have been something to aim for, not to resist. And look where it took them: straight to the court of Henry VIII."

"I wonder," said Giovanni, "if a kind of informal ecumenism existed in Venice at that time in spite of the Ghetto."

"Possibly. I was talking to the English *reverendo* after dinner one evening, and he told me he thought the churches near the Ghetto had been named St. Job and St. Jeremiah—*not* Roman Catholic saints, remember—as a friendly gesture."

"Maybe a person could have an 'aesthetic' conversion," said Giovanni. "A beautiful church, combined with glorious music, especially of his own making, could have a profound effect on a man."

They passed through the great portal of the Marciana Library into a cloistered world that was one of Giovanni's favorite places. Historic, beautiful, civilized, and no tourists—it was almost too good to be true. Professor Faleiro went into the main reading room with Giovanni to order the books he'd promised to have sent down and then continued on his way upstairs. Giovanni walked over to a table near the huge stone effigy of Petrarch, looking down like a god in his temple, and left his laptop and his note pad. He went to the center bookshelves and pulled out Sanudo and Sansovino.

He carried them back to the table, sat down, opened his computer, and pulled up his file on Guidebooks. He thought for a second, then pulled up his file on the Future of Venice as well, just in case anything came to him. Giovanni leaned back and opened one of the early guidebooks: *VENETIA: Città Nobilissima et Singolare. Francesco Sansovino, MDLXXXI. VENICE: Most Noble and Unique City.* He started to skim the pages. He could tell the archaic language was going to make him sleepy; he shouldn't have drunk that wine with lunch. Something caught his eye: *This is the city that astonishes the whole world.* What a wonderful sentence. Would anyone write that today? He looked up at Petrarch's intelligent face and beautiful hands with the long graceful fingers spreading over his book. In Petrarch's day Venice must have been astonishing. Centuries later in Sansovino's time it was obviously still astonishing. But today? No. Centuries ago travelers approaching Venice by ship marveled to see the distant domes and towers rising out of the sea like the birth of Venus. Some people said that the name Venice echoed Venus. Giovanni wondered whether Venice would ever astonish again. What would it take to bring it back? The spirit must still be there hiding among the lost ideas and buried links that Faleiro sometimes found. Venetians still regard themselves as somehow blessed, a chosen people. Petrarch's solemn face conceded nothing. Giovanni returned to the book. *They gave the city the name VENETIA as if to say Veni etiam, come again.* He had never heard that before. Giovanni propped up the book so he could copy the sentence. He typed:

> *They gave the city the name VENETIA as if to say Veni etiam, come again.*

Come to think of it there *was* something he had heard before. Someone had spoken that phrase recently; he could still hear it in his ear. It was that woman on Sunday morning: He will *come again,* she said.

He stared at Petrarch for a long time wondering. *Veni etiam, come again. This is the city that astonishes the whole world.* Giovanni's thoughts drifted to the Accademia Bridge where he had chanced upon Professor Faleiro meditating about Giuseppe Treves and the Jews of Venice. And how was it that Faleiro, a Jew exactly like himself, had been drawn to the window at the precise instant that the sparkling disk flashed across the Venetian sky? Why had so many Jews congregated in Venice and merged from the Ghetto into the mainstream of Venetian life? Why did Venice look to the East? Why did Venice protect Jerusalem? Why did two columns stand in the Piazzetta like a pair of trees? Ideas rushed towards him like stars on the night of San Lorenzo. He couldn't catch them all. He had to think. He put his head on his arms and shut his eyes, but he was still looking out over the Grand Canal with Professor Faleiro. They were watching in breathless silence as the clouds darkened to sanguine and the sky paled to incandescence.

Something strange was happening. This time he was not alone. Would they see the disk again together? No . . . wait . . . the clouds . . . they were parting like the Red Sea; the sky . . . was rolling back . . . and he, Giovanni . . . could see descending between the clouds a perfect firmament, after Tiepolo, with the Titian Christ from San Salvatore on one foot skating down from heaven. Beside him Moses showed his tablets and held his ground ahead of jostling saints and prophets by diverse Venetian hands. Aloft in a fiery radiance all His own, the foreshortened God the Father from the ceiling of the Accademia looked down like a kindly rabbi on the place where Jews and Christians dwelt as one. Venetians cheering and weeping for joy crowded the Grand Canal with trailing banners and fluttering raiment, like Regatta day but without boats. They were walking on water, like the big freeze of 1929 when the glassworkers walked to Murano.

Giovanni sat up and wiped his eyes. He would never again give up hope. Things change. The time of tribulation was winding down, the time of contemplation near at hand. He had been beckoned to side with the angels, no more to jump and caper while the Mayor cranked the tune. From now on he would write as he pleased. Even the Doge didn't tell the Bassanos how to write music. He pulled his laptop towards him and deleted his file on the Future of Venice. He laid his head on his arm again to wait for the guide-books. He closed his eyes to see if he could have the dream again. Later he would go outside and ring Irene to tell her the good news. He would play the monkey only one more time. His fingers tapped on the keys:

qwwerrta Bothnpl in xctrdc onezrced Faithpimehy unanimousmolpi thoughpoikl sad, Withx causejytr for5mkop evils8ycf past,poiu yetxfgy muchAsd moreAZW cheer'd Withzxcvt meditationqweru onsdruy6 the9iuj happy end.

MOBILITY

To *feeel* sharp and be on the ball, du-*dee*-du . . ." How did that jingle go? Donald Flower felt so good he wanted to jig down the lane to his car. But he kept a grip on himself. Instead, he turned and gave a big wave to the crowd that was calling his name from the stands—"Hey, Donner, go!" "Flower Power!" "Dasher Donner!" He stood for a moment smiling with his arm raised like Caesar. Today to conquer Monte Carlo, and tomorrow on to Rome? No. He was on his way to Venice, even though, as he stood there, he would never have believed it.

But the choice was not his to make. Donald Flower didn't know it yet, but he was about to plight his troth. The trip to Venice would be a wedding present from the parents of his Italian bride, Prima Caravalli, editor of the new lifestyle magazine *Fast Lane*. She had a godfather there, Danilo Peto, who was big in local politics and would want to show off the glamorous couple at a dinner party. And Prima would be all for it.

*

As for Donald Flower the first time he set foot in Venice he thought it was the damnedest place he'd ever seen. What was the point of a city without cars? He couldn't imagine how anyone could live there. Brooding about this first visit four years later, when his career got caught with a stop-go penalty and he had leisure to reflect, Flower came up with the notion that the so-called *Serenissima* had been out to get him from their first encounter. Prima didn't believe it; she told him he'd better put on a hat in case a squirrel came by looking for nuts. On the other hand, it was evident that his life took a number of unexpected turns because of that encounter. For example, it was odd from any point of view that after a single night in Venice he should awaken with the unaccountable urge to leave his bride asleep and slip away for what his father called "a little constitutional" before breakfast. Even stranger was the fact that on this early morning excursion he made the profound and unexpected discovery that walking in Venice exhilarated him like a drug—so much so that after lunch he was stirred to send Prima out shopping so he could walk some more. In effect, it was the racing around and around that fascinated him. Losing himself in the narrow alleys that suddenly flared out into campos or cantered up to the Grand Canal only to drop off at the brink, he felt he was on the track of something momentous, even forbidden. The feeling drew him like a siren. That broad, twisting Canal sliding like a boa through a forest was his prey. Curving this way and that, it would give him the slip, then catch his eye from an unexpected spot, glaring between buildings or reclining in gray-green insolence at the bottom of a broad calle where to Flower's mind it definitely should not have been. It was always taunting, always throwing down the gauntlet. At least that was how he interpreted it.

In fact, the great heart of Venice was doing its best to avoid him, but it only succeeded in making matters worse. The challenge spurred Donald Flower; it made him walk faster and faster. He almost ran. It got into his brain. As he hurried this way and that, he marveled at how his distracted mind coursed through arguments, ideas, designs, plans—anything it found stalled in his memory. Something in Venice lurched him into high gear and made him focus on other things. If he could go on like this, he reckoned, he could become a phenomenon. He decided to come back often. This exhilaration, he reasoned, was a mysterious force exerted by the maze, which would drain away as he learned his way around. To put off the inevitable, he tried never to repeat the same routes and avoided so much as glancing at a Venetian map. Still, he knew that after years of driving he had a faculty for subconsciously memorizing patterns, and that he would soon fathom it all, even walking. For him it was a foregone conclusion that Venice familiar would be the equivalent of

Venice futile. But what he eventually fathomed instead was that there was more to this pursuit than first met the eye.

The euphoria that Donald Flower enjoyed in Venice was a feeling not without precedent, though his habitual euphoria sprang from a different genesis. A year to the day before that first compelling walk in Venice he had swaggered down the lane to his car feeling all the power of the god within. In fact his personal manager, Inman Blunckaie, had said that morning when he handed him the powder, "They say the difference between men and gods is the difference between coffee and coke. Let's hope it's so, kid; you need a win." Donald Flower snorted in disbelief. But he soon knew apotheosis when it shot through him in one splendiferous, dazzling rush: Oh, yes. Yes! Being a god suited him. He felt cockier than ever: no self-doubts, no raw edges, and in a flash the laws of feasibility banished to bloody hell. Oh, yes! Not by coincidence, that was the day his Formula One racing career took off.

For Inman Blunckaie this Grand Prix victory came not so much as a joy as a goddamned relief. This Flower klutz was more than his discovery; he was his burden. Blunckaie had been scouting Formula Three for the Formula One alpha team when he fingered Flower as a promising driver and urged the team to give him a contract. But the reaction of Flower to his great break was not to be believed: He turned petulant and behaved like a general bad sport. He was by nature self-centered which put him out of sync with the team culture. At first his teammates excused his behavior as a privilege of genius. However, as he persistently missed the money, he progressively lost credibility. Blunckaie racked his brain to bring out the winning talent he could have sworn was there. By a stroke of luck he complained to his old mother who came up with an unexpected solution. She found among her notebooks from the great house where she had worked the name and phone number of the man who used to deliver the magic powders—as well as various pills and cigarettes for weekend parties—which, according to the butler, gave the master of the house his trademark confidence and cutting wit. In any case it solved Blunckaie's immediate problem with Donald Flower.

When they worked together in Formula One, Flower had no idea that Inman Blunckaie had spent his early childhood in Venice. All he knew about him was that he was a dislikable foreign runt who made himself useful, mainly through his weasel-like facility for popping through windows of opportunity less accommodating than a cat flap. It was he—for the duration of Dashing Donner's meteoric success on the racetrack—who against all odds somehow managed to substitute the sample taken in the morning before the race for the one taken afterwards.

Blunckaie was a child of Venice in the antique tradition—he was a refugee, the posthumous child of a mine-
clearance worker in Czechoslovakia. He and his mother
had escaped first to Italy, where their strange name was invented by a creative clerk at the Italian border. They went
to Venice, where his mother found a job as a maid in the
Bauer Grünwald Hotel and kept a sharp eye out for a
chance to better herself. From the hotel's famous concierge
she learned which guests were most important and soon attracted the attention of the wife of a British peer, who dispatched her back to London as her resident housekeeper.
Lady Longstaff even paid to pack off Inman to boarding
school so his mother should have no distractions. Thus the
Blunckaies found their way. For Inman, boarding at school
was a chance to pick up new survival techniques. For his
mother, looking in from the wings at power and privilege
was a chance to pick up excellent scraps of wisdom which
she passed on to her boy.

Donald Flower was much better placed on Fortune's
wheel. The son of a diplomat, he had grown up with the
opportunity to drop friends every few years and start again
elsewhere. He moved among capital cities and acquired a
taste for glamour. Moreover, he was the baby of the family
and much indulged. Whereas his older brother, Jack, took
up the cultivated interests and manners of his father, baby
Don inherited the sporty cussedness of his mother's big
brother. When the two boys were together at school, Jack

was known as Elder Flower while Donald earned the ironic pendant Cordial. Once embarked on his racing career, Donald Flower also became known by sportscasters and journalists as Dasher Donner, the Donner, or Donny Boy, while the smart alecks around the tracks generally called him Monsieur de Flower or D. Flowerer, but not to his face.

Flower spotted Prima Caravalli when she was working for Italian *Vogue* in Monte Carlo setting up a fashion feature with a photographer during the Grand Prix. She was standing with her hands on her hips down by the harbor. The wind flattened her dress against her six-foot frame and sent her long hair flying out in waves like a mermaid's tresses. She was looking over the scene as though she might send it away and call for another. When Dasher Donner saw her, his blood pressure jumped like a Jack Russell. "Holy Moses, what a chassis!" He sighed. "That is One Classy Number. Wait a minute, Flower," he counseled himself. "Get a grip. Right here in these shoes is another of the same. Come on. You are Canadian," he reminded himself. "You can speak French. You are the son of a diplomat, a citizen of the world. You are almost famous. This could be a match made in heaven."

She seemed to sense his presence and turned. Her gaze spoke her heart: *What are you—last night's fish and chips?* Flower was thrilled. He presented himself to the girl of his dreams and learned what he might have guessed: She was an Italian career girl. She speculated as they talked that she might be able to use a nice-looking driver for the feature. She accepted his invitation to dinner and, soon after, his proposal of marriage. She was half a head taller than he, but they looked smashing together.

Three years and two babies later, Prima Flower struck a deal with her husband. He could have as many traveling secretaries as he might need to keep him happy, but he had to let her concentrate on her career. *And* he had to stay away from the nannies because she didn't have time to find a new one every six months. Don Flower was not the man to accept anyone else's idea of a deal, but he accepted this one. For one thing, she knew his weakness: their sons might have been bastards they looked so much like their father and for this he loved them even as he loved himself. Also, Donald Flower may not have had a noble mind but he had a love of fame. His wife had the means to attract celebrities—there was hardly a soul in the haut monde, the beau monde, or even the demimonde who wasn't longing to be immortalized in *Fast Lane*.

A curious exception was Inman Blunckaie, who from childhood had cultivated that neglected art of being in-visible. Inman wished to have no enemies, no special friends, no politics, no debts, and no principles except to stay out of trouble and out of the spotlight. One piece of wisdom his mother passed on to him, overheard while serving at table, was from a military man who described his favorite advice to junior officers. "I say stick your finger in a glass of water and pull it out. The impression it leaves is a measure of how indispensable you are." Blunckaie listened to his mother and took the idea to heart. Sometimes, even as a grown man when he felt a bit down he would dip his finger in a glass of water, pull it out, and take pleasure in how perfectly the intervention vanished into nothing.

Inman didn't do drugs himself. He was wary as a snake and preferred to stay on the ground. Unlike Don Flower who, once he got a sense of himself fully empowered, never felt like he was himself any other way and resented Blunckaie's cautious control of his supply. For Flower, the new self was the true self, the man for whom the stature of colleagues and competitors diminished like images in a rearview mirror and might as well have been so many flies on the horizon. "As flies to wanton boys, are we to the gods" perfectly described Flower's regard for the mere mortals who got in his way. One day after a bad performance on the track—a humiliation that could easily have been averted by a little generosity on Blunckaie's part—Flower let go with lashings of sarcasm. He found Blunckaie standing in the pit watching the mechanics.

"Oh, there's my wonderful manager. Did you come to enjoy your share of the day's success? Since you put nothing into it, what do you expect to get out of it? I'll tell you what. You can have all the credit for today's performance. All of it. Which is nothing. Which is exactly what you contributed."

"I came by to see how the cars are coming, Don," said Blunckaie who understood his client's mood. They had addressed Blunckaie's rules of supply and Flower's demands before. "Mick and Joe are trying to get the diffuser right." Blunckaie liked the mechanics and admired their constant efforts behind the scenes to improve the cars. They were tireless, always checking their work and never pushing the blame onto someone else.

"I'm glad you're worried about the mechanics," snapped Flower. "Maybe they would like to take you onto their team." He glared at the mechanics, who shook their heads to say they wanted no part of it and walked away. Blunckaie hated to be made a cause of conflict between the mechanics and a star driver. It was an ugly moment, but Flower didn't relent.

"By the way, those photographs you made. I showed them to my wife. She says whoever took them is a has-been. She's sending someone better. What am I paying you for anyhow? I thought you could do some things."

Blunckaie recoiled. Donald rejoiced; he had as good as swatted him flat. It wasn't Seven at One Blow, but he was as tickled as the little tailor anyhow.

In fact, Donald Flower in his physical person was not half as big as he felt. He was barely 5'8¼" tall. For racing, a large physique is not an advantage. Dominance hides in the character. Even so, he took a rare pleasure in towering over Blunckaie who was only five-foot-five. But the difference that those three-and-a-half inches made in their characters was beyond Flower's ken. What Nature had denied to Blunckaie in height, it had made up for in determination—in *grinta*. The little man never lost sight of his objective, and he never changed course without a compelling motive.

Blunckaie was taken aback by Flower's treatment of him. All the more because he had never liked this bullyboy, even though he had launched him himself. He had never gloried in Flower's success. He had stayed the course out of policy. At this point he felt free to move on. He put a cheerful face on it, threw Flower a long-distance high five minus four, and left, wishing he had the means to teach this dude that three inches, six inches, twelve inches—real or feel-real—was not enough to browbeat Blunckaie.

Soon after this falling out, Donald Flower was summoned by the race authorities about an irregularity they didn't want to get into the press. A test had proved positive. What would he like to do about it? He understood they were offering him an ultimatum: "We have to take a hard line even though it is painful to us as well. You know the saying—'If your hand offend you, cut it off.' We have no choice, Don."

Donald was outraged. "You mean 'If your nose offends you, cut it off and spite your face?' Fine, then. I'll take a powder." Later he improved these lines for private circulation: "I told them I was clean and could have sued them, but I was ready to change careers so I let them go. They were grateful, and I still work with them."

He called a press conference and retired from racing. He let it be known that he had the kind of ambition aptly known as drive and made it clear to his audience that as a businessman he would be doing interesting things, even extraordinary things, in the world of Formula One and that they would find plenty to follow in his future movements which would include sponsorship, track management, and talent scouting. The message was: Watch this space. Nobody loved fame more than Donald Flower, and he wasn't going to give it up.

Setting up DF Mobility Ltd. meant changing his life. He put its headquarters in Monte Carlo, with a branch in London, where Prima had her magazine and where he spent as much time as he could. He hired a Spanish beauty, Delia Moor, to help with Spain and South America, and a pretty American civil engineer, Patti Tushman, who had done graduate projects on the Sepang and Bahrain circuits and would manage his proposals for the Monte Carlo improvements. Even more important, he had to find someone for the Italian side. He had not forgotten the good effect that Venice had on him so he planned to spend time there working on important projects, and he also had to build his contacts at Imola and Monza. He needed someone special.

Rosi Rosso was one of those pretty girls with a certain past and an uncertain future. She was a good translator, a moderately efficient secretary, and had so much ambition that she didn't know what to do. Whenever she got a job she had only to look around her to see any number of jobs that she could do better than the present incumbent, especially if it was a man. The anomaly was that it was usually these very men who hired and promoted her.

She had awakened to the fact, and it weighed on her consciousness, that she would soon be on the wrong side of thirty and her long-term prospects were at present nil. Even more vexing, she had so many times posed as a wife, she felt she had practically an enforceable right to become one. So when she applied to Prima Flower for a job with *Fast Lane,* she hardly expected this worldly-wise editor to pass her like a box of chocolates to her handsome husband. The poor girl worried all the way home where she took a hard look at herself in the mirror to see what had gone wrong. But her interview with Donald Flower the following day relieved her doubts. And by the time she accepted the position later that same afternoon as his translator-cum-secretary-cum-travel-assistant, she knew the lay of the land. He, for his part, was also satisfied. Her first job was to make a long-term booking for a suite at the Bauer where they could work on projects.

On one of these working visits to Venice when he was playing hide-and-seek with his great serpent Grand Canal,

Donald Flower came across old Blunckaie in deep reverie sitting outside a bar in Campo San Giacomo dell'Orio watching three little schoolgirls in smocks and a very small boy in a diaper playing a game of hopscotch.

"Well, look at you," said Flower, stopping in front of Blunckaie's table with his arms akimbo.

Blunckaie looked up. He rose slowly to his feet and clasped his hands behind his back. "And look at you. What brings you here?"

"I'm a consultant now. I like working here. I keep a suite at the Bauer. My girls like to come here." He grinned.

"I guess that justifies the expense," said Blunckaie.

"Do you have a place here?"

"I bought one for my mother when she retired."

"And what are you doing now, Blunckaie?"

"I represent manufacturers for the racing market: Michelin, Automotive Products. I work with mechanics now."

"Interesting. Why don't you come have lunch with me tomorrow at the Lido. I'm taking my Italian assistant to the Hotel des Bains. We've got a motorboat from the Bauer at one."

"Yeah. Okay."

"One o'clock," said Flower, looking around the campo, "sharp." He picked a calle and struck out into the un-known for one last time.

*

In the morning Blunckaie rang to confirm lunch. Flower was already up and took the call in the sitting room at the desk. As he talked, he was idly leafing through papers that Rosi had emptied from her briefcase. Flower had forgotten, in their surprise encounter, how much Blunckaie bored him. As he talked he studied a photocopied page of notes scrawled on a busy background, trying to make out what it was. All at once he realized that he was examining a map of Venice. He got off the phone fast and rushed out of the room without so much as a word to Rosi, still asleep in bed, slamming the door as he went. He had to get the image out of his mind and fast. "Damn that girl!" He ran down the four flights of steps, across the lobby and out the front door. He wondered how much he'd taken in. He'd been having the feeling for days that Venice was about to be demystified. He was following the signs to the Rialto, where he planned to cross the bridge and lose himself in the wilderness of calles in Santa Croce, when he came into Campo San Salvatore and found an improvised plywood structure in the center of the campo. It was covered with photographs and posters with bold black headlines denouncing AN OUT-RAGE! A GREAT SWINDLE! They suited his mood; he stopped to look. The text was an elaborate explanation of the MOSE mobile flood barriers—which had long been in the news as the best way to save Venice from the increasing tendency to flood—only to denounce them as unworkable and fraudulent. As he read, something clicked. He realized that he didn't care anymore about the map and the mystery of Venice; he had seen the track of the Grand Canal. This MOSE project was just the thing he was looking for. It was bound to be expensive, and it was right up his street. He was having dinner with Avvocato Peto that same evening. Peto would know all about this project and could set him up with the Mayor. He went back to the Bauer to have breakfast with Rosi.

Paolo Grandi, Mayor of Venice, claimed Venetian descent through his children. He paid his first visit to Venice's town hall, Ca' Farsetti, while still a law student at the University of Bologna in order to marry Silvia Trevisan. On that occasion the parents of the bride gave the newlyweds a small palace all their own in Venice, not far from the Fondamenta Nuova where Grandi and his colleagues on the town council hoped one day to be able to board a subway train to the mainland. On the ground floor of this palace Grandi set up his law offices and from this base launched his career as a prosperous notary and a bounding political force. In due course his talent for business and his many contacts in that world made him an obvious choice for mayor at a time when there were big projects in the offing. His detractors maintained that his talent for large projects extended only to the bidding and to the assignment of contracts, that he had little interest in their actual execution; whereas his supporters maintained, in his defense, a discreet silence.

As Mayor of Venice, Grandi lived up to his name: He got big. As a rising power he had been svelte, nimble, and occasionally acerbic. Now, after a record-breaking ten years as mayor, he was swollen, shuffling, and almost always genial.

When Donald Flower went to meet the Mayor of Venice, he had prepared his lines and felt at the top of his form. He couldn't help strutting like a seven-foot cowboy as he swung into the *androne* of the *Municipio*. He saluted the guards *en passant* with "The Mayor is waiting for me" and took the steps three at a time. When he arrived at the Mayor's office, the secretary was being alerted by the guards; she put down the telephone and stood up to intercept him. She walked in front of him to the office door. "Mr. Flawvor," she announced with studied boredom, and stalked out.

Donald Flower strode halfway into the room and stopped. Mayor Grandi gripped the arms of his chair, leaned forward and rose with effort to his feet. It might have been a meeting between Zeus and Buddha.

"How do you do, Mr. Flower," said the Mayor, sinking back into his chair and waving towards the nearest armchair.

"How do you do, Mr. Mayor," said Flower, too energized to accept the offer to sit. He addressed him standing like a great genie with his arms crossed. Nevertheless, the historic encounter went surprisingly well. They had more in common than they might have expected. The Olympian was enticed by this scheme to subdue the sea. His Amplitude saw votes in it, plus he owned a ground floor compromised by high water. The Soaring Potency had access to large sums of money. The Enthroned Power had access to the experts making the plans. Emboldened, the Visitor admitted that his interest in the floodgates was less altruistic than financial. The First Citizen acknowledged this common ground between them and arranged for him to meet some specialists.

From the experts Flower learned what he needed to know about how the movable gates would sit invisible, deep under the water until called to perform and how they would rise. He went back to England and put Patti Tushman in charge of a group of engineers familiar with the Thames Barrier, which was just as good, already working, and more accessible. Also, if he was going to win the financial backing he needed, he wanted consultants who could speak English. He told her to put it on a fast track, not to let it hang around. There were already too many people involved in Venice who might slow it down. He asked Blunckaie to come on board practically in the role of factotum for the girls. He needed Blunckaie's steadiness. In ac-

tual fact, the job was beneath Blunckaie, and Flower
thought he was going to have to offer him something better, but for some reason—Blunckaie himself couldn't say—
he accepted the job without demur and worked hard to get
the study finished in a hurry.

Bouncing across the Lagoon in a water taxi from Venice airport, Flower opened his laptop and started clicking through
his PowerPoint presentation. He turned to Blunckaie.

"Can you remember the names of the government
people who are going to come to this?"

"Sure."

Flower took a pen and a notebook from his pocket.
"Shoot."

"Delmuro, D-e-l-m-u-r-o; Marchiori, M-a-r-c-h-i-o-
r-i; Calmar, C-a-l-m-a-r; Russo, R-u-s-s-o; Bullo, B-u-l-l-o;
Puppo, P-u-p-p-o; Volo, V-o-l-o. Then there will be the
local industrialists, the ones with the venture capital, who
may want to join the ones you already have in Monte
Carlo and England and so on."

Flower sat reading the names. "Are these the only ones
I need to know?"

"Yeah. The industrialists will want to stay in the background until they're sure they're interested. Remember,
they don't know anything about how you're going to work
this miracle salvation."

"Yeah. You know Grandi had that idea of putting the barrier in private ownership and leasing it to the city. I think he talked about an operating fee as well. Anyhow, we're on the same wavelength."

"What, money?"

Flower laughed, "Sounds good to me." He tore off the sheet of names and put it on the seat beside him. "I want you to take some photographs. Prima said she'd put some snaps in her news montage for me."

"Hey, that reminds me," said Blunckaie pulling a brown envelope from his briefcase. "Here are some photographs I took of Rosi and you at the Lido. She looks like a movie star. You both look like movie stars." He handed him a sheaf of photographs. Flower went through them, smiling. "She's a looker isn't she. Not as classy as Prima, but nice. You can see how she won Miss Swimsuit in the Miss Italia contest. She almost married a Venetian count."

"Why didn't she come today?"

"Oh I dunno. She didn't feel well. Something bothering her. She said she had to see her doctor. I wasn't pleased about it. I need her here. She flirts with these guys and it does me a lot of good." He closed his laptop and put it back in his shoulder bag. "She does me good in other ways too," he muttered as he pulled the zipper shut and put the strap on his shoulder. "You're quite helpful, Blunckaie, but there's a limit to what you can do for me. I mean you don't turn me on, Blunckaie."

"The feeling's mutual, Don," said Blunckaie, looking out the window at the passing palaces. "The feeling is quite totally mutual."

"Here." Flower handed him the photographs. "You keep these. I've got this other stuff to think about."

"They're for Rosi anyhow. I left a set for you back in London if you want them."

The taxi was pulling in at the Rialto.

"Here we are," said Flower. "This is it. *Twenty billion euros.* Gimme a headache powder, Blunckaie. I couldn't bring any because of the dogs."

"Sure." He reached in his pocket and pulled out an envelope labeled Nodolo Headache Remedy. "Take this one. Hold it up like this. The others are okay, but I couldn't get that one to stick shut again."

Flower got up to leave. Blunckaie picked up the notepaper from the seat. "Hey, what about these names?"

"Naw. I've memorized them."

"Well, you don't leave this stuff lying around. People don't like their names left in taxis," said Blunckaie putting the paper in his pocket. "You ought to learn a little consideration. I may have said that before."

Inside the meeting room a crowd was already milling around the broad dark boardroom table. There were twenty chairs arranged in a horseshoe around it. The front ones were already occupied. The table was set up with glasses and water bottles, note pads and pencils. At the end was a large screen and lectern. Blunckaie stayed long enough to check the electrical connections, take a few photographs, and see the presentation begin. He had seen it twice before but had been sworn to secrecy until today. The first time he saw it he couldn't believe his eyes. He decided to stay long enough to catch the first impact. Donald Flower went to the lectern and opened his computer.

"Hello. I asked Mayor Grandi to let me introduce myself so we could get straight into the presentation, which I might add, contains surprises for him as well as you. My name is Donald Flower. I first came to Venice on my honeymoon with my beautiful Italian wife. For a Formula One pilot, as I then was, it was a strange sensation being in this city, but somehow it fascinated me. I found I could come here and work as in no other place. I began to like it as much as my present hometown, Monte Carlo, where I won my Grand Prix and where I have been consulting on the upgrading of that fascinating urban track unique in the world. Here in Venice I keep an apartment at the Bauer and come with my staff when I have work to do. Recently I began work on a new Asian track. In my wanderings one afternoon I came upon a denunciation of the flood barrier MOSE. Luckily, I happened to be having dinner that evening with my good friend Avvocato Peto, who is here today. He explained to me the means by which the flood dams rise and lower and reassured me that the project is indeed viable and has a good name. I came to see Mayor Grandi about my interest in this project, and that is why we are all here today. I decided to pursue my researches in London, where a movable flood barrier is already in place. In the course of our discussion, Avvocato Peto also explained the problem of assuring for Venice an economy equal to the demands of these extremely costly measures of *salvaguardia,* of safeguarding the city. Without funding, nothing follows. I think that is true the world over. I have now completed a project with the help of engineers familiar with the Thames flood barriers and have adapted it into the much more elaborate and costly intervention that I recommend for Venice. I have in my travels for my work come across a number of contacts willing to underwrite this project and hope that some of you here today will add your support. I think this project answers all the needs of this fascinating but struggling city. Here begins our virtual tour."

When the lights went down and the first image flashed on the screen—a silvery rising highway flying out towards a lake then turning in a beautifully banked wide curve to the right—the politicians and the venture capitalists couldn't fathom at first where they were. Almost simultaneously they identified the white façade of the Salute where the low road in the foreground rushed towards the basin then curved up and around towards the Giudecca Canal, but the strangest reaction came from a journalist Blunckaie often saw in the *Municipio,* who put his hand up as if to shield a blow and gasped *"Christo!"* The gasp, the exclamation, these were just what Donald Flower wanted to get him started. After a quick lap over the entire circuit, he came back by the grandstand at the Pescheria where the virtual crowd rose and cheered. He took his auditors flying under the Rialto Bridge, down the Grand Canal with cheering crowds on the balconies, past the Peggy Guggenheim Collection with virtual people having lunch on the roof terrace as if it were a racecourse clubhouse. Around the bend in a stomach-churning swing with monks waving from the campanile of San Giorgio. Then along the Giudecca in front of the longest grandstand in the world giving a Mexican wave all the way down to the Molino Stucky. Then a glorious pass over the causeway through a beautiful chicane, then on and down into a virtual pit stop, up and out again onto the Grand Canal, past the railway station with its own grandstand, under the bridge past the casino, and back to the Rialto.

Flower showed the hydraulic systems, which raised the track from its resting place on the canal beds, as part of the same system that managed the floodgates. He showed the separate raising and lowering of the votive bridges for the Festa della Salute and the Festa del Redentore. He took them on a tour of the boxes at the Tronchetto. He showed the palaces, already the property of the city, that would enclose the mechanisms. Then he explained how much it would cost, and last of all he revealed how much money such an enterprise could bring to Venice. He had commissioned many studies. He brought in figures from Monte Carlo as the most comparable example for this incomparable project.

Blunckaie slipped out after the first gasp and went to join the bodyguards and security police in the security office. To give them a laugh, he told them what the VIPs were looking at in the auditorium. They couldn't believe it.

The racetrack isn't the best part, said Blunckaie, sharing their amusement. Ever since Flower had taken him into his confidence about this project, he had been secretly looking forward to watching Venice give this bully his comeuppance. "Do you know how much venture capital has to go into it?"

His audience stopped laughing. "How much?"

"Twenty billion euros!" said Blunckaie, waggling his head like an idiot.

But his auditors didn't laugh; they didn't even smile. They looked at each other.

"Guess what," said the policeman sitting behind the desk. "With that kind of money sloshing around, it's a shoo-in."

"No stopping it," said one of the bodyguards.

"For sure," said another.

They were all shaking their heads.

"That bastard," said the policeman watching the monitors. "He ought to go to jail."

"Not bloody likely," said one of the bodyguards. "It's the same old story: *Rubi poco, vai in galera; rubi tanto, fai carriera*—Steal a little, go to jail; steal a lot, make a career. Why'd you let him do it?" said one of the bodyguards.

They all shook their heads.

"I had no idea," said Blunckaie. "Not that I could ever stop him from doing anything. I can't believe you think he'll succeed. That makes me sick. I counted on Venice to trip him up. I never thought for one minute that he could get away with it.

"That Dog as a devil deified," murmured Blunckaie half to himself.

"The converse is more like it, from the looks of it," commented one of the bodyguards sitting next to Blunckaie.

They sat in silence each thinking about how powerful people can get away with anything in Venice; it was the Marghera Industrial Zone all over again.

"They'll be coming out soon," sighed Blunckaie. "I'm going down to the men's room." He picked up his briefcase and walked down the corridor. Inside, he balanced his briefcase on the basin and took out the envelope of photographs. He took the remaining powders from his pocket and dropped them inside. He had no use for them; better to get rid of them. The list of names he had picked up in the taxi was among them, but he didn't bother to pull it out. Let him have it. He sealed the envelope and slipped it in his pocket behind the newspaper. He walked back to the security office.

"Flower should be finishing," he said, looking at his watch as he sat down again.

Just then the door of the meeting room opened. The bodyguards jumped up and moved towards the open door. Noise filled the corridor. There was laughter and banter. The mood was festive. The policemen were right. Flower had won them over. Blunckaie's heart sank.

Donald Flower was approaching, surrounded by women chattering breathlessly, each one trying to hold his attention. Several of the men were chuckling and reaching over to pat him on the shoulder. The security police and the bodyguards threw Blunckaie a sullen look. Blunckaie swallowed and shifted in his seat. He got up.

Flower saw him. "Blunckaie, I'm going straight to the airport. I've decided to catch the next flight." That was typical. Flower always lammed it on an upswing. "There's something via Paris or Frankfurt. I want to get away. It's been a great day. I'm coming back to do the presentation again next week."

Flower was shaking hands with one industrialist after the other. "Ciao." *"Benissimo."* "My pleasure." "Ciao." "Looking forward to it." *"Grazie."* *"Molto gentile,* very kind." Mayor Grandi was beaming in the background, nodding his head in admiration and talking sotto voce to Marchiori and Volo.

Blunckaie wiggled in beside Flower as he moved towards the elevator. "Give me your briefcase, Donner. I'll check your tickets." Flower continued to shake hands as Blunckaie took the briefcase and turned around. He looked over the tickets and put them back. He slipped the photographs in the side pocket and worked his way to Flower's side. "Listen, Donner," said Blunckaie, handing him his briefcase, "those tickets are fine, and you've got that envelope of photographs for Rosi. I won't go straight back. I've decided to visit some cousins in Belgrade."

Flower ignored him. He stepped into the elevator still lecturing a group of men on issues of parameters and feasibility, sexy design, thrilling transformation, cutting edge, state of the art, new departure, modest projections, profit margins, and handsome returns. He still had his back to Blunckaie when the door rolled closed and he began his journey downward without bothering to say goodbye.

Blunckaie turned and walked back towards the security office. He addressed the policemen from the door. "You guys got friends out at airport security?"

"Yeah. Lots of 'em."

"He's on his way to the airport. Tell 'em to check out a brown envelope," said Blunckaie. He stepped forward to put a scrap of paper on the desk. "Here's my number. I'm turning off my cell, but you can leave a message if you need anything. Ciao."

"Ciao," said the policeman at the monitors watching a water taxi pull away. "There he goes."

"Bene, bene, bene," said the policeman at the desk, picking up the telephone.

FORTUNE

On the precise instant that Dieter von Thurigen turned the handle on the bedroom door, an explosion of Charleston music ripped through the house, making him jump back like he'd triggered a booby trap. *What in hell's name . . . ?* He stood for a minute straightening his back and taking three measured breaths before continuing his transit into the *salone*. *"We're all alone; no chaperone can get our nummmber."* The jazz tune jumped along the walls to the ceiling; it jived along the floor and capered like a gang of demented fauns. Dieter put his hand over his eyes. He deplored the desecration of this austere Venetian space, so reminiscent—as he'd observed on his arrival the day before—so reminiscent of the Capulet ballroom of his first *Romeo*.

"Bingo is working on his sound system," explained Beau from the settee.

"Bingo is a *pessst*," hissed Dieter as he crossed to the

credenza, trying not to mince in time to the music. *"There's something wild about you, child, that's so contaaagious; let's be outraaageous; let's misbehave!"* Dieter dropped ice cubes into a glass and poured out a double, then made it into a triple scotch, before arranging himself at the other end of the settee. *"And,"* he went on with energy, *"a prick*teaser!" Beauregard Benson raised his Old Fashioned glass and smiled, but he didn't like the remark. In fact, as much as he loved Dieter he wished he didn't feel quite so much at home here. But he didn't want to make an issue of it since he himself felt a little uncertain how to behave.

The truth was that Beau's beloved son, Bingo, had never in all his twenty-three years incurred his father's serious disapproval—not even when Beauregard and Carmenina were divorcing, and Bingo, merrier than ever, romped back and forth between his parents proffering useful information in exchange for praise, affection, sports cars, holidays, apartments—in short, anything his tiny heart desired. Now, at the express invitation of Bingo, who had barely a year ago claimed the family house in Venice for his primary residence, Beau and Dieter were in Venice on their first visit since assuming the public status of partners.

It was a difficult setting for Beau. Returned to the ambiance of his married life, he found himself once again stalked by the very demons he'd left to die in the closet. It was a grim surprise for him that they had, if anything,

gathered strength from their repose. As he sat waiting for
Dieter to join him for a drink before taking Bingo out for
dinner, he was wondering what had happened to the joy-
ous relief of five years ago when Bingo turned eighteen and
set his father free. And then, as if being back here in the
vitrine of Venice wasn't uncomfortable enough, Beau had
learned at lunch that Bingo was planning a dinner in
honor of his houseguests for the following evening that
would include Carmenina and her suitor, a Count Barbaro
from Rome, where she now lived. That pair too were coming at the express invitation of Bingo, but staying in a
hotel. Unlike Beau, Dieter was looking forward to the
dinner: he had no doubt that he was going to adore Carmenina. He seemed to be savoring the prospect of weaving
himself into the torn fabric of Beauregard's family life as
some sort of invisible mend. Beau counseled himself that
these ambitions probably stemmed from Dieter's not having a family of his own. His parents, the only family he
had, died decades ago when he was so engrossed in his
dancing career that he hardly noticed. But whatever the explanation, the whole situation made Beau feel exactly the
way he used to feel when he lived in Venice—like a mari-
onette hanging in a toy shop, jerked into frenzies by any
passing brat. Ever since they arrived, Beau had sensed
trouble brewing, hovering like an impending hand.

Beau and Carmenina had timed their divorce to coincide with the start of Bingo's university career at Harvard—an illustrious placement made possible more by the prolonged efforts of his excellent school at Gstaad than by any effort on his part. By that point, Carmenina was at the end of her tether from the strain of keeping up appearances for so many years while her errant husband plied between Venice and his special friend in Berlin. Yet Dieter von Thurigen was a name she never knew until Bingo enlightened her during the divorce. The information was welcomed by her lawyer as helpful for the settlement. But in fact Beau was so elated, and guilt-ridden into the bargain, that he was more than happy for her to have almost anything she wanted including—rather, *especially*—the family residence in Venice.

Carmenina could see his point. She too would have been more than happy to offload the scene of so much disillusionment: she would have put it up for sale before the ink dried on the new deeds, had not Bingo claimed to be deeply attached to it. This was an argument from a source she could not resist; nevertheless, she was determined to put all that bad karma behind her. She left the house in the custody of her faithful housekeeper, Fernanda, and followed Bingo to the New World.

She settled in an agreeable apartment on the Upper East Side overlooking Central Park and to keep Bingo happy, she bought him a commuter pass so he could come to New York with the greatest of ease whenever the whim took him. And take him it did, far more often than she ever realized.

Bingo was routinely on the prowl for amusement. His degree course in Modern Languages was a disappointment. Intended to be an easy option as he had virtually three mother tongues—English, Spanish, and Italian—it didn't turn out to be easy at all. His professors were not satisfied by the mere fact that he could chat more fluently than they could themselves, and even less so by the evidence that his brain was as full of tag ends of information as a Christmas tree is full of balls. They were unrelenting in their expectation that he should read books and write essays; even worse, they scolded him for not taking his Harvard opportunity seriously. Their complaints did not fall on deaf ears. Bingo was no longer a child. He was catching on to the virtue of addressing a problem. He saw that the only person who could get the professors off his back was himself. He accepted their ultimatum or, to put it his way, he stuffed it. Bingo went to New York. This time he stayed with his mother long enough to explain that at Harvard he had already learned the most important thing he could learn there.

Carmenina was pleased that the Harvard professors had done their job so well, and she didn't mind that they had managed it after so few rounds of fees. Above all she was proud of her clever boy. Of course she didn't understand—because he didn't explain—that what he had learned at

Harvard was quite simply that he wanted to embrace as his life's work what he had been doing all along—showing off. What he told his mother was that he wanted to realize his potential without delay. At school his languages were a cause for admiration, but so too was the fact that he was a quick study, capable of subsuming the outer trappings of almost any subject in no time. In a world of appearances, the dilettante is king. All signs pointed home to Venice.

Bingo set up a travel business for rich people who wanted something romantic and chic yet, at the same time, clearly "cultivated." He called his company Gotha Tours, or rather he *named* it Gotha Tours. In actual practice, after seeing one of his advertisements defaced in an Alitalia magazine, he adopted Gotcha Tours for in-house use. Bingo wasted no time in New York. He threw his all into finding an agent to do the Stateside work; he personally set up an advisory committee of poor royals and rich arrivistes to spread the word among the two top-end groups who like to travel together; he devised a roster of lecturers— most of them selected from the better behaved of his for- mer professors, who promptly forgave his sins and blessed his enterprise; and most importantly he enlisted the sup- port of Beau and Carmenina. Only then did he hustle back to Venice, where the great ladies, now very old ladies, put down the drawbridge and welcomed him with the adoring fascination they had accorded him ever since he was a baby lisping indiscretions through his ice cream.

On his way back to Italy, Bingo followed up a lead from a friend who was a contributing editor at *Vogue* by stopping in London to see Prima Flower, the founding editor of *Fast Lane*. He hoped to convince her to do an article that would promote his travel company because *Fast Lane*'s readership was exactly the market he was targeting. Better yet, Prima Flower was an Italian with friends in Venice.

Hardly a month had passed when a letter from Prima Flower dropped into Bingo's letterbox introducing "an interesting young man" by the name of Cadmus Argus Peacock who was writing an article for her. This Peacock, as Bingo instantly perceived, was an Oscar Wilde wannabe who worked his passage as combination lounge lizard and freelance journalist. To avoid his hated given names, he signed his articles CAP and strove to establish himself as Cap Peacock. But with the case-hardened indifference of her profession, Prima Flower presented Peacock to Bingo under his full name. And with the heart-hardened glee of an enfant terrible, Bingo presented him to Venetian society as Cad Peacock—and under this *nomen omen* he earned his reputation. His official brief was to write a wicked article about Venice but to avoid politicians and industrialists because his editor's husband had hopes of reviving some projects with those two centers of power. That left the visitors, the foreign residents, and the aristocracy—or, as Cad called them, the itinerant, the immigrant, and the impotent. He wasn't pleased about the strictures, but he soon recognized that the services of Bingo Benson were going to make the project not merely doable, but fiendish, and fun.

"Caddie?" Bingo was pushing crates of bottles around on the pantry floor, while Cad was trying to make scrambled eggs in the kitchen. "Caddie? Does bourbon go off? I've got enough in here to float a liner; it's been here since Papà flew the coop." He pulled a bottle from one of the cases and walked into the kitchen holding it up to the light. "My mother used to buy it for my father every holiday, every birthday—especially when she was trying to save the marriage. We Bensons believe that bourbon makes babies. That is why my father is Beauregard van Dongen *Bourbon* Benson and I am Bingham de Bienville *Bourbon* Benson Bolivar. Mamma started to give me bottles too, when I turned eighteen. She wants grandchildren."

Peacock looked at him. "Does she really believe you'll come through?"

"She believes in bourbon, stupid. *I'm* here, aren't I?"

Cadmus Peacock didn't like this conversation. He liked Bingo as he perceived him and he liked living in the maid's apartment on the floor below. Lately he had been wondering about staying on with Bingo and making Venice his home. "Do you put milk in scrambled eggs?"

"A splash, and some salt and pepper. Anyhow," said Bingo wandering back into the pantry, "I'd better find a way to use up some of this bourbon. Papà and Dieter have agreed to come and stay here next week. I could give a party and make some kind of bourbon punch, like whiskey sour punch. That might be good."

"You mean a bowl of whiskey sour?" asked Cad. "Is that quite . . . *comme il faut?*"

"*Chi ne frega?*" Bingo came out of the pantry with a bottle of tonic water. "Who gives a damn?" He unscrewed the cap. "Someone told me Ezra Pound liked a splash of fizzy tonic in his omelet to make it fluffy. See what it does to scrambles. We're the makers of manners, Cad."

"Nice customs curtsy to great queens," allowed Cad, putting toast on the plates. He splashed some tonic water into the mixture and poured the eggs into a saucepan.

"Stir it up," said Bingo. "Keep stirring."

"My profession," said Cad.

"My real problem," said Bingo, "is that Venetians don't drink whiskey like Americans do. For one thing it's expensive so they don't get the habit. For another, it's strong. People lose their decorum."

"And make babies. Someone should tell the Mayor."

"Maybe I should invite my mother to come with her Count while Papà and Dieter are here, so they can be friends again, for *my* sake. That Count is after her money for sure. I don't trust Dieter either. It guess it was a mistake to let my parents get a divorce. Live and learn. Should we make some mischief?"

"Bingo, this is fate! Remember the woman my editor sent me? The one I had lunch with yesterday?" Cad plopped the eggs onto the toast, dropped the pan into the sink and sat down. "She used to work for my editor's husband, Donald Flower, that race-car driver who had some drug trouble at Venice airport, implicating all sorts of politicians, so he had to give up his project here. She's called Rosi Rosso. Prima Flower told her that it would be awhile before her husband had another project for her and she should take a break and get married. Maybe we could get her interested in the Count."

"That's an idea," said Bingo, getting up from the table. He surveyed the recipe books on the shelf over the sideboard. He took down three cocktail manuals: *Six O'Clock and All's Well, Promising Preludes,* and *Low-ball Highballs.* "Time for some research," he said, putting the books on the kitchen table and sitting down again. "Could you make me another espresso, Caddie? The cups are still in the dishwasher. Maybe you could empty it while you're at it. Bourbon . . . bourbon-based drinks. There's no punch in any of them. Here's a good one: mint julep. Papà would like those; he's from the South. Oh, look at this—Scarlett O'Hara. My mother would love that. But it's not bourbon; it's Southern Comfort. Wow. That's one hundred proof.

Why don't we just double the bourbon? We've got plenty of it. What's a jigger? Is that the same as a shot?"

"What's a shot?"

Bingo went to the bookshelf and took *The Joy of Cooking* back to the table. "This is the Bible of the kitchen," said Bingo. "It has everything, even measurements. But I can never find them. Skip the measurements, we'll improvise. This book was an unwanted wedding present: never used. Nanda couldn't read it. She wouldn't have trusted it anyhow."

"How come it's so filthy, then?"

"*Filthy? I* use it. Those are souvenirs of delicious meals."

"The lily that festers . . ." sniffed Cad, putting the book on the table. He turned and lifted the cutlery basket from the dishwasher. "Am I the replacement maid because I live in the maid's apartment?"

"Not at all," said Bingo. "You're the temporary maid. When I got rid of old Buttinski, my mother took her to Rome, but now she says Nanda wants her Venice job back again."

"So I'm evicted?"

"No. You can stay until you finish your article. Nanda can stay in Rome a bit longer. It might grow on her. Fetch that plastic basin from the sink. We'll mix six quarts of Scarlett O'Hara and six of mint julep and put them in the fridge until the party. Scarlett O'Hara seems to be more or less two measures of cranberry juice to one of

Southern Comfort, so make that two juice to two bourbon. Pour these two bottles of bourbon into the basin and add two cartons of cranberry juice from the fridge. Then taste it."

Cadmus poured and stirred, then tasted. "It's good, but it lacks something."

"Pretty color, though. Here's a recipe that calls for Amaretto. See that bottle on the sideboard. Pour it all in. Now taste it."

"Mmm, smoooth. Perfect. You taste it."

"Mmm. You're right. Bottle it, Caddie, while I do the mint juleps. While you're at it, Cad, divide one of the Scarlett O'Hara bottles between two and fill them up with water. You and I will drink from those until we get dinner on the table. Then we can switch to killer blend. The point is: how does that poem go? If you can keep your head when everyone around you is losing theirs—it's the water in the drink, my son. Hide our bottles in the little fridge under the counter."

"I hope the bourbon works. If I can get the Count off with Rosi, Prima will be so pleased with me."

"You know, Caddie, we could do an aphrodisiac dinner. I could seduce Dieter. Even better, I'll bet I could get him to seduce me. Papà would go *crrraaazy.*" He went back to the bookshelf. "Here's something." He took a book and looked at it: *"Food of Love."*

"That's supposed to be music," said Cad.

"It's aphrodisiac recipes. Some are good. Ha! Here's the article I tore out of a magazine at the barbershop in Cambridge." He pulled some folded pages from the back of the book. *"And So to Bed."* He cackled.

Cad was looking at *The Joy of Cooking.* "Listen to this: 'Dried peas and beans, being rather on the dull side, much like dull people respond readily to the right contacts.'"

"Why are you looking at beans?" asked Bingo.

"Food of love: music. You know—

"Beans, beans, the musical fruit,
The more you eat, the more you toot.
The more you toot—"

"Put a sock in it, Cad. We're doing an orgy, not a concert."

The morning after Dieter and Beau arrived, Cad bounced up the stairs from the mezzanine apartment envisaging a big family breakfast with witty chat and copious gossip. Instead he found Bingo standing alone in the kitchen wearing a striped butcher's apron surrounded by crates of groceries.

"Ah! Cad. Just the man. Papà and Dieter have gone to Vicenza to look at the theater. The stuff for our aphrodisiac dinner just arrived." He stepped over a crate of vegetables and sat down at the table. He picked up a sheaf of papers.

"I'll read the ingredients for each recipe, while you find them and sort them into piles."

"Aren't we going to have any breakfast? I could make my scrambles with tonic."

"After, after. I have to be sure we've got everything. Here's the cocktail snacks: toasted almonds, smoked oysters, crackers, cream cheese to lace with Tabasco and top with canned asparagus tips, pesto dip with extra pine nuts, sesame crackers."

Cad rummaged through the crates then stood at the counter sorting the cans, cartons, jars, and bags into islands; then bent over the crates again, then back to the counter, up and down. "I'd love to have at least an espresso," said Cad, straightening his back.

"Later. The first course will be that Casanova pasta. I got that long spaghetti because it's such fun to eat. Then anchovies, *peperoncino,* black olives, and tomato sauce. All there?

"Then for the main course. The shrimp are in the freezer. There should be mushrooms, sesame seeds, parsley. There's sherry in the pantry. Put it out on the counter. Did you find a lemon?

"Now dessert: Cream Passionel. For the zabaglione we already have the eggs, sugar, and Marsala. There should be three envelopes of gelatin. Is there a whipped-cream squirter? Some maraschino cherries? Done.

"Throw the crates in the pantry, and then you can make yourself some breakfast; I've already had mine, but I'll take an espresso. I'll start on the Cream Passionel. It has to sit in the fridge all day to jellify."

Luckily, Rosi Rosso and Cad were already sitting in the *salone* chatting with Dieter and Beau and drinking mint juleps and Scarlett O'Haras when Carmenina and Count Barbaro arrived. Bingo was in the kitchen putting the finishing touches on the snacks when the doorbell rang, but everyone rushed to the door to meet *La Mamma* and the Count with the important name. Carmenina couldn't have asked for a warmer welcome into an ambiance she didn't fancy and a society she rather feared. For his part, Count Barbaro was completely disarmed; he had prepared himself for a situation altogether more demanding. This was going to be a walkover—easy, casual, unbuttoned: *la vie Améri-caine.* Rosi immediately devoted herself to her fellow Italian, the Count. Beau decided to do his duty and sat down beside Carmenina, striking up a conversation about how strange Venice seems to a person who once lived here but doesn't anymore. Bingo and Cad stood together beside the credenza, giving Dieter a refill of mint julep.

"This is good," said Dieter, "but I want to try the Scarlett O'Hara next." Bingo had established a half-teasing, half-flattering relationship with Dieter since his arrival which kept him in a confused state about his footing.

"I had to start you out with mint julep to please Papà. But Scarlett O'Hara is probably more *you*," said Bingo, with the slightest hint of a wink. He turned to Cad. "We have to go to the kitchen now, but refill the glasses before you come." He turned to Dieter. "You come too."

Cad filled Rosi's glass last. "We're going to the kitchen now," he said.

"Oh, I'll go with you," she said, getting up. "You come too," she said, turning to Count Barbaro, who rose with a puzzled expression and followed her.

Bingo had put on his apron and was stuffing mint sprigs into a glass pitcher and some lime slices into two others. He filled them, one with mint julep and two with Scarlett O'Hara, then handed a jug each to Rosi, Dieter, and Count Barbaro.

"Could you take these out to the table, please?"

Alone in the kitchen, Bingo and Cad filled their glasses from the small fridge under the counter and then filled glasses for Dieter and Rosi and Count Barbaro from the pitcher on the sideboard. While Bingo cooked, Cad fetched serving bowls, counted out plates, and sliced bread. Dieter, Rosi, and Count Barbaro chatted by the sideboard. The kitchen was rather warm and the drinks

were cool and refreshing. Bingo refilled the pitcher and refilled their glasses.

"Are you a dancer?" asked Rosi.

"I *was* a dancer," said Dieter.

"Oh," said Rosi, "that's a *little* bit better."

"Anyone want to test the spaghetti?" said Bingo, flinging a strand at the ceiling. "They say if it sticks it's done,
but I can never get it up there; sixteen feet is a long way."
He tried again.

"Why don't you just taste it? Can't I help?" said Count
Barbaro, putting his glass on the sideboard and walking
towards the stove.

"The party seems to have moved to the kitchen," said Carmenina. "I guess we're the only ones who don't feel drawn
there."

"It beats me why Bingo doesn't get help when he enter-
tains," said Beau. "It's fine to play at cooking, but it's awkward when you have guests."

"I couldn't agree more. I don't know where he gets this
eccentricity. And I wonder about Lodovico. I can't imagine
he feels at home in there."

"Oh, that girl, Rosi, asked him to go in the kitchen.
Maybe he fancies her," Beau said, winking to show that he
was only joking.

"He might. She's awfully good-looking. Is she a model?"

"No. She was a runner-up for Miss Italia and has some connection with the magazine that Cadmus Peacock works for. I wouldn't think they're together, though. He doesn't seem to be the type."

"How does Bingo know him?" The concern showed in Carmenina's voice. "Is he staying here?"

"No, no. He seems to be using Nanda's apartment. Bingo says he wants him to give a puff to his company. As far as I can see there's nothing more than that."

"You know I want grandchildren someday."

"Does Lodovico have any?"

"Six."

"Have you met them?"

"Of course. He wants to marry me. I think that's why he went with that girl; he thought she might be Bingo's girlfriend and he wanted to be a good sport."

"Are you going to marry him?"

"Beau, I'd love to be married again, but you know I'm Catholic."

"Are you asking me to die?" He intended to be jocular, but it sounded bitter. Carmenina sensed that he was a little jealous about her making such a good match. She was thinner than she had been when they were married. She still wasn't model thin; she was what Bingo, who was a keen cineast, called *1950s thin*. Beau had said how nice she looked.

"It isn't your problem," she said.

"Of course not."

"Lodovico is a widower, but I would have to get an annulment. My sister says I could; she asked the priest who married us. But Bingo hates the idea. I do too, really. Marriage isn't something you just erase."

"Do you live together?"

"Heavens, no. We don't even stay together in hotels."

A loud crash in the kitchen gave way to a shriek and a burst of laughter. The swinging door opened and Rosi appeared, holding on to the weaving door with both hands to steady herself. She bowed like a footman, but didn't straighten up. She addressed the floor.

"Doan worry." Her speech was slurred. "Ever'thing is okay. Nothing broke. The Count slipped on some spaghetti. That's all." She let go of the door and turned, still bowed, back to the kitchen. The swinging door caught up with her backside. There was another crash, another scream, and more laughter.

"Oh, dear," said Carmenina. "What is our little angel cooking up?"

"Here," said Beau, filling her glass. "Have another Scarlett O'Hara. I started on the mint juleps, but these are better. We might as well enjoy ourselves."

"It's a delicious concoction, isn't it," said Carmenina. "So light!"

*

A hand swinging a dinner bell emerged from the kitchen door, followed by Bingo, who stood beside the door still ringing the bell. Cadmus held the door open. Rosi appeared horizontal in midair holding out a bowl of spaghetti as though about to place it on an altar. She was being carried by Dieter, who was struggling to keep her balanced.

"*OooooOOOOwa!*" cried Rosi. "*Aiuto!* Help!" The bowl was tipping and spaghetti was rising over the rim. Bingo rushed up and caught the bowl as Rosi and Dieter sank to the floor, convulsed with laughter.

Count Barbaro stood leaning against the kitchen door, looking pale.

"Do you need to lie down?" asked Cad.

He nodded. Cad helped him to the chaise longue and put his feet up.

"Do you want anything?"

Count Barbaro shook his head. He closed his eyes. "Oooooh," he said.

Beau came over. "Try this." He dragged one of Count Barbaro's feet off the chaise longue and placed it flat on the floor.

"Oh, that's better. Thank you."

*

So they were only six at table. Bingo put Carmenina and Rosi at the head and foot, himself and his papà flanking Carmenina, with Dieter next to Bingo and Cad next to Beau.

"Did you organize any of your dance festivals in Venice?" Cad had hardly had a chance to speak to Beau.

"I once brought a production of *Don Juan* to the *Teatro Verde,* the open-air theater at the Cini. It was good, but I was so stressed out by the end I never wanted to do anything in Venice again."

Carmenina started to giggle.

Beau smiled at her. "You're remembering that ridiculous accident."

Carmenina nodded, giggling.

"She," said Beau, nodding towards Carmenina, "was worried about mosquitoes, so opening night we put out those smoldering coils. As people were coming in, one of the coils flamed up. Someone kicked it to turn it over and it rolled under a chair, but it went out, so that was fine— except that during the performance it flamed up again. The weather was hot—total sirocco—so poor old Count Boscolino who was sitting over it didn't think twice about the heat until someone pointed under his chair at the exact moment he felt his pants about to catch on fire. He jumped up shouting 'Fire! Help! Fire!' just as Don Juan was about to meet his fate so everyone thought at first that it was a bad joke."

"Was he furious?" asked Cad.

"He was apologetic. He was completely old school: modest, retiring."

"Unless his pants were on fire." Carmenina giggled again.

"Exactly," said Beau, "which I'm sure didn't happen often."

"He probably didn't drink enough bour—" Cad broke off as Bingo kicked him under the table.

"When people saw who it was," continued Beau, "they knew it was no joke."

"Was that why you didn't do any more ballets in Venice?" asked Cad.

"Not really," said Beau, catching a look from Dieter that said he was not enjoying this resurrection of Beau's former life. "Working in Venice is difficult, and I was getting so much valuable help from Dieter in Germany that I found it easier to work there."

Bingo squeezed Dieter's thigh under the table before he got up and pushed the pitchers of mint julep and Scarlett O'Hara towards Cad. He collected the spaghetti plates and put down clean ones while Cad filled the glasses.

"That was delicious, darling," said Carmenina. "Just the way I like it: so *piccante*."

"As in *Fire! Help! Fire!*" said Beau.

"Sets your pants on fire," said Cad, receiving another kick under the table.

"Speaking of stories, how is your article going, Cad?" asked Carmenina, still giggling. "Fernanda keeps asking me."

"*Mamma!*" said Bingo. "That's unlike you. Have some more Scarlett O'Hara."

"What's your article about?" asked Dieter.

"Venetian society," said Cad, "as Venetians see it."

"I marvel that you can get them to talk," said Dieter.

"I can. I do."

"How? Charm?"

"No. That doesn't get you anywhere. Mainly I catch them off guard talking about vague things that don't concern them much. Then I sometimes quote someone. That works best if I can hit on a pronouncement by someone they don't like. Bingo is very helpful in that department." Cad had the sense that he was giving too much away, but he couldn't stop himself. "Venetians have to have the last word on any subject."

"Didn't take you long to find that out," said Rosi. "That's why we all love them."

"Thank you, darling," said Cad. "That's my job. Tell Prima how great I am."

"Do you record your conversations?" asked Dieter.

"Oh, you have to!" exclaimed Cad. "People are so treacherous. I have a recorder that looks exactly like a cell phone."

"Hey, Bingo!" said Rosi. "That spaghetti was great. I

just noticed: I got over my whirlies and my hiccups and everything."

"Now eat up the shrimp sesame, everybody. It soaks up bourbon like a sponge. That's why I made it. Like I said, we've got this bourbon overstock we're trying to correct tonight."

Carmenina looked at Beau and laughed. Beau felt Dieter looking at him and looked at his plate. But he pressed Carmenina's knee under the table so she knew he shared the joke. He couldn't see any point in being cruel after all he'd put her through.

"Now I have to get the dessert. Cad, will you collect the plates when they're finished?" Bingo started for the kitchen.

"What *is* dessert?" asked Carmenina.

"It's called Cream Passionel, Mamma," he answered over his shoulder.

"Crime Passionel?" asked Dieter.

"Someone told me about a school dessert they used to have called Tragedy in the Alps," mused Cad. "I wonder if it's the same."

"It's *c-r-e-a-m*," called Bingo from the kitchen, "not *c-r-i-m-e*."

"Tragedy in the Alps? What could it be, I wonder," said Beau, stifling a yawn.

"Here," said Cad, filling his glass. "Have some more Scarlett O'Hara to wake you up."

"It sounds like strawberry shortcake to me," said Carmenina.

"As school food?" asked Cad. "Not my school."

"In Gstaad," nodded Beau.

"And that's in the Alps," added Rosi, making everyone laugh.

Bingo put a tray of parfait glasses on the table next to Carmenina. "Caddie, I filled some more pitchers in the kitchen. Can you keep serving the glasses?" He put a parfait glass at his mother's place. "I brought out the Count's glass as well, if anyone wants it."

"His name is Lodovico, darling," whispered Carmenina; "not Count. You know that." She looked over her shoulder and saw that he was still asleep on the chaise longue.

"And now," said Bingo, putting a pack of Camel cigarettes on the table, "the best cigarette of the day. Anyone care to join me?" He waved the package around the table giving one to Rosi and one to Cad.

"I love camels," said Rosi, blowing smoke high into the air.

"They're nice, but they're strong," said Cad.

"Maybe," said Bingo, "I like the picture."

"That's what I mean," said Rosi. "The picture. The animal."

"Me too," said Bingo.

"I know an English poem about a camel," said Rosi.
"Recite it, recite it," urged Bingo. "Let's be literary."
"I won't stand up," said Rosi. She took a deep breath.

> *The sexual life of the camel*
> *Is stranger than anyone thinks,*
> *For when the urge comes upon him—"*

Carmenina looked at Bingo, worried.

> *"He climbs on the back of the sphinx."*

Carmenina looked at her plate.

> *"Now the sphinx's remarkable rectum—"*

Carmenina folded her napkin in her lap.

> *"Is filled with the sands of the Nile."*

Carmenina's glance flew to the ceiling, slid despairingly down the wall, and landed on the floor beside her chair, where it rested.

> *"Which accounts for the hump on the camel*
> *And the sphinx's inscrutable smile."*

Bingo's laughter exploded first, followed by a chorus of loud hilarity from Dieter and Cad and Beau. Dieter put his arm around Bingo and laughed some more; Cad and Beau gazed at him with affection, sharing his mirth. Rosi flushed with pleasure.

Carmenina was the only one not laughing. Her lips were trembling and her eyes were brimming with tears. She put her napkin beside her plate and started to rise to her feet, keeping her hand on the table to steady herself.

"Oh!" said Bingo, jumping to his feet. "I forgot. Poor Mamma gets sentimental when she drinks." He squeezed her shoulders and kissed her forehead. Beau too stood up, swaying slightly, and squeezed her hand; after all, it was an emergency. She started to sob. She turned to leave the table, taking careful steps. Beau walked with her, weaving towards the chaise longue. Drunk though he was, Beau understood that she was looking for refuge so he dragged up a chair so she could sit beside Count Barbaro.

"I think it's time we go," she murmured to Beau. "I'm going to wake him up. Lodovico, *caro*?" She shook his shoulder gently. "How do you feel?"

He opened his eyes. *"Ooooooo,"* he said. "I'm better with my eyes closed. I still feel like . . . I'm in a gondola . . . in a storm."

Cadmus was standing beside Carmenina. "I'll take care of him. I'll make him some toast and coffee. Then I'll walk him back if you want to leave."

"I can't leave her to walk back alone," said Count Barbaro, trying to sit up, "but I can't quite stand up yet."

"Don't worry," said Cad. "Beau or Bingo will walk her back to the hotel, and you can rest for a bit longer."

He lay down again with a sigh. "I've never been so drunk in my life, not even when I was young. But then we only drank wine."

"Bring your glasses," called Bingo, taking two pitchers from the credenza and placing them on the coffee table. "We have two more pitchers of mint julep and one of Scarlett O'Hara to finish."

Cad went to the kitchen to make toast and coffee for Count Barbaro.

Lodovico Barbaro was grateful for Cad's offer to walk back to the hotel with him.

"To tell the truth, I don't feel very steady on my feet even after coffee and toast."

Cad made conversation. "Luckily we don't have to drive. I suppose lack of practice is why Venetians have crashes; the young ones especially. They drink and drive."

"My cousin's son died like that. Poor woman. It's destroyed her. And ruined her financially, too. The *Gazzettino* wrote heartbreaking things about him. They don't care."

"Did they write lies?" asked Cad.

"Maybe not," said the Count, "but that's not the point. The family shouldn't be made to suffer like that."

They went into the hotel and asked for the key. The night clerk smiled and informed them in a chatty way that Mrs. Benson had returned earlier, then decided he had been indiscreet. To make up for it he assumed a stony aloofness.

The Count interpreted his demeanor as a criticism for letting Mrs. Benson come back without him. He returned it with a demeanor that might have been cut from a diamond—a sharp reminder that the Count could give names to his ancestors for five centuries whereas this upstart would be lucky to know who his father was.

Cad thought a pot of tea would be a good idea. Lodovico agreed. They found some comfortable chairs in the *salotto,* and Cad went back to the concierge to order a small snack from room service.

Cad sat down opposite the Count. "They're going to send us some more tea and toast. I asked him to order a boiled egg and a banana as well, but he wasn't sure. Bingo says that when they make an exception they never quite meet your demands as a matter of principle. Anyway, you should be fine after you've had a bit more to eat."

"I can't thank you enough. I hope you said I'll pay for it myself."

"Oh, yes. I knew you'd want to do that."

"Good, good. Thank you. Thank you."

"You were saying that your cousin had been mistreated

in the *Gazzettino*," prompted Cad, placing his pocket recorder on the table.

"Someone is suing them about the crash. I wish I could help, but my father lost almost everything, gambling and drinking. My sister helped herself to the rest. By the time he died, there was nothing. My wife wanted me to get a lawyer, but I didn't want a scandal. About all that's left of the old Venetian families," he confessed, "is their good names."

The tea came, with the boiled egg and toast but no banana.

"It's disillusioning how little people help each other," said Cad, as he poured the tea. In his experience interviewees were often reassured by the introduction of a philosophical note.

Count Barbaro tipped his head and then nodded. "I see what you mean. You think the little people get in the habit of helping each other through the hard times, whereas with people like us, there's less call to help and people lose the instinct?"

Cad tipped his head. "Mmm."

The Count continued on the themes of treachery and family intrigue. Details swarmed like relatives following an immigrant, first the wife and children, then parents, cousins, nieces, nephews; they joined the story like dry streams rising in spring to flow to the river and thence out to the open sea. Cad watched with fascination as the tired old man burst his timeworn bastions of reserve. Cad saw with jubilation his own star rising in the wake.

"Rosi Rosso enjoyed your company very much."

The Count looked surprised. "No. I don't have success with that kind of girl. But she's very nice. Is she a friend of Mrs. Benson's son?"

"No, no. She's a friend of mine."

"Well, congratulations. She's a very attractive young woman. Full of spirit."

Cad let it drop. This wasn't going to work. But Prima would be happy anyhow. He felt a bit sorry for the old Nob sitting over there mumbling his egg. He'd be unhappy when he heard about the article. But *I told* him I was a journalist. At least he's learned a priceless lesson.

Carmenina awoke early with an aching head and a sinking heart. She wondered how wildly beyond all sane limits she must have strayed in terms of carbohydrates. She slid her hand under the covers and squeezed her hips. They didn't feel as big as they once had, but she would have to make this a day of penance: carpaccio and raw prawns. She didn't even feel like getting up. She turned over, but as she was closing her eyes she caught sight of something that woke her up—it was a man's back, and one she recognized. What on earth was her former husband doing in her bed?

"Beau, Beau?" She tapped his shoulder. "What's happened? You must slip away."

When Beau walked through the lobby of the Bauer, he felt the porters and the concierge staring at him. Damn their eyes, he thought and wondered whether they would think less, or more, of Carmenina as a result of his attentions. And Dieter? What would he think? The worst. Dieter was madly jealous. There was sure to be a fight. As Beau crossed the bridge into Via Ventidue Marzo he looked down the broad avenue and saw his old friend Oskar Weisman talking to a fellow professor. Five years ago he would have doubled his pace to catch up with him for some amusing chat, but today Beau was too preoccupied to talk; on top of that he felt like an invader, as if he had changed identity now that he didn't live here. He dodged into Bar Borsa for a coffee.

Standing at the bar drinking his coffee, he continued to rue, and to marvel, that on his first visit to Venice with Dieter he'd been such an egregious fool as to spend the night with his ex-wife—the first time he'd seen Carmenina since the divorce. It gave completely the wrong impression. She was utterly resistible. To tell the truth, he had never been attracted to her. So why had he tumbled into her bed?

As he walked through San Stefano, he decided to spare Dieter's feelings and pretend that he had merely sat chatting with her to make her feel better until she fell asleep, but he was so tired that he dropped off in the chair without realizing it and didn't wake up until morning, when he slipped out. He could speculate that she didn't even know he'd fallen asleep in the chair because she was still asleep when he left. Anyhow, it was a fact that he had been kind to her because Bingo wanted them to be friends, so, he could say, there was no point in making a bad job of it by leaving her in distress. Dieter would swallow that; he knew how much he loved Bingo and even confessed to feeling a twinge of jealousy about him. Dieter's life as a dancer hadn't channeled him into marriage the way Beau's life had. He probably would have liked to have a son, all things being equal—which they weren't.

Beau opened the gate with his own set of keys that Bingo had restored to him immediately on his arrival. As he walked through the courtyard he looked up involuntarily to the balcony where Bingo used always to greet him, sometimes waiting for hours, sometimes appearing when he heard the gate clang shut. There was baby Bingo on his knees behind the railing dropping a cookie to him, which he miraculously caught, to the boy's delight; then there was schoolboy Bingo waiting for him behind a whole city of Legos ranged along the railing, where he'd stood for hours building and building; there was Bingo back from school in Switzerland dropping an examination paper to him which he missed, to the boy's delight as it spilled its pages all over the path; then there was Bingo, almost grown up, leaning on the railing smoking a cigarette and drinking a glass of Prosecco, dropping some ash on him as he passed underneath. What a boy. Beau shook his head.

He stopped at Bingo's bedroom to say good morning, but he wasn't there. He looked in the kitchen. What a mess! Dirty dishes piled helter-skelter everywhere. Pots and pans on the stove and on the floor. Bingo must have gone to meet his friends for breakfast at the Gritti. He couldn't blame him for running away from such a sight. He *had* to get a maid. This was ridiculous. He was about to conclude that he should talk to Carmenina about it, but canceled that thought as more reprehensible backsliding.

As he crossed the *salone* to the master bedroom, he wondered whether Dieter might have gone out with Bingo and was surprised to feel a twinge of jealousy himself. But opening the bedroom door he found the room still shuttered in darkness and felt reassured. He followed the light gleaming around the shutters, kicking a pair of shoes and stepping on something that felt like a pair of trousers as he went. He almost laughed. Dieter must have been completely drunk to be so careless; it was unlike him. Anyway, he wouldn't have difficulty understanding how Beau could fall asleep in a chair. He opened the shutters partway, so as not to be too cruel, and turned smiling, ready to get things back on an even keel as fast as possible.

But his smile went slack and his eyes blinked in disbelief. There, stretched out like loaves on a baking sheet, were

Rosi, then Bingo, and behind him, rising up on his elbow and scowling in the light, was Dieter. There were clothes strewn everywhere. Beau shut the shutters tight and followed the light from the open door back out to the *salone,* getting tangled in the trousers, which he now knew with a stab in the heart to be Bingo's. Out in the *salone* he marched up and down waiting for Dieter to come out. He had never been so agitated in his life. He buttoned his jacket, then unbuttoned it. He rubbed his hands, clapped them together, closed and opened his fists, shook his hands as if to dry them, all the while marching up and down, up and down. He bit his lip and shook his head. Why? Why? Why?

Finally the door opened. Dieter came out in his dressing gown with his hand shielding his eyes. "Beau darling . . . what a night! I can't remember anything."

"Get your clothes on. We're leaving for Berlin. I'll send a courier for the suitcases. And don't wake them up again. Let's hope *nobody* remembers *anything.*"

The day after the party, it wasn't until almost lunchtime that Cad climbed the stairs from the mezzanine. He had plenty to report about the Count but was wondering how much to fudge it about the Count's reaction to Rosi.

He soon perceived that he needn't have worried. When he entered the *salone* he found Bingo was sitting at what Cad supposed was still the breakfast table with Rosi. He seemed to be explaining about his business, while she—she was taking notes, and making suggestions like it really mattered what she had to say.

"Cad!" called Bingo. "Sit down. Meet the new CEO of Gotcha. Rosi has the most amazing executive talents. From now on I am the éminence grise, and she will make money, win friends, and influence people." For Cad, it was like coming back to a chess game and discovering that somebody completely unqualified had sat down in his place—and worse—was *winning* the very game that had flummoxed him.

Beau and Dieter were drinking coffee in the bar at the Berlin Four Seasons. Nearly four months had passed since their cataclysmic Venetian sojourn and they were, at least superficially, back to normal. They were waiting for Beau's old friend from Venice, Oskar Weisman who had just finished a series of lectures at Humboldt University around the corner from the hotel. Beau looked at his watch. For some reason he was excited about seeing Oskar, who didn't know Dieter but knew who he was: Weisman had seen Dieter dance years ago when he was *the* rising young star.

"I'll go out and wait for him in front," said Beau. "I'm so glad I found out he was here and didn't miss him. He's flying back today."

Beau had barely turned the corner from the corridor

when Oskar's Johnsonian girth and ebullient character emerged from the revolving door.

"I'm here!" said Oskar, throwing his arms around Beau. "I'm here. Where's your dancer?"

"He's waiting for us. Are you in a hurry?"

"Yes. I can't wait. I am so bored with Berlin." His voiced boomed through the lobby. "All these new buildings and the East German taxi drivers who miss the old days when they didn't have to work. I would rather have my diabolical Venetians any day."

As they came into the bar, Dieter stood up and pushed back his jacket to rest his hands on his hips; his feet slipped into third position; he summoned an enigmatic smile and wondered what on earth Beau saw to like about this wrinkled bundle hurrying towards him.

Weisman stood at last before the poster boy, now middle-aged man, that he had admired in his youth. Dieter proffered a limp hand. Oskar ignored it and passed behind him, slapping the back of Dieter's Armani jacket rather hard as he went to the chair Beau was offering between them.

"Our apartment is five minutes away," explained Beau ruefully. "I could have come to your lectures if I'd known you were here." He stood with his hand on the arm of Oskar's chair waiting for him to sit down before sitting down himself.

"I gave them in English—the new lingua franca," said

Oskar, sitting down and picking up his napkin. "I love the way the French get so annoyed when I say that. The university is going to publish them: *The Modern European Novel.* I'll send you a copy. Do you come back to Venice?"

"No," said Beau quickly. He and Dieter had never spoken about their abrupt departure from Venice and he considered it to be a mutually agreed Closed Issue. He tried to turn the conversation to safer ground: "Do you ever see Bingo now that's he's moved back?"

"I do," said Oskar. "I caught a glimpse of him in Via Ventidue Marzo just before I left, but I couldn't stop. He was with a striking young woman. They looked very happy."

"Yes," said Beau. "I've met her. She's his business partner, I gather."

"And more, I should say. He seems devoted to her, and she looks . . ."

"There *is* more," said Dieter, waving his hand to silence Oskar and leaning forward to engage Beau. "Rosi phoned me. I wasn't supposed to say anything before Bingo talked to you, but if it's going to come out, I'm the one who should tell it. She and Bingo are getting married. She's having a baby. Bingo's waiting to tell you until they find out whether it's a boy or a girl. She wants me to be godfather. After all, it could be mine for all I know."

Even as he heard the words, Beau was aware that he was

hearing them with a sense of detachment, as though he'd slipped his moorings without noticing and had for some time been drifting on a current that was only now beginning to carry him away.

Oskar looked from Dieter to Beau, and he gloried in the Jamesian expression on Beau's face, it might have been reflected from an iceberg. Oskar grinned. He was jolly glad to have been a party to all this. "I would never have ventured," he murmured to Dieter in apparent admiration, "that you were so . . . versatile."

Dieter smiled.

"I've always wondered," continued Oskar. "Where did you acquire that *von*?"

"My agent," said Dieter, still confident, "when I defected. It suited my roles."

"You must have had so many over the years," said Oskar. He turned to Beau and stood up. "I have to go."

Beau put down his napkin and walked out with him.

At the door, Oskar put out his hand. "Thanks for inviting me, Beau; I'm always glad to see you. Will you be coming back to Venice?"

"Not to live," said Beau. "I might go to Rome until Bingo's baby is born. And then I'll come up to Venice. I wonder if Carmenina knows. She'll be over the moon with joy."

"Weren't you alarmed by Dieter's . . . bravado?"

"I was surprised that he said what he said, yes, but I'm not worried that it's true. It comes under the same heading as the *von*—vain pretense. Let's just say I know he drank a lot of bourbon on the evening in question, but I also know it's a taste he never acquired."

INTEGRATION

Splashed with color like a plastic toy, the blue Cornu-copia shuttle bus popped into view on the crest of the causeway and began its descent from the Ponte della Li-bertà, the Freedom Bridge that fastens Venice to the main-land. Laden with abundance, the bus rolled down into Piazzale Roma, its flanks cartooned with red and yellow letters dancing the names of the supermarket and discount shops at the American-style mainland shopping mall. This was the way to the new life; this was the modern transport of delight. The bus plied back and forth between Cornu-copia, a few miles behind the Industrial Zone, and Piazzale Roma every half hour, six days a week, as a service to the dwindling population of Venice's historic center, whose local butchers, bakers, grocers, and fruit and vegetable merchants were all but extinct. The service had rapidly es-tablished itself as a basic tool of workaday Venetian life, but for some, like Contessa Giulia Panfili, it languished undefined in the peripheral vision of a diverted gaze until a force majeure rearranged the scene.

Happily at home in the Venetian hinterland, Marco and Natasha Panfili made a point of always having breakfast with Bumbi, their eleven-month-old son, before they set off to their law and architecture practices. Each had an office in Padua, not far from their farm, and also in Venice, half an hour away. Today Natasha was meeting clients in the Venice office of Fallon-Fierazzo Architects, and Marco was meeting his father in Piazzale Roma to take him some clients of Natasha who were interested in buying his father's Veneto villa for their food and real estate interests.

Marco's parents, Conte and Contessa Panfili, no longer had their own car in Venice. Marco's younger brother, Bobino, had demolished it coming home from a party on the mainland. The insurance company was continually raising issues to delay replacing it; but that was of no consequence in comparison to the fact that Bobino had been killed in the accident. So had Matteo Patristi. A girl who had inveigled Bobino into letting her ride back with them because she fancied Matteo had escaped with injuries. She had recovered, but her uncle, a lawyer known for his imbroglios, had filed a suit on her behalf against the Panfilis because the car was theirs. At first the case seemed so tenuous as to be almost frivolous, but eventually Marco con-

cluded that this Avvocato Doghoni had some ulterior motive and intended above all to undermine his parents' financial stability. He was succeeding, but only because he
was greatly assisted by the fact that for decades Bobo and
Giulia Panfili had been living as their parents had lived
only by dint of slipping ever more beyond their means and
into mounting debt with the bank.

For Conte and Contessa Panfili, mired in grief and mis-
fortune, Doghoni's attack was bewildering. They recognized the disadvantage of never having played a part in the
world of affairs and perceived that they were, despite their
heritage, outsiders in modern Venice. They appealed to
Marco to rescue their finances. They appealed to his wife,
Natasha, too. Like all architects she was well versed in real
estate, and virtually all the Panfili capital was tied up in
land and buildings.

Marco, as a lawyer, was well aware that there were no
secrets in Venice and guessed that Doghoni must know of
his parents' financial vulnerability. He concluded that he
had to get them somehow inside the palisade, so he went
practically on bended knee to Corrado La Strada, who
even though he was retired from his legal practice still
presided over the most influential law firm in town, and
urged him to take on the Panfili defense. La Strada agreed,
but only on condition that Marco recuse himself. It
wouldn't, La Strada maintained, be credible for a son to de-
fend his parents.

*

Marco continued to work on their finances. He concluded that they had to raise some cash to pay their debts and to put a nest egg in Switzerland where Doghoni couldn't find it. A positive aspect of the otherwise bad situation was the advantage, as Marco pointed out, of their wealth being in property. He based this on the fact that real estate, by long tradition in Italy, changed hands on the basis of a white price, which is declared to the tax authorities, coupled with a black price, which is paid under the table. By selling one of their properties they could raise this secret nest egg, the sum of the black price, to hide in Switzerland. The villa was the only possibility. Though old and handsome, it was not of sufficient historic importance to be listed as a national treasure, which meant that the government did not have the automatic right to intervene at the moment of sale and claim it by simply paying the white price—ignoring the black price and thus obtaining the property for a fraction of its market value. This "right of preemption" was a real danger when a listed building was put up for sale, so the sale of the Venetian palace, which like virtually every other building in Venice was a listed national treasure, was too risky.

Bobo resigned himself to giving up his villa. Nevertheless, he drove the old station wagon he kept in the barn up and down the lanes, wondering why he and his farm manager, Gino, had never been able to turn a profit on this good land and wishing he could have a few more years to try to make it work. For almost a decade Giulia had been too busy with her Venetian causes and her social life to come to the country. Ironically, Giulia had lost interest in all that since the accident and they had plenty of time, but now it was too late. A big agricultural concern would buy it and earn the profits that had eluded him. It didn't seem fair.

Natasha was sitting opposite Marco at the breakfast table, peeling orange sections as fast as she could, but not fast enough for Bumbi, who was pounding the tray of his high chair beside her.

"Give me my breakfast," said Marco, pretending to bring his fist down on the table.

The maid appeared at the kitchen door. "It's on the table."

"I'm teasing her," laughed Marco, indicating Natasha.

"Pay no attention to him," said Natasha. "You can see where Bumbi gets his character." She dropped four pieces of orange on Bumbi's tray and turned to Marco. "I'm sure these people you're meeting with Papà are going to make an offer today, so it's just as well that you're the one going with him. They're going to drive a hard bargain. I wonder if your mother will come to Piazzale Roma with him. I'm pretty sure I've convinced her to try shopping at Cornucopia."

"Are you serious? She'll hate it. It's so déclassé."

169

"I'm beginning to think she needs shaking up. I thought she'd be so happy when Bumbi arrived, but instead she practically bursts into tears every time she sees him. Is he really so much like Bobino was?"

"I can't remember that far back. Maybe you're right; maybe she needs a shock."

Nanny came through the breakfast room carrying a basket of laundry from the nursery. "I'll come back for him in a second," she said. Natasha and Marco went to put on their coats. As they filed out the door, Nanny held out Bumbi for his hugs and kisses. Walking down the gravel drive to their cars, Marco said, "Papà wants to stay at the villa all day. He said Gino will take him to the train. I'm coming to Venice as soon as I finish with your Agricoltura people. I want to talk to Irene del Banco about converting the mezzanine in Venice into tourist apartments. I need to know how much money Mamma and Papà can earn from an investment like that. Shall I invite her to meet us for lunch?"

"Sure. Let's meet at the Monaco."

Giulia had found her way hit-and-miss through the scrambled bus lanes of Piazzale Roma and arrived at the Cornucopia bus stop with twenty minutes to spare. This expedition was a leap into the wild unknown, and she was doing her best to rise to the occasion. She knew she was becoming a burden to her family, and she knew she had to find a way back into life.

The shuttle bus had not yet returned from the mall, but it was awaited by a steadily growing crowd of men and women, many with shopping carts. Giulia had the Vuitton shoulder bag she carried when she went to the few remaining local shops near San Stefano and Sant'Angelo. All at once the mood of the crowd changed. She looked up and saw, swinging around the corner from the causeway, a sky-blue bus painted like a fairground trolley.

As it came near, the crowd surged tentatively this way and that, swelling and contracting like a paramecium in travail, until the bus, swerving into its parking lane, triggered a sudden division into three crowds: one for each door and one with shopping carts for the luggage portal. The bus sidled back and forth, back and forth, wiggling into its place. The three crowds moved in time with the bus, back and forth, a little bit this way, a little bit that way, each one targeting its door like a cat mesmerizing a mouse, never letting the quarry out of range. Suddenly the bus lurched sharply forward and stopped. The groups lunged.

The people getting off pushed to break through the ranks of the people trying to get on, complaining and casting aspersions on the intelligence of those blocking their exodus. But there was a certain resignation in their grumbling. Only a few hours before, they had been in the same position and knew that these would be in their present position a few hours from now.

The driver got down and opened the luggage compartment which was full of shopping. Once again, the people waiting to stow their empty shopping carts crowded in so the returning shoppers had to struggle to clear away their bags and carts. It made no sense to Giulia. The last person to get off had hardly put a foot on the ground before an old man on the right and a young woman on the left had thrust a foot onto the step and swung themselves up, engaging in a scuffle on the stair. Why was there such urgency? The bus wouldn't leave for another ten minutes. Giulia waited and climbed aboard last. Looking up and down the bus she saw a number of empty window seats but no aisle seats. She asked as she walked along the aisle whether this or that seat was free, but most were being held for people stowing shopping carts. Finally a man let her have the window seat next to him. When she hesitated to climb over him, he stood up. She offered him the window seat but he looked at her in disbelief. "I need to get out fast," he said.

Contessa Panfili sat bolt upright in her seat, wishing she could be anywhere but where she was—between a smudged window on one side and this man she had never seen before slouched with his knees apart in the seat beside her. She couldn't help wondering at the dismal state of affairs that had conspired to put her here. She looked around at the dirty upholstery bursting at the seams, ashtrays half ripped from their sockets, and graffiti on the seat backs. Today she would travel with her back to Venice in the company of Filipino maids and houseboys, immigrant Slavs, thrifty housewives, gypsies, and even some opportunistic shopkeepers and tour operators who left their cars in the shopping center's free carpark to commute gratis.

The bus was filling rapidly. Cell phones were ringing. People were speaking languages she had never heard before. The man next to her was Italian. He talked to a man across the aisle. "I wouldn't go home for lunch but that new parking lot attendant is after me. When I park in the morning I have to go in and buy something to leave on the car seat. Then I have to take the car away at lunchtime and bring it back to a different place. If he sees me, I have to go in and buy something again. I have more razor refills and batteries than I know what to do with. Still, it's the best commuter service you can get: free parking and a free bus every half hour each way. Maybe I'll just start tipping him."

"Yeah. Think how much it costs to park in Venice, and how much time you'd waste getting in and out."

A woman walked up the aisle looking for a seat. A man pushed past her and took a seat near the front. The woman shook her head and looked around. It was the last seat in the bus. She turned and got off. The passengers murmured among themselves.

"I'm on a tight schedule!" the man protested to the person next to him. "She can afford to wait; I can't."

Another woman boarded the bus and walked up the aisle looking right and left.

"It's full, dear," said a woman near her.

The woman in the aisle looked around. "Aren't there any seats at all?"

"It's full," said a man.

"Okay," she sighed. "I'll have to stand."

"You can't stand!" shouted a man angrily. "Can't you read the sign?"

"It's against the law," called another. Confirmations sounded from different parts of the bus. The woman took one last look around and moved towards the door. The driver climbed into his seat and watched her in the rearview mirrors until she reappeared on the pavement outside.

The bus labored to break away from the tangled traffic of Piazzale Roma, twisting and turning until it achieved the foot of the causeway and began its journey to terra firma following the slow, steady exodus across the Ponte della Libertà.

The Contessa stared at a seasonal message scrawled in red marker, now two months out of date, defacing the seat back in front of her: *Babbo Natale Stronzo*—Father Christmas is a piece of shit—and below, in black, scrawled in another hand: *Befana Troia*—the Epiphany witch is a whore. Two months ago she and Bobo had passed their first Christmas without their younger son, Bobino. His sudden death had trapped her like a jar over a bee. The frenzy of beating against his unreachable nearness had worn her out. Doctors offered sedatives, but she left them on the bedside table. She wasn't ready to forget.

Babbo Natale Stronzo, Befana Troia. Someone had hatched these sentiments in the very seat where she was now sitting. She wished she could rise and float away from the writing, from the bus, from her whole life as it was now.

Looking from the Ponte della Libertà over the shallow waters of the Lagoon, Giulia's memory flashed back to a scene from her childhood. She was six, at a birthday party; her best friend's mother was raising her blindfold to show her, amid screams of laughter, where she had pinned the tail on the donkey. She had got it completely wrong. And she had felt so sure of what she was doing. It was happening again, but this time she had sensed the revelation creeping towards her, even before Bobino's death sent an ominous craquelure chasing into every corner of her life. *She had no place in this world.* She was the merest passerby, and so was Bobo. And so were their children, Marco, Bobino, and Carolina. Bobino was already gone. She and Bobo would probably be next, but who could tell? And what did it matter? Once upon a time she had felt that her Venetian birthright made her special. But she saw now—as clearly as she was seeing for probably the thousandth time in her fifty-eight years the white boat club marking the mainland—that this assumption was false. Venice had come uncoupled from its past and now looked desperately to the mainland like a cat clinging to a perilous branch. Now this Ponte della Libertà was the true bridge of sighs. Years ago people carried their delusions with them to the grave. Nowadays a person had to face the truth.

Marco said that to maintain your illusions you need a fortune, but to make a fortune you have to shed your illusions. His wife, Natasha, had urged her to go to Cornucopia because everything was so cheap there. But Giulia understood that she was trying to shift her mind from the sadness about Bobino. Natasha said it would be something new, with no memories. More than a year had elapsed since Bobino died. Natasha and Marco's baby, Bumbi, would soon be learning to walk. But Giulia still couldn't look at Bumbi without thinking of Bobino and how—had she foreseen his fate—she would have swept the whole family away to live anywhere in the world, even in a tent in the Sahara, to save him. The thought of meeting him in heaven in a white robe, a pious angel, her most amusing, mischievous child, was almost worse than consigning him body and soul to dust. The priest promised that prayers could gain passage for the unshrived spirit to enter the Kingdom of Heaven, but he offered no assurance that Bobino could continue for eternity as his funny bad-boy self. She had drifted away from the church and hardly went to Mass. What did Santo Stefano matter now? Carolina would never be married there. Her boyfriend was still waiting for his divorce. They had decided to start their family anyhow. The young had no time to waste.

Giulia watched through the cloudy glass their passage among the empty buildings and broken windows of the industrial zone, then along the back streets of Marghera, and past tenements with cluttered balconies. The bus wound this way and that way, down one street and then another, until it seemed the driver was trying to confuse them so they could never find their way out. Finally, at the end of a narrow street, a vast parking lot spread before them and behind it a long, low building with an entrance capped by a gaudy horn of plenty. A restless air ran through the bus: This was their destination. Giulia waited and followed the last person along the aisle and down the steps. She had already forgotten the peril of being last off the bus. The waiting crowd was so eager to get on to the bus that they nearly threw her from the step. One thing Natasha had warned her about was that she would need a one-euro coin to rent a shopping cart. But she hadn't mentioned the urgency with which the shoppers grappled to get their hands on one.

The carts were almost as large as trash collection carts in Venice. The Contessa felt like a circus clown pushing it over the forecourt and through the automatic doors. When she passed the entrance barrier the guard stopped her and asked for the Vuitton bag. At first she didn't understand and hesitated. He said he had to seal it in a plastic bag so she couldn't shoplift. Giulia blinked and handed him the bag.

Once through the barriers she stopped to look around. The place was as big as the airport. In front of her people were crowded around troughs piled with shirts and halters. She pushed on until she found herself in the midst of cascading hills of apples and bananas, lettuces and tomatoes. Every kind of fruit and vegetable imaginable was heaped before her in fairy-tale abundance. She marveled; the place could not be better named. People were picking and choosing from the piles and putting their choices in plastic bags. They wore plastic gloves. She found the glove-and-bag supply and went to work. She felt a little guilty picking the best, but no one was paying any attention. Old Vianello, her local fruitseller, would have taken the bag from her, saying something like, "Cara Contessa, allow me. I have some better stock in the back," and returned from the stockroom with a bag that she wouldn't have had the nerve to open until she got home. It was understood that everyone had to take the bad with the good. Here you only had to take what you wanted. She looked around. This was a new world of opportunism and *benessere* that had nothing to do with her. Under pressure from the lawsuit, she had started to take account of prices. Everything here was a bargain. Soon she had covered the bottom of the cart. She went on to the meat department, and the canned goods, olive oil, detergent. The prices were ridiculous. She could see why people made this terrible journey. And she could see why the carts were so large. If you could get enough, you wouldn't have to come back for a long time.

Natasha was right. Everything was going big. The little shops couldn't keep up. For a while the palaces of Venice were being divided and subdivided into smaller and smaller units so generations of families could stay together. "But now," just as Natasha always said, "everything is going big again—not for families; for business." Practically every day her architectural firm was asked to arrange bids on a new contract to convert a private palace into a hotel or holiday apartments. Every week they got telephone calls from hotel chains asking for properties to buy or lease. "A decree went out from the Mayor of Venice," said Marco, "that all the world should pay to visit, and no one should live there."

When Giulia had passed through the checkout and was packing her plastic bags, she realized how much she had overloaded herself. She could get her four bags to the bus with the cart, but how would she get home? She pushed her cart to the bus stop, parked her bags on the curb, then returned her trolley to the nearest station. The bus arrived as she rejoined her purchases. The rush to deposit groceries in the luggage compartment was frantic. She thought it better to hang back and let them battle without her, but by the time she got to the luggage compartment, it was full. A man noticed her predicament as he swung onto the bus

and called over his shoulder, "There's another compartment on the other side." Giulia staggered around the front
of the bus with the bags beating against her legs and found
a place to stow them. As she walked back to get on the bus,
she passed the driver hurriedly shutting the luggage compartment and rushing around to close the other side.

Giulia climbed onto the bus relieved to have completed
the first stage of a difficult journey. She looked around for
a seat. People were wagging their fingers at her.

"It's full."

"You can't stand up."

"There are no seats; you have to take the next one."

She looked down the aisle and saw the driver looking at
her in his rearview mirror as he started the engine. She
turned and went back down the steps. Her foot had hardly
touched the ground when the bus began to move, while
the door was still closing. She stood on the curb watching
the bus snaking through the parking lot heading for the
main road. Her groceries were gone, disappearing like a
lost child.

She sat down on the bench under the canopy. Why was
everything against her? She had tried to save herself; she
had tried to save money; she had come to this godforsaken
shopping center in that terrible bus. It was all very well for
Natasha; she came here in a car. Anyhow, she was rich and
came only to save time. Why didn't the world give her any
help? She cried for a little while until people began to

gather for the next bus. She wiped her eyes and looked at them. These people knew how to look out for themselves. She was too old to start learning a different way of life. Carolina and Marco and Natasha knew how to take care of themselves. Her grandchildren would be okay. Even Carolina's baby, born with unmarried parents, would be able to cope. They would learn to survive in an ugly world right from the beginning.

Marco arrived late for lunch at the Monaco and found Natasha sitting with a glass of Prosecco looking through a sheaf of floor plans.

"I'm sorry I'm late," said Marco. "Irene del Banco phoned just as I was leaving to say she couldn't come to lunch after all, so we had a quick chat. What are you looking at?"

"This is a palace that someone wants to convert into a hotel. They've asked me whether it's feasible. It's not very promising. You need something like your parents' palace. A courtyard opens so many possibilities."

"Funnily enough, Irene was asking me whether Mamma and Papà would ever consider selling or leasing their palace for a hotel. She said there was a hotel chain asking her to find something in place of a palace they've been trying to get. But it's taking too long—even though they've got La Strada trying to get it for them. She said Palazzo Panfili is just the kind of building they want. I told her that at this point I wouldn't even mention it to Mamma. It's insane how much demand there is. I'll bet that in ten years thirty percent of the new hotels will be closed."

"How's this for something strange," said Natasha. "When I came in I saw that dreadful Doghoni over at the corner table with one of La Strada's people, talking to the acquisitions manager of Hotels International, the same one who keeps in touch with me about the property market. When he saw me, the manager came over to say hello. But I noticed over his shoulder that the two lawyers had stopped talking and were staring at him. They looked very strange. Do you think they're holding something against me because of the lawsuit? They got up and left without having lunch."

Marco didn't say anything for a minute. "I wonder," he said eventually. "You know Vittorio told me that Doghoni used to ring him about palaces for hotel conversion, but stopped after the accident. He was putting consortiums together and needed property. I wonder if that has anything to do with Corrado's insisting that I recuse myself from the case. I can't believe it. Have I been gulled?"

"What kind of offer did Agricoltura make on the villa?"

"It's difficult. They plan to sell or develop the frontage for residential and commercial use and then sell the villa and farmhouse as well. All they really want is the farmland, and that maneuver would virtually pay for it. There's still the problem you're worried about—the brutalization of the countryside. But that's not the worst part. They refuse to keep Gino as manager. They wouldn't tell me why, but the older guy took Papà aside and asked him who supplied the figures for the accounts and who did the audits and who filed the taxes."

"Oh, no. Gino's been cooking the books—stealing from Papà all these years?"

"That's what they seem to be hinting. The man warned Papà that anyone comparing the results they expect to get and the results he's been showing the tax authorities could raise some questions. Gino told them the figures came from Papà and of course Papà signed the declarations. They were interested that the auditor was a friend of Gino's and did the accounts as a favor. But somehow Papà's own accountant seemed not to be paying much attention either. You can imagine how Papà feels about it. The one success he might have enjoyed, stolen from him."

"So he has to get rid of Gino?"

"They won't buy it otherwise. But the man who took Papà aside suggested that he talk to the tax authorities about inviting an investigation and agree on terms in advance. He would have to pay a fine for his carelessness. But Gino could go to jail. They think that the mere mention of the authorities will force him to cut a deal and leave voluntarily."

"Poor Bobo. And Gino keeps his ill-gotten gains."

"Life is short," said Marco.

*

Giulia wondered whether anyone in the store could help her. She went back inside and stood at the Customer Service desk.

"Yeah?" A woman behind the counter addressed her while she continued shuffling and stapling papers.

"I couldn't get on the bus," said the Contessa, "because there were no seats."

"You'll have to take the next one." The woman chewed her gum thoughtfully as she looked at her watch. "There should be another one out there in a couple minutes."

"But my groceries were on the bus that left without me."

The woman stopped chewing and looked at her. "In that case you'll have to wait for that same bus to come back. So go over there to the bar," she pointed across the lobby, "buy yourself a coffee, and go out again in about twenty minutes or so."

Giulia went back to the bus stop. She waited while one bus loaded and left and watched as the next bus arrived. She recognized the driver as he opened the luggage hatches. He glanced over his shoulder as he hurried away towards the café.

Giulia waited until everyone had unloaded their shopping carts, then went to the other side to reclaim her groceries. But they weren't there. She hadn't expected them to be. She wondered who had figured out that her groceries were orphans. Maybe it was that man who had told her there was space on the other side.

She climbed onto the bus and took an aisle seat near the back. She hid behind the tall seats wiping her eyes. The tears wouldn't stop coming. Everything was against her now. She realized that she had been on the descent for most of her life. It was impossible to get on top of life at this point. Bobino's death had not changed things but only hurried them forward. Her life was futile. Bobino had, in a way, caused the misery by bringing on the lawsuit, but the truth was that he was the only person who could have sat here with her and made her laugh about her hopeless situation.

The bus was filling up. A young girl with a blue jewel in her nose asked whether the seat beside her was empty. Giulia nodded without speaking and stood up so she could pass. The girl sat down and looked at her with frank curiosity. "Are you crying? Is something wrong?"

"No, no," said Giulia, but her voice caught on a sob. "My son died, that's all."

"Aw," said the girl, "that's tough. Did it happen just now?"

"Oh, no. It was more than a year ago, but I can't forget."

"I know how it is. Everything reminds you. I was like that when I got divorced. What made you cry now?"

A man in a leather cap who appeared to be a pensioner looked around the seat in front of her, then stood up and bent over her. "What's wrong, Signora?"

The driver climbed into his seat and looked in the mirrors. He called out. "Listen. Everyone has to be seated. You there." He stood up and looked down the bus at the man. "Do you have a seat?"

"Of course I have a seat, but there's a lady here who's in distress."

"Get in your seat or I'll make you get off."

People were leaning into the aisle looking back and forth between the driver and the man in the leather cap.

"You're keeping everyone waiting," said the driver.

"Wait a minute," called a woman, getting up and going to the back of the bus. She looked over the man's shoulder. "Hello, dear. Did you find your groceries?"

"No," said Giulia, shaking her head and wiping her eyes.

"What's this?" asked the man.

The girl with the blue jewel said, "I don't know anything about the groceries, but her son died. That's why she's crying."

But the woman said. "Maybe so, but she also lost her groceries on this bus. I heard her telling them at Customer Service. They seemed to think they would still be on the bus."

The man in the cap straightened up and walked down the bus towards the driver.

"You sit down," said the driver, "or I'm calling the police to take you off."

"You sit down," said the man. He leaned over behind the driver's seat and lifted a newspaper, then pulled one, two, three plastic bags and a Vuitton bag from underneath. "What's this?"

"I have no idea," said the driver. "They were left in the compartment. I asked everyone, and no one knew anything about them. I was going to turn them in to the lost and found."

"That's why you put them under the newspaper?" The man shook his head, then carried the bags up the aisle and placed them near the Contessa. "Are these the ones, Signora?"

She looked at the bags. "Yes, yes," she nodded, wiping her eyes.

"I'll leave them here," said the man, "and don't worry. We'll help you get them off. The driver said he'd asked everyone who they belonged to." He smiled at her and shook his head. "You know how it is." He patted her shoulder. "We're all sinners." He went back to his seat.

When the bus arrived in Piazzale Roma the people around her picked up the bags and carried them down the steps, lining them up along the far edge of the walkway. The man in the leather cap joined her with his shopping cart. He balanced one bag on his cart and carried the other two in his hand, leaving her to shoulder the Vuitton bag.

"We'll try to leave a couple of these bags over at the luggage check, so you can make two trips. My wife always buys more than she can carry. Then she rings me to come and get her. That's the life of a retired husband—always at-your-service."

At the luggage deposit the man heaved two of the bags onto the counter. The attendant behind the counter looked up.

"Whataya got there? We don't take perishables."

The man in the cap looked at him. "Come on, mate. You can see that she's got a problem. Help her out for heaven's sake. She's not used to this kind of thing. Can't you see that?"

The attendant stood up and tore off two claim checks. "That'll be four euros. And you better be back in an hour. I can't be responsible for this stuff."

The Contessa and her good Samaritan walked together towards the vaporetto.

"Which way do you go?" he asked, putting down the bag he was carrying for her.

"I take this one," she said.

"I take the one farther on."

"I can't thank you enough," she said.

"*Madonna*. It's nothing. I was glad to save your groceries from a thief. There's too much of that around."

The Contessa nodded.

"Did you really lose a son?"

"Yes, in a car crash. It was in the *Gazzettino*. The one where the car turned over and burned."

"Oh, I saw that. It was a while back. With the young boy Patristi. Terrible. Was he your son?"

"No. My son was the driver."

"Ohhh. So you've got that lawsuit."

"Yes. It's a terrible burden."

"Stay away from lawyers, stay away from doctors . . . they used to say to stay away from priests, but I guess they're harmless now. My daughter's going to be a lawyer. I guess it's better to be one than at the mercy of one."

"My son wasn't on drugs like they said in the newspaper." The instant she said it she recognized Bingo Benson and his journalist friend staring at her from a distance like vultures on a cliff. She felt like crying again. The journalist had been collecting gossip for months for a magazine article about Venice. He went everywhere questioning people about Bobino and the car crash and the lawsuit. Marco had even noticed him at the hearings.

"I can believe it," said the man. "The newspapers write any damn shit they please. Excuse my French, Contessa. But you know what I mean: Stay away from journalists."

For the first time in a year, Giulia Panfili laughed in spite of herself, just as she would have laughed with Bobino. It was exactly his kind of naughty remark.

"I remember the article," he went on, "because I used to hear about your boys and the Count, your husband, from my brother-in-law. He was a gondolier. He used to help his son-in-law teach rowing and look after the boats out at the club where your husband and sons used to row. My brother-in-law used to talk about them. He held them in high regard."

"So he knew Bobino? Does he know how he died?"

"*Può darsi.* Maybe. He's dead himself. That's another story. He had a bad back. He thought it was from heaving boats in and out of the water. He went to the hospital. They decided it must be his kidneys so they stuck him with a needle to take a sample. From that one kidney got infected and they had to take it out. But he still had the backache, so they loaded him up with painkillers, which ruined the other kidney and that was the end of him."

"Oh, dear. Did his family get any redress?"

"Ha! We went to a lawyer and he more or less said that he didn't want to make any enemies at the hospital. He said we would be better off ourselves to stay on the right side of the doctors. I don't know. We felt like they killed him, but there was nothing we could do. That was one of the reasons my daughter decided to become a lawyer. My brother-in-law used to argue like a lawyer. He was a smart guy. They used to call him Volpòn, the Fox, when he was a gondolier. The children got all fired up about it. They joined the Communist Party to get some help, but it turned out that the hospital has strong ties with the Communists so it was the same story as the lawyer. I think sometimes it's a hand-icap to be in the right. Even my daughter says it can be an advantage to have some fault on your side. It makes you normal. Like I said, we're all sinners."

He helped her to the *pontile*. As he left her, she saw Bingo and the journalist approach him. They would never let her have any peace. The man was talking to them, animatedly. She could imagine him making things up to seem important, to be in the newspapers. So many people she had thought were friends had done it. This man had no reason to be loyal to her.

The boat arrived. The sailor helped her lift the bag nearest to him as she struggled aboard. The boat pulled out. Looking back, she got one more glimpse of the man talking to Bingo and the journalist. The man turned and started away from them but they followed him, gesticulating. Suddenly he turned, leaned forward, and spat like a goose. The journalist jumped back and wiped his face. Bingo's crowing laugh howled across the water. Giulia Panfili was aghast. Then she put her hand over her mouth and laughed for the second time in ten minutes.

Walking home with her shoulder aching from the weight of the bulging Vuitton bag and her fingers numb from the weight of the plastic bag, she crossed the last bridge then put down her bags to rest. She hoped not to see anyone she knew so she interested herself in some writing on the building beside her, scrawled in blue marker and written like a verse or an incantation:

Mago Alexander
Dio ti punerà—
Ladro!

Wizard Alexander
God will punish you—
Thief!

She could imagine the story. The wizard would have stolen money, but he would have stolen the person's hope as well. That was what caused the bitterness. As she turned to pick up her bags, she wondered whether God ever did punish such thieves. But her bags weren't where she'd put them. Someone had picked them up. She raised her eyes in alarm and saw the delivery boy from the florist.

"*Buona sera,* Contessa. Can I help?"

Her heart was pounding. Why? Was it because money was so important now? Or was she afraid of everyone?

"Oh, I couldn't ask you to do that."

"Don't worry," he said, turning to lead the way. "I'm going by your house. My mother used to carry bags like this before we moved to the mainland. Now we have a car. You're brave to try it." He carried the bags all the way up to the kitchen and wouldn't even accept a tip. She supposed he knew about the lawsuit. She was no longer the Contessa she had been. She felt touched by his generosity but humiliated too.

As she unpacked the first load she realized that there would hardly be space for all she had yet to bring. The kitchen would be as piled with food as it used to be when they gave dinners for twenty or thirty people. They would have to eat like farmers. Anyway, it would be fun cooking, and she could freeze some of it. Her mother used to talk about cooking and canning as a young bride during the war and about how her father used to dream of her cooking when he was in Africa. They had moved to the country when the war started so they could grow food and get fruit from the orchards. Now we are in our own war.

She was thinking as she went down to the mezzanine to look in the maid's storeroom: In the end we are all human. Even that willful maid, Maria, who had quit her job at the age of fifty-two to marry, had turned out to have a sympathetic side. Her childhood sweetheart, after his wife died, came back to woo her by fishing every day on the opposite bank of the Grand Canal, where she would see him each time she shook a duster or cleaned a window. Bobo used to say the windows overlooking the Grand Canal had never been so bright. After the accident the Panfilis had stopped trying to replace her. Instead, they hired a girl who came in twice a week. Behind a cupboard, Giulia found what she was looking for: the maid's shopping cart. "Wheels make the world go round"—that was Marco's mantra about living in the country. She remembered the families in the parking lot at the shopping mall loading their groceries into their cars and imagined them unloading in front of their houses—instead of struggling to a boat and then from the boat stop struggling for fifteen or twenty minutes more on foot. Contessa Panfili marveled at how everything had changed since she used to speak out for the old ways and the old institutions. And she had thought herself a champion of Venice.

When the children were young and they used to go to the villa, she'd never done the grocery shopping. Later, when the children were studying in Rome and Milan, she was too busy to go to the villa, and now it had to be sold. She would go once or twice to help Bobo decide what to keep. If they stayed for a few days she would take Bobo to the shopping mall so he could see it. She didn't think she would ever go back from Venice and carry her groceries like she was doing now. Of course there were supermarkets in different parts of Venice as well. Soon there would be no shops and only supermarkets. In the end, she would be carrying groceries willy-nilly.

On the vaporetto to Piazzale Roma with her shopping cart to pick up the two remaining bags from the luggage deposit, Giulia rang Marco on her cell phone.

"Marco?"

"Ciao! How was your trip to Cornucopia?"

"Epic."

"Did you like it? Will you go back?"

"*Forse*—maybe. But not on that bus again."

"But even if you had a car in Venice, Mamma, you wouldn't take it out to go shopping and then have to unpack the car and get your groceries down to the boat. It would be worse than the bus."

"I'm thinking of something else. How's Papà? I can't reach him. Is he on the train?"

"Probably. Agricoltura made an offer for the villa and the farm, but it's complicated. Papà will tell you."

"Marco, would Natasha be annoyed if we didn't sell the villa?"

"Don't worry, Mamma. Papà is reconciled to it. There's no alternative. We'll work it out."

"But I'm thinking that maybe we should live in the country. We'd be nearer to you and Natasha, and it would be more convenient for Carolina to come from Milan. Do you think Natasha could find a hotel chain that would lease the palazzo?"

"Are you just saying that? Natasha has any number of people looking for hotel property. In fact, Irene del Banco was talking about something as well. You can certainly find someone at this point, but I think this madness can't last. On the other hand, you might get a nest egg, more income than you've ever had before, and in ten years get your palace back again."

"Papà would be so happy if we were solvent."

"It could be more than that. In fact, it just occurred to me, Mamma. If you put that palace out of reach, you might get rid of Doghoni."

Marco put down the telephone. He picked it up again and rang Natasha.

"Ciao, *cara*. I've just talked to Mamma, and you won't believe it: She sounds like she's back among the living."

"How can you tell?"

"She's making plans. She's talking about moving to the country. It sounds like you're going to get another hotel project. I'll tell you about it tonight."

"What caused it?"

"She went out to Cornucopia to do the shopping. She couldn't explain much; she was on the vaporetto."

"Fantastic! I'm so happy. Didn't I tell you? She only needed to get out and see a bit of life."

ART

Cinzio saw human actions as shapes altering them-selves against a blank canvas and only later, if at all, attached significance to what was going on. For example, if someone extended his hand, Cinzio might be so impressed with the squareness of the paw or the backward swoop of the thumb that he might almost forget to shake it. Even something so important to his emotional life as the ap-pearance of the top of his daughter's head getting bigger and rounder as she came into the world was entertained as a visual matter for quite some time before it became asso-ciated with love and joy. His memory was a caravan of moving shapes. He had little skill in putting thoughts into words. And what entered through his eyes rarely found its way out in the form of speech. If it came out at all it usu-ally emerged as a form on canvas. He preferred staring at people and things to thinking or talking about them. He understood little about human nature and was himself generally misunderstood. But he had a nice affable grin that expressed, better than anything else, the truth about his strange uncomplicated nature.

Cinzio Calabron, with his gorilla shoulders and moose jaw, looked more like a boxer than an aesthete. Nevertheless, on this clear day under the blue Venetian sky, he was up on top of the Accademia Bridge, squared off in front of his easel, palette and brush to the fore, unconcerned that he was attracting a considerable crowd of amateur critics. He was only sketching the underdrawing for a painting, but the animation around him vouched for its startling quality. Hardly a passerby glanced at the canvas without flinging himself on the parapet to scan the nearby palaces. And not a few of them, frustrated, came back to indulge another hasty squint. They murmured among themselves.

"Do you see it?"

"Damned if I can make out anything from here."

Two American men sauntered over to have a look. They glanced at the canvas and then at the nearest palace.

"Reminds me of the one where a guy says 'Hey, look at the ladybug,' and the other guy says, 'Gad, what eyesight!'"

The crowd continued to grow. Each new voyeur stepped in for a look then stepped back a seemly distance and strained to see over the heads of those hanging over the parapet. A continuous commentary murmured through the crowd.

"You couldn't see anything from here anyhow."

"You'd have to have the eyes of a hawk."

"It must be a joke. *Sta scherzando.*"

"Maybe we should call the police. *Chiamiamo i vigili.*"

Cinzio Calabron continued to paint. He worked fast, ignoring the chatter except to stick out his chin and assume a stubborn look. He was thoroughly accustomed to his wife crisscrossing the room behind him, twittering like an angry blackbird every time he started a new painting. That was the reason he was out here today. He couldn't take any more of her squawking.

Meanwhile, at the C & D Campana Gallery near Piazza San Marco, Dottoressa Cara Campana had no idea of the excitement her most promising discovery was creating as she stood gazing at the middle Calabron in a row of three. She spoke without taking her eyes from the work. Her audience, Dottor Emilio Zambon, was a dentist from the Friuli who believed that art bought in Venice had a special cachet. Cara Campana never disabused him; in fact, she thought she might have been the one who gave him the idea in the first place.

"These are the only three paintings we have left from the twenty—*twenty*, mind you—we bought from the artist, less—just imagine, *less*—than two months ago." She was telling the truth. She made it a point always to start with the truth; it made, by far, the best base for who-knows-what claims might spring into her improvised discourse. Her pitch was bright and mechanical.

"We bought heavily into Calabron," she continued, "because his work has those rare—*rare*—qualities that make a modern master. We were happy with the purchase as a long-term investment, but the response—*response* is really an understatement—has been incredible; our most savvy collectors have been snapping him up, just *snapping* him up. This week my husband has to negotiate another purchase. It will be much—*much*—more expensive. But that's the way it goes with important discoveries. *This* painting is the masterpiece of the entire group, and of course the most expensive. I wanted to keep it for the gallery, but my husband convinced me that for the sake of the artist we should let it go, as long as it goes to a collection of the highest—the *very highest*—quality."

Dottor Zambon stood with his arms crossed and his head tilted, looking like the connoisseur he aspired to be. The object under scrutiny was an abstraction in tones of ocher that might have descended from that famous work once compared to an explosion in a shingle factory. Calabron seemed to go in for lyrical titles. He claimed they floated to his ears as he walked through the crowded streets. This one was called *Love Is Where You Find It*. Zambon's gaze wandered to the two paintings flanking it: *Hidden Passion* and *All Animals Are Sad*. He thought he could see why the center picture was more important and more expensive.

"I'll take it," he said with a sharp nod.

Cara Campana nodded slowly; she never hurried at this stage. "I am almost sorry to let it go, but I know your collection. This Calabron will fit into it perfectly—*perfectly*," she nodded again. "Shall I have it sent by courier?"

"No, I'll take it with me. I want to show it to my wife."

"Of course. And if she doesn't like it, you know we wouldn't mind at all having it back. Would you like us to bill you?" This exchange was part of the purchase ritual they executed every time he bought a painting.

"No. I'll pay with my credit card."

"Very well." She called through the door into the corridor of offices and storerooms. "Gino? Could you come out and package a Calabron for Dottor Zambon, please?"

As she processed the payment and waited for the painting to be packed, she passed the time praising the collector's earlier purchases and admiring his uncanny eye for quality.

After he left she went back to her office to indulge in her favorite pastime: adding up the weekly sales, then the monthly sales, then comparing sales for the same period in the year before, and every permutation and projection she could imagine. This week had been almost, but not quite, a record week. The Calabron sale would put her over. She and her husband had opened the gallery only two years earlier, and they had already opened another gallery where they were showing Calabron's drawings. Cara Campana had decided to support Calabron's show of abstract paintings with a companion show of his stunning academic drawings. The contrast made a good talking point.

She seemed to be getting better and better at the selling game. She had come up with the bright idea to target the professional classes—doctors, dentists, lawyers—people earnestly cranking the winch of art to hoist themselves into the establishment. Her success in the gallery left her husband, Dino, free to do what he was best at—wheel and deal: He was a demon networker. That was his forte. He got the lease on the new space around the corner at a huge discount because someone told him that the glass shop there was failing, and this morning he'd managed to get a radio interview for Calabron slipped into a cancellation slot. Cara had transmitted the message to Calabron's wife, Rina. Cara was a little displeased not to find the artist himself at home working. She was going to need a steady supply of his work. He would have to keep busy to stay ahead of her.

Cinzio didn't know his paintings were in demand and didn't feel at all under pressure. He painted because he wanted to. But he never painted after dinner; instead, he sat alone on the fat sofa in the rough ground-floor room that doubled as studio and sitting room, watching television or rather, staring at the moving images. Rina didn't join him because she couldn't stand the way he flicked from channel to channel without ever getting interested in any program. It was like a nervous habit that he couldn't stop—*click, click, click, click*—until he got so weary from the flashing images that he shut his eyes, threw back his head, and within two seconds let rip with a snore no motorboat could better. Rina busied herself putting the baby to bed and clearing away the dinner. Then she sat and watched television in the kitchen until she got bored and went to bed herself. Once in bed, she liked to pretend that she was back in the mountains, but it was difficult because of the echoing footsteps in the calle, the roar of passing motorboats, and the ensuing splash of waves against the house. She was beginning to feel that Cinzio might soon be successful enough to buy a cottage where they could go in the winter.

When they had met in the mountains as ski instructors and he said he was a painter, she had assumed that he had a normal trade. Her father exposed him when he asked him to paint a door. It was perfectly natural for a father to appraise a suitor. He wanted to know whether the young man was likely to be able to support his daughter. But the test raised more questions than it answered. When it finally came out that Cinzio knew no more about putting enamel on a door than he knew about mending a clock,

Rina's father was nonplussed. In the end he told his daughter she had to decide whether to take a chance on that kind of painter. So she waited to marry Cinzio until he finished at the Accademia. Somewhere along the line he promised to take her back to the mountains as soon as he could afford it. He couldn't remember the occasion, but she did. He thought living in the mountains sometime might be nice, but he had no idea when he would have that kind of money to spare so it wasn't a pressing issue.

Since there were almost ten small local television channels to every large national one, more often than not Cinzio woke up in the small hours to find himself tuned in to one of the local channels that lapsed, after prime time, into sex videos. Sometimes he sat there blinking for a long time before he could figure out what was happening on the screen. The camera angles were so strange—"art shots," they called them. The odd arrangements of flesh were something remarkable. He tried to remember the best shapes so he could transfer them to canvas. Rina, having nothing of the artist in her, had no trouble at all recognizing what was happening with the shapes he was painting. She scolded him and called him a pervert. But he went right on painting and painting until the forms were lost under a complex veil of lines and drips and patches. Rina never doubted it was her nagging that drove him to obliterate the underpainting, so she never relented. But for Cinzio the shapes were only the initial phase, the inspiration, the substructure. They worked a kind of magic; the method got him going. And it made him prolific, too. The downside was that it made his wife into an awful harridan.

One afternoon Cinzio put a clean canvas on his easel and started to paint. He had only covered a few square inches when Rina started her lament.

"What is wrong with you that you have to paint such smut? I think you're sick and need a doctor. Normal people don't think like you. Where do you get this nasty stuff? Is your head so full of trash that it has to spill out onto the canvas. I never knew you had this disgusting side to you." She rattled on and on, hardly drawing breath, never at a loss for words. It was her part in the creative process, and today she was a speaker taken by a spirit.

Cinzio was stolid and resistant as a Venetian foundation, impermeable as Istrian stone; he could shut out rivers of drivel, torrents of aggression, but today something cracked. Maybe he was tired. He jumped up like a man in danger, grabbed the canvas, folded his easel, swept his paints and brushes into a rucksack and ran out the door. He staggered along San Vio with his easel sprawled under one arm, his canvas in his other hand and the rucksack on his shoulder. When he got to the top of the Accademia Bridge, there were already two artists eking out their poetic renderings. One was rendering the Grand Canal towards the Salute, and the other the façade of the storied Palazzo Barbaro. He got as far away from them as he could and set himself up. He started to paint. This was much better. He had almost finished the basic shapes when he realized that people behind him were trying to find his models in the windows of the nearby palaces and were muttering among themselves about public places. But he was used to worse babble than this, so he painted on and on, just the way he did on a normal day at home.

While Cara Campana was sitting in her office amusing herself by working out her weekly averages and thinking about what angle Dino might use to get another consignment of Calabrons without having to pay a lot more for them, the doorbell rang. When she came out of her office and saw who had rung the bell, she could have spit tacks. Standing outside the door was Dottor Zambon with the Calabron painting under his arm. Damn! Sometimes these novice collectors were like children. She went to the door smiling and called through the glass, "Please wait a minute. I have to go shut down the alarm system. I was getting ready to go out and my assistant isn't here."

She went back to her office and sat down at her desk. She lit a cigarette. What a damned bore. It was pretty clear that he had changed his mind about the picture. She would have to be completely relaxed and persuade him that it would be a mistake not to keep it on approval. She would get him to take it home for a week or two. She had been through it all before with these earnest neophytes. At the end of the first week she would ring and tell him that an important collector from Austria or Switzerland had come asking for that very painting, and she was just ringing to find out whether she could let him have it and when. No one ever let go under those circumstances. She thought it was partly the fun of depriving the foreigner. She always shared their joy saying how happy she was to keep that particular work in such an important collection in Italy. She finished her cigarette and went back to open the front door.

"So sorry about the delay. It's such a complicated system and it doesn't like to be turned off so soon after it's been turned on. I had to wait. Tell me. Have you had some second thoughts?"

"Yes," said Dottor Zambon. He was a little sheepish. On the whole that was a good sign: he would be pliable. He shrugged, "My wife and I were talking about collecting some artists in depth, and I think Calabron is a good one to start with. I've decided to buy the other two as well."

Cara Campana did a quick calculation and felt like hugging him, but she had the professionalism not to show any excitement. She substituted concern.

"He's a good artist for that," she nodded, "but it leaves

me with no Calabrons in the gallery. Would you mind letting me mark them as sold and keep them on show until my husband can arrange another purchase with the artist? It's in your interest as well."

"No problem. I can't carry three paintings anyway. But could you give me photographs to show my wife?"

"Of course. Should I send a bill?"

"No, I'll pay as usual."

Cara's weekly average was something amazing.

Cinzio was enjoying painting on the bridge. The crowd of onlookers had dispersed. He was left with only a pair of *vigili* staring at his canvas. They looked puzzled.

"What are you painting?"

"I don't know yet. I could call it *Academy Piece.*"

"Does it have something to do with the Accademia?"

"Sure. I'm on the Accademia Bridge."

"Are you painting something you see?"

"Sure. Everything. I look around. If you stand there, I'll have something about you in it too."

"Listen, maestro. You've been denounced for showing pornography. Where is it? Is it in your bag there?"

"No. But go ahead and look. This is the only painting I've got."

Two young men had come up behind him and stood looking at his canvas, speaking English between themselves. One turned to the *vigili* and asked why the picture had been denounced.

The older *vigile* looked at him. "You live here, don't you? Didn't you used to ride a bike down there in the campo when you were a baby?"

"Yeah. Small world, isn't it. I've come back. But what's wrong with the painting?"

"That's the mystery. Something strange is going on here. We had about five calls all excited about a man painting obscene acts and we ran all the way. What do you see?"

"*Bò!*" said Bingo Benson. "I don't see anything but odd shapes, but I'm not looking for anything. I have a satisfactory life at home." He grinned.

Cinzio laughed and nodded excitedly. Both *vigili* also nodded and smiled. The younger one said, "That's a thought. Maybe that's why none of us can see it."

Giovanni del Banco from the *Gazzettino* had joined them. A security guard at the *Municipio* had crossed the bridge on his way to work and hurried up to Giovanni's office to alert him to this exciting new artist. "Abstract art is meant to be suggestive," he said to the *vigili,* who listened because they knew him from seeing him around the city offices. "Sometimes it's planned, sometimes it's subconscious. There are some shapes that typically evoke certain ideas. Those ink-blot tests revealed that."

Bingo Benson's companion asked him whether the Italian talking to the *vigili* was talking about the Rorschach.

"Yes. He's a journalist too. Maybe you should put this artist in your article for *Fast Lane*, Cad. Give me your card. I'll set up an appointment with him."

When Cinzio got home, he was in a good mood. He'd finished the painting and felt like starting another. His wife was glad to see him, and especially relieved to see that the finished product belied the underpainting. He gave her the card of Cadmus Argos Peacock, the *Fast Lane* journalist, to give to the gallery. She too had good news. The gallery had rung to say that he was to go to Palazzo Labia the following day to do a live radio interview. If it was successful, they might be able to arrange a television interview later. Also, they wanted to buy another lot of paintings. Dino Campana had played it cool on the telephone, but Rina figured they wouldn't be buying if they weren't selling. "Did you notice, Cinzio," she said, "it was so clear today you could see the mountains?"

The next morning Cinzio crossed Campo San Zuan Degolà entertaining a vague image of the campo's namesake, St. John Beheaded, as he plodded along. He didn't feel like doing a radio interview; he felt like painting today. A gurgling neck would be an interesting way to start.

As he entered the lobby of Palazzo Labia, Cinzio held on to the C & D Campana Gallery catalog that Rina had handed him when he went out the door. He wondered whether he couldn't just leave the catalog for the interviewer. She could just read from it. He went to the desk and started to offer the guard the catalog.

"Do you have an appointment with someone?" the guard asked.

"Bella Bontà," said Cinzio.

"She's not here," said the guard. "She's in Rome."

"Fine," said Cinzio, turning to leave. "She might have let me know."

"No," said the guard. "Come back; she's never here. She works in Rome. She does her interviews long distance. Hardly anybody works here anymore." He called upstairs for someone to come down.

A blond girl in a halter top and miniskirt appeared on the grand staircase. *"Allooo. . . ."* She hailed Cinzio so she didn't have to come all the way down. He hurried over and followed her up the stairs. Looking up, he felt a rush of inspiration. He so wished he didn't have to do this interview; he could have started a painting right then and there.

The girl led him into a large office. "This is the interview for Bella," she said, to a man who was sitting on the floor stacking tapes. "Where should I put him?"

He turned. "You can put him in Studio D. I've set it up for recording this afternoon, but it will be fine."

She took him into a dark room full of electronic equipment like a cockpit. She sat him at a table, put a microphone in front of him, and clamped some earphones on

his head. She told him not to get too close to the microphone when he spoke. She said he would hear the interviewer over the earphones in a little while. She left.

Cinzio looked around at all the little lights. Maybe his
mother was right. She had speculated for years that when
she snapped off her radio or television as an expression of
dissent, a light went out in the studio where the program
was being transmitted. He could see what she meant now.
He wondered how she'd worked that out. She always said
it was only a tiny light, like a single pinpoint in a great big
LED, something that didn't interrupt but gave a little fillip
to the broadcaster. He wished he'd told his mother to listen
to the program. He might have been able to figure out
which one she was.

"Good afternoon, good friends, wherever you may be!"
A brassy voice poured through the earphones straight into
the middle of his reverie. "It's Bella Bontà with news and
amusements for the Now Crowd. Our first guest today is
the latest discovery of the famous Campana Gallery of
Venice—Cinzio Calabron. Hello there, Cinzio! Welcome
to the Bontà Hour."

"Hullo," said Cinzio. He was pretty sure he didn't like
this woman.

"Tell us what you do, Cinzio."

"I paint pictures."

"Yes. Beautiful, interesting pictures. We are looking at

some here in the catalog. The one called *Love Is Where You Find It* tells me that you are an abstract painter."

"Yes."

Bella was not enjoying this. Why hadn't someone warmed up this creature? "I guess it would be pretty hard to find love in what I see here."

"It's there."

Damn those lazy tarts in Venice, she thought; damn this arty-smarty. "Do you believe that people see what *you* see in what you paint?"

"I don't care." Cinzio looked up as he spoke. He was just concluding that this was a terrible bore when he saw a little light go out, then another, and he realized—*he* was the bore. He had to retrench. "What I mean is that people can see what they want to see, but the ideas are there nevertheless." One light came on.

"Do you mean that your paintings are just a starting place?" Another light came on, and another. He could see that this Bella Bontà really knew her business.

"I guess so. In fact it's all a joke, really." Several lights came on. He was catching on.

"You mean your art is just a leg pull?"

"Oh, more than just a leg pull." Several lights flickered; he wondered what that meant—borderline exasperation?—delight? "It's an everything pull." More lights came on. He had to keep looking around. It was like tracking a mosquito. More lights flickered. It was hard to keep up. He could just about manage because Venice is such a small place, but she must have hundreds of thousands of lights in her studio. Her head must be spinning after five minutes. He was beginning to admire her.

"Maestro. These are fascinating revelations for our audience. Have you ever spoken so frankly about your art before?"

"No, I never talk about it." One light flickered. "The truth is, I do it for fun." The light went out. "No. That's not the truth. The truth is that I do it for money." Three, four, five lights went on and stayed on.

"What inspires you, then? Only money?" The five lights went out.

"Television." Lights flickered here and there. "I watch television. Every night." He was struggling. More lights flickered.

"Thank you, Cinzio Campana, for your frank revelations about the art of today."

"Calabron!" he shouted. "I'm Calabron!"

"You're off the air, sir," said a man's voice. "This is the engineer."

Cinzio was sitting at the dinner table watching the baby try to eat a *banito* in the manner of a monkey. He had bought the *banito* at the Rialto on his way home from

Palazzo Labia. "A baby banana for baby Barbi," said Rina, as Cinzio watched her peel the skin back then place it like a nosegay in the little hand. The baby couldn't get her mouth on the right part and was beginning to feel cross. Her face looked like a dirty plate. Cinzio felt pretty disgruntled himself. Everybody was mad at him; they said he'd ruined his career. He wished he'd stayed home and painted. The Campanas had been horrified by the radio interview. Then the *Gazzettino* that same morning had published an article about his being denounced to the police for showing pornography on the Accademia Bridge. The journalist had written more about the power of suggestion than about pornography and had hardly mentioned his art, but the Campanas had taken it badly nonetheless. Rina said it had been a struggle getting them to buy some more paintings even at the same price as before.

"They said there was a journalist from an English magazine as well worrying them about the pornography question. I think it must be that Cadmus from *Fast Lane* who gave you his card. The strange thing," said Rina, as she started clearing the table, "is that they are giving this English journalist an interview and said they would do it with you there at the gallery. They said they wanted to guide you through it and avoid mistakes."

"I was just getting the hang of that radio interview when they turned it off," said Cinzio. "Strange, isn't it; my mother was right about those lights all along and I never believed her. I wonder how she ever came to know about something like that."

"She told me she just guessed," said Rina, "because they're always telling you how many people watch a program on a particular night so there has to be something like that."

"*Uffa.* I wouldn't want the job of counting those lights. You can hardly keep up with them. I guess I wouldn't have made a very good showing. It's a good thing there was no one there to count."

"Never mind, Cinzio," said Rina with a sigh. "We have to stop thinking about it. Tomorrow morning Dottoressa Campana wants you to take as many paintings as you have ready over to the gallery. She says you should come to the back door. She'll look at them and see if there's anything she might be able to sell. But she says you've practically ruined all her good work." Rina stood up and started stacking the plates. "They shouldn't have just sent you over to Palazzo Labia like that. You're an artist. What do you know about interviews?

"Oh, and there was another thing. I almost don't want to tell you. They're putting up your drawings in that new space they're opening around the corner from the gallery. She says the contrast between the academic drawings and your abstract work might help to give you credibility. She said she knew you hadn't intended to show them, but she had to do everything possible to try to retrieve the situation."

"I hope she's not going to try to force me to start painting like Canaletto," said Cinzio, sticking out his chin. "I'm not going to do that."

"Can you paint like Canaletto?"

"No."

Rina gave a little shrug and returned to rinsing the plates.

"More like Bellotto," said Cinzio thoughtfully.

Rina had her back to him so he couldn't see the expression on her face when she heard what he said. After a few minutes she turned around. "I've seen Bellotto's paintings," she said thoughtfully. "Sometimes he painted in the mountains. He must have had a house there."

Cinzio pulled his luggage cart loaded with nine paintings down the calle that led to the back door of C & D Campana Gallery. He had ideas from his adventures of the day before for two more paintings and he wanted to get back to work. He rang the bell. Gino the factotum opened the door.

"Ah!" said Gino, when he saw Cinzio. "I'd better tell the Dottoressa at once. She's waiting for these paintings to arrive. She keeps asking if you've come yet."

"I don't have time to wait for her to sort through them," said Cinzio. He didn't feel like being scolded. "I want to get back to the studio. I'll pick up the cart and the ones she doesn't want when I come for that interview." Instead of going back the way he came, Cinzio went down the side calle that led onto the *fondamenta*. As he came out, he looked along the shops towards the gallery. He could see people milling around, but turned in the other direction towards the gondola ferry. As he cut across Campo San Fantin, the journalist from the *Gazzettino* hailed him. Cinzio looked at him. There was something in this man's face that looked uncertain, like he wasn't quite finished.

"Did you read my article?"

"No."

"I was hoping you liked it. I'll do an interview with you someday."

"I'm no good. I don't like to talk. I had a bad interview yesterday morning."

"You mean the one on the radio? I heard it was very funny. People said you sounded like a real artist."

"The gallery's not happy."

"I wonder what they want?"

But Cinzio just looked at him. He was thinking about how this man's eyes were like two different shapes of almond and how they weren't even the same shade of brown. He liked them.

*

Cara and Dino Campana were having dinner at Da Ivo to celebrate Cara's record week.

"That *Gazzettino* journalist, del Banco, the one who wrote about Calabron's painting pornography on the bridge, did a really wonderful article about the drawings. I've already sold the drawing he used to illustrate it."

"I saw it but I didn't have time to read it. He used the drawing of the Patristi broken arch, the one you have in the window."

Cara pulled a folded newspaper clipping from her handbag. "I've got it here. He says the drawing of the arch is an example of Calabron's peculiar way of seeing. He says, 'The draftsmanship is strangely delicate in a way that makes the arch seem to be almost alive with the window, like an eyeball looking at something so intriguing as to merit its cramming itself right into the arch to get a better look.' He goes on, 'Only an artist of the first quality could identify and then capture the haunting beauty in an image as universally decried for its ugliness as this broken arch.'"

"That's a good advertisement. We should get to know this journalist."

"Everyone is so *taken* by that drawing. I could have sold it three times—*three times*—in one morning. Signora Fallon saw it in the *Gazzettino* and rang up immediately. Of course you can see why she would want it—her new husband is the architect for the Patristi restoration and she's divorced from Barone Patristi. She used to live in that palace. Marda Segusio caused the divorce, remember? She was having an affair with him. Marda was another one who wanted to buy it, but I didn't want to waste it on her. I think she planned to give it to the Barone as a way of getting in touch with him now that he's divorced. She still talks about him. She says he was in love with her and only married Sofi Fierazzo for her money. According to Marda, Fierazzo is a truly vicious woman. She's making Patristi sell his palace because she paid for the restoration, which means that her architect husband will get a lot of the money from the sale. Marda thinks she was having an affair with the architect all along and she's sure that when the Patristi boy died she was secretly happy because she was having another baby anyway and it gave her the chance to pull the Barone's palace out from under him."

"My God that's diabolical," said Dino with disbelief.

"It shows you the power of money in a marriage. She's a clever woman, and I want to keep her as a client."

"Sounds like she's inherited her father's acumen," said Dino.

"But there's something strange going on. She insisted that no one should know that she bought it and we have to hold on to it until she tells us to whom she wants it presented. It's a gift. She wants Calabron to present it himself. I haven't told Cinzio yet."

"That will take some convincing. I wonder what she plans to do with it."

"I think I can guess. I'll bet you anything she's going to give it to her ex-husband to blow him a raspberry. Your friends the Padoanos are buying the palace. In fact, someone tried to buy the drawing for the Padoanos as well. He was called Daniele; he was with Cantiere Italia. He asked me who had bought it and said he'd pay double, even triple what they paid. He said Signora Padoano wanted it taken out of the window."

"That sounds like a good deal. Can you convince Signora Fallon?"

"No. I wouldn't try. Believe me, she's worth more as a client. She told me she's starting a modern art collection. I see Cinzio as a long-term investment for us. Remember when there was that Picasso exhibition and everyone was so interested that he could draw so well? It's an important distinction for an abstract painter."

"But I would never," said Dino, "have picked Cinzio Calabron to turn out lucky. He looks like a fall guy to me."

"*And how,*" said Cara. "But there it is. He gives an interview so ridiculous that the interviewer cuts it short and everyone thinks it's a masterpiece of artistic personality. He nearly gets arrested for pornography and the public rushes to see his paintings for themselves. A journalist from an English glossy just happens to show up in the middle of it all to give him an international reputation. He's a lucky one."

"All he needs is good management," she added.

"From now on the big collectors will begin to buy him," said Dino, "which means we won't be able to keep the kind of control we have now, buying stock outright and selling to the new collectors from the professional classes. If we want to keep him, we'll have to put him on a contract and sell on commission."

"Why? He's in a world of his own. He won't know the difference."

"His wife will. And if she doesn't figure it out, some gallery that wants him will explain it to her."

"Maybe she won't listen. What if we were to lend them our cottage in the mountains? It's a bit rustic for us now. We could sell it to the gallery and buy something big where we could do promotions."

"Antonio!" Dino hailed the waiter as he squeezed Cara's hand. "Would you bring us another bottle of Prosecco?"

It was another clear day under the blue Venetian sky, and Cinzio Calabron was once again up on top of the Accademia Bridge, but this time he was as tranquil as a Sunday painter, seated at his easel on a folding camp stool, with

Rina's blessings at his feet: a box of sandwiches and a bottle of water on one side and, on the other side, where people passed, a sign: PLEASE DO NOT DISTURB THE ARTIST. IF YOU ARE INTERESTED IN HIS WORK, PLEASE PHONE RINA AT THIS NUMBER. It gave the number of a cell phone. Once again, Cinzio was attracting a considerable crowd, but this time the comments were more attuned to the traditional.

"Look at that. It's Canaletto all over."

"Not exactly, but it's close."

"Bellotto?"

"I wonder if it's for sale."

"We're not supposed to be talking here. Read the sign. It disturbs him. I've got the telephone number."

"Look at that. He's even got a hint of the mountains in the background." Everyone was writing down the telephone number.

Rina was lining up commissions at the rate of three or four a day, and she began to worry that the experiment was getting out of hand: Cinzio might never get back to the kind of painting he liked. She reduced the canvases to the size of a tray cloth and put up the prices. But the demand had shifted into overdrive. The telephone rang continuously. If she turned it off, she found a dozen messages when she turned it on again. After only a week, she had the names and addresses of thirty tourists who said they would buy any painting of Venice he had available to sell. A shop in the

Frezzeria wanted to put him under contract. The mounting saga reached its turning point when the Padoanos rang to commission a portrait of Palazzo Patristi. Everyone knew how lavish they were with money. Rina had an idea; she demurred: the demand for Calabron views was too great. Carina Padoano was not going to be put off again. She had begged the Campana Gallery to let them buy the Calabron drawing of the broken arch and offered to pay double or triple, but it was too late. She kicked herself for not finding out in time that Calabron wasn't under contract to the Campana Gallery. She might have been able to insist about the drawing. She would damn well insist about the commission. They finally agreed on a price that brought within easy range the end of Calabron's *vedutista* phase.

This agreement also afforded the Padoanos the pleasure of informing Cara Campana that her star artist, with whom she had no contract, now had a lucrative contract with them to paint a picture of their new palace. Cara Campana had been delivered a raspberry. She flushed with humiliation and fury. It crossed her mind that someone had intimated that the Patristi arch had the evil eye. She would have taken the drawing out of the window and hidden it in the safe had she not remembered that Carina Padoano had pleaded with her to do just that. It could stay in the window and screw up the whole of Venice for all she cared. Cara Campana was not going to do Carina

Padoano's bidding. Instead, she rang Dino, who was on the train coming back from Lugano.

Dino came to meet her directly from the train station. They were walking along the Rio Terà dei Assassini on their way to the Osteria Assassini for a working lunch. Cara was explaining to him what his former friends the Padoanos had done and, even worse, what Calabron and his wife had got up to.

"You were right," said Cara. "We should have put him under contract when we had him in a corner, right after the interview."

"Live and learn," said Dino. "We're still new at the business."

"Wait," said Cara. She put her hand on his arm to stop him and stood looking at him while she organized her thoughts. "I've got it. We'll give him our cottage in the mountains—just *give* it to him—on the condition that he goes back to abstract painting and signs a contract."

"Do you really mean that?"

"Yes, I do! I don't want to lose him. He's a winner. We have to keep him with us *a tutti costi,* at *all costs.*"

"Then what are we waiting for?" he said, turning back towards Campo Sant'Angelo. "It's early for lunch; let's go see if he's up on the bridge."

DESIGN

Giuseppe Padoano stood behind a sturdy, squat column. Over the years he had grown to resemble the column and was somewhat sturdy himself. One day the realization came to him that everyone in the world was not similarly placed. Those speeding past him on both sides, for example, were not behind columns. After years of sneaking little peeks around it, he had a sudden rush of courage and threw it over. He waited to be crushed, then realized, slowly, that his world was not going to fall on him. It had fallen on his wife. He was truly sorry. He offered several hundred million pardons (in lire) plus the house, stepped over the rubble, stuck out his chest, and started to run. Beside him, setting the pace, was Carina Tosetta.

Not two months before they set off on their private marathon to Venice and the best society money can buy,

Carina Tosetta was in Giuseppe Padoano's office. She was sitting in his chair smoking a cigarette and composing, in her mind, her letter of resignation. He was in London. They had had a major disagreement.

Carina had joined the Padoano T-shirt firm, near Padua, P&PTs, Ltd., straight from the Institute of Graphic Design. She was twenty-two. He had hired her to realize shirts for the hundred or so museums and other organizations he supplied, but she had reached far beyond her brief. First she introduced dark colors, then T-shirt cocktail dresses with scooped necks, half sleeves, or dipped, fluted, or beaded hems, even swallowtails. Designers took up her ideas and commissioned branded T-shirts from P&PTs, Ltd. At that point, she approached Signor Padoano and asked him whether he thought she should move on to work with a major fashion house, or did he think she had a future with P&PTs, Ltd. That time he hadn't hesitated for a minute. He raised her salary, invented a title—Director of Product Development—and encouraged his wife not to work at the factory anymore. The moment had finally arrived, he said, when he could offer her a life of leisure.

Carina Tosetta was quite a phenomenon. She modeled her own designs. She was built for T-shirts with a robust top and slender bottom. She even made fashion news with one of her inventions, the full-length skin-tight maternity T-shirt, or NEL, the New Expectant Look, which became known in the trade as the SBL—Snake after a Big Lunch.

She worked hard, she worked late, and she led the way. She went with Giuseppe to local trade fairs. She supervised the workroom, managed orders, checked supplies, and kept an eye on the accounts. One evening, addressing him from the opposite side of his desk, she revealed her latest design. It wasn't for a T-shirt, or for managing the business; it was for him. She thought they should get married.

"I can help you," she said, "to get where you want to go. There is no door we can't unlock together. We are a good team."

Giuseppe's eyes opened wide. He felt stripped, naked as a goldfish. His mouth opened and closed, but no words came. Finally, he found his voice. "I don't think Signora Padoano would be happy about that, nor would our son and daughter, even though they are almost grown."

"Okay," said Carina, dropping her notebook and pen into her handbag. "That's fine." She stood up.

"But," Giuseppe Padoano stood up as well, "we can talk again when I get back from London. I'm expecting to make a lot of new contacts for the fashion lines."

"We'll see. Have a nice trip." She left.

From where he stood, he could see her through the window unlocking the door and swinging up into the driver's seat of her third-hand white Toyota SUV parked alongside his new silver BMW. She backed out, swung around, and shot gravel all over his car as she peeled out.

Giuseppe Padoano sat down. This was most disturbing. She was certainly big and tall and attractive. He wondered what doors she meant when she said, "there's no door we can't unlock together." She had certainly made a difference for the company. The bank was ready to open its deepest coffers to him. He had moved his family into a big villa and drove a fancy car. He took them on two short and two long holidays every year. Now that he thought about it, he remembered mentioning to Carina one day when they were driving to a merchandise fair that he wished he could join an exclusive golf club. And he remembered exactly what she said: "What's stopping you?" She made everything sound so easy. He felt weak and thought he'd better sit down. But he *was* sitting down. What was happening?

Giuseppe was rumbling along in the tube heading for Baker Street. There was a museum shop he wanted to visit; he had it written down somewhere. He liked traveling. He enjoyed being in England on business. He had been coming for years, but this was one of the most productive trips he'd ever made. Perhaps he was spurred on by the knowledge that Carina was in the game with him, creating a winning line of products, ready to meet every challenge. He was sorry he'd annoyed her. He couldn't imagine how

awful it would be if she went away. One day he would
bring her to London. She was vain about her English and
spoke it every chance she got. He too was pleased with his
English. The man next to him had opened a book.
Giuseppe let his eyes drift onto his neighbor's book and
tested his skill:

*Our aim in this book is simply this: to show you the
road to success.*

That was simple enough; interesting, too. Giuseppe shook
his Italian newspaper in front of him to give the impression that he was reading it and continued to peruse his
neighbor's book instead:

*Everyone could be in sight of success. If you cannot see
it from where you are, you are standing behind a pillar. That pillar may well be the thing which you regard
as most central to your life. If it is taken away, you may
think, the ceiling will surely fall in. But it won't.*

The man turned the page. Giuseppe caught another
statement.

*Let us be quite clear about one thing: what we are aim-
ing for is success and success alone. By way of definition:
roughly speaking, success and money are synonymous.*

The man turned over a sheaf of pages to a bookmark. *"Marriage or Success: Totem or Taboo"* was the chapter heading. Giuseppe could read only the far page.

> *First the success loves his mother: her cooking and her warm, selfless love will never be equaled.*

This book must be translated from Italian, thought Giuseppe. If I can find out the name, maybe I can get it in Padua.

> *She thinks,* he read on, *that he is the peer of any man or woman in the world; she shares his ambition. When he returns to his boyhood home (he will of course not make the mistake of living there) it will be, as it were, to refuel (and to use the telephone); he will find there the loyal admiration which he so desperately needs and that kind of life which, throughout his own existence, he will do everything to avoid.*

Giuseppe blushed. He scrutinized his newspaper, feigning avid interest, and turned the page. He eyes strayed once more toward the book.

> *The success thinks only of the future. He never regrets anything he has done, for what is done is in the past: it may be used as a weapon against others, but you should*

never hold it against yourself. That would be to drive
with the brake on, when to succeed is to move freely.

The train pulled into a station. It had been a long time
since the last one. The man looked up and jumped from
his seat. Giuseppe looked around. Where was he? Golders
Green. Where is that? Giuseppe jumped up too. He followed the man off the train. He had to stay near that book.
He had to find out its name. The man was taking the steps
three at a time. Giuseppe's legs hammered like pistons. The
man was walking fast. Giuseppe jitterbugged through the
crowd after him. When the man got to the guard at the
turnstile he waved a card and strode on through. Giuseppe
pulled out his ticket. He'd ridden far beyond his stop. He
showed his ticket to the guard without looking at him. He
was keeping his sights on the man.

"This ticket doesn't cover the fare."

Giuseppe glanced at the guard, but he was compelled
to watch the man who was almost outside. The man
paused and dropped the book in a trash can as he passed
by. Giuseppe started to go after it, but the guard put out
his arm.

"Hey! I told you this ticket isn't valid for this journey."

"I made a mistake," said Giuseppe. "I rode too far. But
that man just threw a book in the dustbin that I need.
Can't I just get it and then go back to where I was trying
to go?"

"Where's that?"

"Baker Street."

"You fall asleep or something? You stay here. I'll get the book. What's it called?"

"I don't know. It's about success."

He went and got the book.

Giuseppe could still see the man standing at the curb.

The guard handed him the book. "Where you from?"

"Venice," said Giuseppe grandly. For some reason he felt inspired to lie.

"You speak good English," said the guard.

But Giuseppe was watching the man get into a black limousine. "Yes!" he said, running down the steps back to the trains. "Yes!"

Cavaliere and Signora Padoano were being shown through a Grand Canal *piano nobile* that had come onto the rental market only a few days before. Actually, Giuseppe was not yet Cavaliere Padoano and wouldn't be for another six months. For that matter, Carina was not yet Signora Padoano and wouldn't be until Giuseppe's divorce was finalized. But they were practically unknown in Venice and those were details. More important was the hard fact that Giuseppe had bought a shirt manufacturer which, added to his T-shirt business, more than doubled his workforce. In addition he had hired a hundred new workers to sew labels onto imported Asian shirts and blouses, which were presold to major fashion houses in Milan. Carina had made sure that the Minister of Employment was aware of this contribution to Veneto prosperity. The recognition had already been confirmed. The title was already theirs as far as she was concerned.

The *salone* where they stood with the rental agent was vast. The chandeliers could have graced Versailles. Carina looked around and nodded; this was the right kind of place. She glanced at Giuseppe who just then remembered he wasn't supposed to be impressed and closed his mouth.

"This was, until two months ago, the seat of a consortium of international banks," said Dottoressa del Banco, "but with all the mergers in the sector, the consortium fell to pieces. The owners want to rent to another organization of similar standing." The Dottoressa looked searchingly from one to the other for reassurance.

Carina stared. "The Minister of Employment will be our reference. Would that satisfy the owners?"

Giuseppe was learning to keep cool; he shut his mouth the instant it dropped open and gave the Dottoressa a curt nod in agreement.

"That would be perfect," said Dottoressa del Banco. "There are not so many companies that can afford this kind of public relations expenditure. For one thing, renting the venue is only the beginning."

"Can we see the living arrangements?" asked Carina.

"Living arrangements?" A sudden chill hung in the air.

"Of course." Carina had locked onto a vital piece of information: This property targeted a severely limited market.

"I thought you and the Cavaliere understood that the owners don't intend to rent for residential use. Because that's the whole point of this kind of rental: residential use is too compromising for the owners."

"I don't mean to *live* here. We have our own residence in the country. But we would certainly have to be able to stay when we entertained for the company."

"I can see that," said Dottoressa del Banco. "I think they would agree to that."

The terms of the Padoanos' lease required them to entertain with dogged regularity, which is what they had intended to do anyhow. The Venice that lay before them like a land of opportunities was both more open and more closed than it had ever been before. In the open sector, the *borghese* and many, though not all, of the nobility passed through the same turnstiles in and out of the large parties organized in the service of some cause or enterprise unrelated to the noble traditions of hospitality. There were parties to honor business clients, parties to celebrate celebrities, parties to pander to politicians, and parties to launch commercial interests and even products. One tier above, there were parties to promote good causes, humanitarian and cultural, one of the most important of these being the safeguarding of Venice itself. Celebrities often figured in aid of good causes as well, as did businessmen with deep pockets. But more important to Carina, this sector of the party scene drew one step closer to that exclusive part of society and sometimes even touched it. Of this latter, closed, sector, many were not even aware. It took even an acute observer like Carina Tosetta a considerable time to divine that there was more to Venetian society than met the eye; there was some aspect eluding her. She studied magazines and memoirs and asked the hairdressers. Though many would have been tempted to do so, she didn't console herself that she had never met those grandees because they spent their evenings in darkened drawing rooms reading Agatha Christie under a bare bulb. She guessed they probably amused themselves together pretty well, coddled in their common heritage. She didn't deceive herself that she could enter the sanctum sanctorum of aristocratic society. She only wanted to have a look at it. She needed to know these things. Knowing was part of her mission. That old society, she knew beyond a shadow of a doubt, was gone forever, and her society would take its place. All she wanted was the chance to rake through the detritus to see if there was anything worth saving.

Giuseppe was more wistful about the past. He followed the game plan and got himself elected president of one

cultural and one humanitarian charity and savored his occasional encounters with the real nobs, but most of all he
savored recounting for his old mother the banter he exchanged with these storied names, telling her about the designer shirts, with their initials embroidered on the front,
that he had sent over to them afterwards. She was, by now,
on the verge of forgiving him for leaving his wife.

When Bingo Benson came back to Venice he was a little
out of touch, but he didn't bother about finding out what
was happening and who was who. He left that to the journalist, Cadmus Argos Peacock, who was living in the
maid's apartment on his mezzanine while he wrote an ex-
posé on Venetian society. From time to time Cadmus
leaned on Bingo to give him tips or interpret information,
a service that he performed in his offhand, careless way,
giving in every case more weight to a good story than to
fact. In a way, he was a journalist himself, but sometimes
he simply didn't know the facts and didn't feel like saying
so to a visitor. He inclined to be almost Venetian on this
point.

One morning around ten, Bingo was sitting with Cad
Peacock having a late breakfast at the Häagen-Dazs bar di-
agonally across from Paolin's in Campo San Stefano, when
Giuseppe and Carina Padoano crossed the campo. It was
unusual to see a couple dressed to the nines strolling arm in

arm at this hour on a weekday morning and Bingo exercised his native right to stare. Cadmus followed his example.

Giuseppe Padoano never wore glasses for long distance. He thought they made him look older. Anyhow, he was content to move through the streets of Venice in a mist. He was happy. He had just learned that he would soon be starting a new family, and he was making money hand over fist. In any case, Carina told him what there was to see, and she never missed a trick.

"Oh, look," she said. "There's that Bingo Benson with that *Fast Lane* journalist CAP Peacock. I want him to interview us." She threw them a big smile and gave Bingo just the hint of a wink.

Bingo was used to this and knew exactly what it meant. With her broad shoulders, narrow hips, and copious rack, teetering over the stones in stiletto heels, she was the stereotype drag-queen glamour-puss.

"Ooooh," said Bingo, returning the wink. "Him-her is giving me the eye. You don't see much of those types when there's no biennale."

Cadmus grabbed his notebook and started scribbling. "I've seen them around. I'll have to find out who they are. He doesn't look gay."

"He's probably very much in the closet," said Bingo, with mock seriousness. "His poor old mother is probably still alive. Surely you have no doubt about his companion."

"No, no," agreed Peacock.

Of this impression, Carina remained happily ignorant, just as she remained unaware that her first appearance, not long after, pregnant in her black SBL, sent five beautifully crafted pages of insider analysis flying with expletives into the shredder—and made Bingo Benson howl with delight.

At this sighting, the Padoanos were on their way to Palazzo Patristi to meet that most revered nobleman, Edmondo Patristi. The Padoanos had been negotiating for several weeks with Architetto Fallon about buying the palace in its present state with the restoration incomplete. The transfer was somewhat complicated because Fallon had refused to carry on the restoration with the Padoanos because of his close relationship to the whole drama that precipitated the sale after the young Patristi heir died in a car crash. He was married to the mother of the boy who died, Patristi's former wife who divorced him because he had an affair. It fascinated Carina how one man's infidelity ran like a crack in a frozen pond right through the town. This was the difference between being noble and being normal. In contrast, her affair with Giuseppe had been interesting to—how many? She could count them on her fingers: the employees, her mother, Giuseppe's mother, Giuseppe's wife, his children. That was all.

The palace, with all its noble history, was exactly what Giuseppe and Carina had been hoping to find. Carina had complete faith in vertical mobility. She believed in transformation stories like *My Fair Lady* and *Pretty Woman;* she believed in the power of clothes. She believed in attitude as well, in walking like everyone is looking, and maybe acting a little like some people are trash. She was watching and learning, and she had admonished Giuseppe to watch and learn from Barone Patristi. If they were going to be the new masters of Palazzo Patristi, they should do it in style.

Carina turned her creative skills to party planning. She experimented and tallied her results. She brought in new caterers from far and wide (a winning formula that created an upscale version of soup-kitchen lines at the door), and worked hard to build her invitation lists to include the big names from every field (a strenuous effort that delivered many disappointments). Her early parties followed the few-hundred-close-friends formula until she realized that she and Giuseppe gained little personal identity from these extravagant displays. She began alternating large and small parties and inserting occasional carefully crafted dinners that put the Padoanos more clearly in focus. Sometimes that didn't help. She measured an event's effectiveness by the invitations they received in return. But it was so much like planting seeds known for capricious germination, from the easier Primula up to the hardest giant sequoia, that she sometimes considered giving up on the giants. The problem was that getting the giants was the whole point of entertaining.

After they met Barone Patristi, Carina grasped a principle that had been lurking on the fringes of her consciousness for some time: In society there was no substitute for having a mystique or specialty all your own. Giants socialize with other giants. She and Giuseppe couldn't be great nobility with historic ancestors; she had more or less accepted that. She noted that Venetians paid great obeisance to musicians, but it was really too late for Giuseppe to learn to play the cello. The only thing she might like to learn was the harp—but she thought there would be time for that later. No, the right course was to become known as an intellectual, as an expert on something, and that meant writing a book. She found a graduate student at the Bocconi who was willing to write, rather act as a research assistant for Giuseppe on a book defining the Venetian businessman. For herself, she hired the journalist husband of her real estate agent, Giovanni del Banco, to help her write a small handbook on the Venetian mercantile palace—or something along those lines. She wanted to be able to speak with authority on the Great Tradition of Venetian Palaces in their function as centers of Venetian business. After all, they were on expense accounts most of the time.

Taking over the restoration of Palazzo Patristi was gratifying for the Padoanos because it gave them the chance to put their imprint on the oldest documented residence of the oldest documented family in Venice, but there were irritating pockets of resistance to their efforts. For one thing, the broken arch over the landward portal was a famous eyesore that cried out to be restored to its original dignity, yet the officials at the Belle Arti were blocking the project. Her father used to shake hands with the priest after Mass with a banknote concealed in his palm. She discussed this method with Giuseppe before they went to talk to the Belle Arti people, but he was afraid to make such a direct approach. They spoke to the contractor about ways of getting through to the Belle Arti. Then there was the business of the famous historic table, which Barone Patristi had allowed to be damaged after they had insisted it should remain as part of the house.

Virtually the only restoration she still had hopes for was the ceiling painting in the *salone, The Triumph of Venice,* a slightly abbreviated version of a painting on the same theme in the *Sala del Maggior Consiglio* in the Ducal Palace, and generally thought to be a preparatory study for the larger painting. Its restoration had not been included in the Patristi project. The Patristis had encouraged the Belle Arti to agree that a restoration was not urgently needed. The Padoanos, however, were of the opposing opinion: An intervention was needed at the earliest possible moment. Scholarship, they maintained, needed the opportunity to study the work up close and to document its history on the basis of a proper examination. Giuseppe cited his presidency of a committee for the safeguarding of

Venice as the spur to this enlightened commitment. The Belle Arti was very pleased indeed and, instead of imposing a restorer on them as they might have done, favored them with a list of authorized restoration laboratories from which they could choose for themselves. Carina visited and examined them all, but there was only one with whom she was able to strike the perfect understanding. The agreement was reached, a contract was drawn up, and money changed hands. The painting would be given the highest priority and returned to the palace in time for their first reception. It was a delicate matter for the laboratory and entailed several follow-up visits from Carina and Giuseppe, but in the end the objective was achieved and the scene set for a certain day in February:

Cavaliere and Signora Giuseppe Padoano
At Home
Palazzo Patristi
Venezia

It happened to be during Carnival that the Padoanos launched themselves as master and mistress of the most historic palace in Venice. In the normal run of things, no Venetian paid much attention to Carnival except to deplore the congestion in the streets, but this promised to be an exceptional occasion, so they went the extra mile and dolled themselves up in costumes as requested (costumes, *please*) on the invitation. Everyone wanted to have a look at the Patristi Palace under its new management, and everyone wanted to take a peek at the damage to the Patristi table, which had incurred fines for both the architect and the Patristi family and been written up in the newspapers.

Carina and Giuseppe met their guests in costumes so elaborate that their guests could hardly greet their host and hostess fast enough, so eager were they to get away and exchange views on their hosts' braggadocio with those who had entered before them.

"Welcome to Palazzo Patristi-Padoano," beamed Carina to each guest.

"Please make yourself at home. Have a look around," boomed Giuseppe.

"Grazie!" cried each person in turn, skipping away from the entrance and around this or that corner, anywhere, just to get out of sight to whisper their first impressions among themselves. New arrivals joined the first crowd of hilarity they came upon, regardless of old feuds and snobberies. They all laughed together. The house was filling up with laughter; the party had hardly begun and it was already a huge success. But not the success that anyone had expected, least of all the Padoanos, whose wildest dreams had not projected such a payoff.

Carina's costume was gray-blue silk with a brocade skirt and a velvet hooded cape of an indeterminate brownish color attached with some kind of giant beads. The bodice and sleeves were squeezed and fooled about with what most people identified as the ridiculous invention of a T-shirt designer. The reaction may have been somewhat prompted by resentment at the displacement of the venerable Patristi family, but there was also truth in it: The outfit was pretentious. Giuseppe looked possibly even more got-up in body armor with a ruff to match his wife's dress and a red cape. He even wore a laurel crown that kept sliding over his ear. As he welcomed people to the house, he gestured with a laurel branch the size of a small tree.

The party had found its wheels right from the beginning and was rolling merrily when the waiters interrupted the fun to herd everyone into the *salone* for a toast. The hundred or so close friends gathered under *The Triumph of Venice* to watch Giuseppe and Carina step onto the plinth where a quartet had been playing Vivaldi in the background.

"Welcome, friends," cried Giuseppe, waving his laurel, as he opened his arms in greeting. "Welcome, friends. We brought you into this room for two reasons. One, you may wonder who we are."

A fleeting exchange of incredulous glances greeted the remark.

"I am," he bowed and gave a flourish with his branch, "Honor! that fundamental virtue of a Venetian businessman, as you know from my book on the subject."

In the center of the crowd, Professor Faleiro was looking at the ceiling through opera glasses. He stopped and looked at Giuseppe for a minute. He looked through his opera glasses at the ceiling again, then looked at Carina. He handed his opera glasses to an eighteenth-century lady in a white wig beside him and whispered in her ear. As she looked at the ceiling he whispered to another companion.

"My wife," Giuseppe continued, "is dressed as Venice, as she appears in *The Triumph of Venice* . . ."

Eyes widened at this most heavy-handed piece of self-aggrandizement. It was cheek to beat all cheek, but a whisper was moving though the crowd.

"—which you will see above your heads in the painting that has just come home after a painstaking and brilliant restoration."

The crowd leaned back to look. There indeed was the classic gray-blue dress they had admired earlier on Carina, and there too was the handsome armor, ruff, and rich red cape of Giuseppe. There was even the laurel falling over the ear. And there too, as the whisper affirmed, were the faces of Carina and Giuseppe.

From that moment the perception of the Padoanos became blurred with history as it suddenly became clear that they were the perfect heirs to the Venetian tradition.

ENTERPRISE

Bella Grana was that very special thing, a rich Venetian, and she made no effort to hide it. In fact, she welcomed the little signs of jealousy that surfaced in murmurs from other tables in restaurants, from the staff at home, or from the secretaries when she went to see her husband at the office. The pure fun of being the target of envious looks was as good a motive as any for dining in restaurants, frequenting the golf club, going to cocktail parties, or even riding the vaporetto, when it passed with all eyes looking at her house. Unfortunately, the effect was at its best only in Venice. Elsewhere it was limited to the well-informed or the bribed—like maître d's and concierges. At least once a day she wondered how it would feel to be one of the almighty Zecca family, the richest family in Italy, one of the richest in the world. They were in another realm. And this was the damnable part of the whole business: There was always someone richer. Bella tried to imagine who the

Zeccas might envy but always failed. Envy could eat up a person who thought too much about it. There was even a small irritation right here at home: The money belonged to her husband.

Vitale Grana, Bella's husband, was that very normal thing: the heir to a business empire who would rather do something with the money other than husband it. It wasn't that he was frivolous or that his wealth didn't please him. The problem was that he hadn't earned the money, so that having it didn't give him a sense of achievement. Instead of seeking a name as an astute businessman, he wanted to be known as a serious botanist, which is the profession he would have followed had he not been destined to look after an international chain of shopping malls. He never compared himself to the Zeccas, except in assuming that the scions of that family suffered from the same restrictions as he did, if not more so.

Ironically, it was Vitale's father himself, Aldo Bruno Grana, who launched his adolescent son on this distracting avocation when he brought back from a trip to his companies in North and South America a variety of *Droseraceae* plants which ate insects. Vitale was an overprotected only child, headed off from adventure at every turn, and the plants were the first hobby he had ever been allowed to pursue all by himself. He focused on the plants his vast accumulated reserves of energy and the great force of concentration born of his relative isolation. In the shrinking society of Venice he was practically in a class by himself.

The plants flourished in his care. Encouraged, he decided to breed and develop them. He reasoned that by gradually expanding their diet, he could make them grow huge, like prize-winning pumpkins, to the point where they could eat like real pets—canned dog food, or table scraps. His motive was not merely the wistful desire for a pet. He had a higher purpose for his plants. He meant to evolve them into rat catchers to take the place of the demoralized pussycats that sit blank and useless all over Venice like so many parlor palms. His failure in this enterprise was what spurred him to study botany at university. He still hoped to do something historic in the field.

Bella, in contrast, was not academically inclined, but she was as alert and bright-eyed as a poodle. She had studied business at university, but not very hard, and eventually gave up without taking a degree. There seemed no point in continuing. Most of the courses appeared to deal with matters that were perfectly obvious. The remaining courses dealt with matters that she didn't understand anything about—not even their relevance to the workaday world. What really interested her was business as she saw it being conducted around her. She read magazines and newspapers and listened to the men who sat next to her at dinner parties. They answered her questions willingly, often in copious detail, glad for a chance to talk about something that interested them—and never gave it another thought. They may even have been indiscreet on occasion. But then, Bella was pretty and, accordingly, not a threat.

In spite of her maddening wealth, people couldn't help but love Bella: she was so gay and unpredictable. Unanchored by fixed principles, she blew in the wind—not like a flag on a mast but more like a dandelion fuzzball borne here and there by even the lightest of vying currents. And just as a fuzzball promotes its own progeny in lawns and borders, she sowed surprising results for people who couldn't figure out what current she was riding, or paid no attention.

Vitale too loved Bella for her unfettered taste for amusement. She was one of the pleasures that his wealth provided, the rapids that gave his raft such an exciting ride; she was the wild, peppery arugula that could take root and flourish anywhere, even in the crack on a windowsill. His two sons observed their contrasting parents from the happy hothouse where their mother placed them, cultivated like the plants that their father tended in his tidy quasiscientific borders, which flanked the walk from the courtyard portal to the landward entrance of the family palace.

At the hairdresser in Lugano one day, Bella was reading an article about the Zeccas in a new magazine called *LUNA* that she'd never seen before. The young girl who was drying her hair was looking at the magazine over Bella's shoulder.

"Do you know the Zeccas, Signora?" asked the girl.

"No," confessed Bella, a little vexed that she'd been exposed. "I think my husband does."

"They have a house near here," continued the girl, as she combed through the tangles. "People say they have a lot of money in Banca Bernardo. I guess they like to be near it. I had a friend who worked there once. He was the doorman. He said they used to come in for meetings upstairs, but their names never appeared on any door lists or security files. He said that they have everything in companies that don't belong to them, and that these companies have shares that are owned by other companies, and at the end there is someone who has a contract to be their agent and he organizes all the people who represent them in all the companies along the way—he's called a nomination or something. You have to be an expert to figure it out."

Bella was interested; she folded over the page of the magazine article and closed it to encourage the girl. "Why do you think they did that? Everyone knows what they own, don't they?"

"My friend said they did all that when they put the Zecca Company on the stock market a long time ago. That's all I know. My friend doesn't work there anymore. The staff complained that he was always asking questions."

Bella nodded in sympathy.

"The owner of this salon does Signora Zecca's hair; Ottorino goes up to the villa at least once a week. He always takes someone to help him. I went once, but I was terrified." She removed the towel from Bella's shoulders and turned to tell Ottorino that Signora Grana was ready.

"No, wait," said Bella. "Could you comb it out a bit more; I think it's good for it. Did you like the house?"

"Oof. It's like the Louvre or something. Like a museum." She put the towel back on Bella's shoulders and continued to comb. "There's a doorman, like a hotel. But if you're going there to work you go in by another door where there's a little office with a window and you have to show your ID. A boy in a striped jacket takes you up the back stairs. They have their own little salon up there. I never wanted to go back. It made me nervous to wash her hair. The whole time I was afraid I would do something wrong and she'd fire my boss."

Bella had to smile. She too had a boy in striped jacket who did errands. But in Venice everyone came in the same door. There was no possibility of another door unless you came by water. She wondered about having a hairdressing salon put in her house, but only for a minute: she liked going to hairdressers. For one thing she liked reading the magazines. In fact, she often tore out the subscription form and sent it in. As a result, she knew a great deal about celebrities. In the airport lounges there were business magazines. She subscribed to those, too. As a result she knew a great deal about what started the Great Imbroglio that changed the future of her husband's company and brought about the very thing he most feared—feared with such an irrational dread that he couldn't even bear to think about it, let alone avoid it. This head-in-the-sand aversion sprang directly from the guilt he felt at not wanting to be a businessman. The issue was so sensitive that Bella never dared to bring it up, let alone share her expertise.

So she always floated in at an oblique angle, as she had done about taking up Swiss residence.

"I think it's time that I and the boys became resident in Lugano," she announced one evening after dinner. "I was sitting next to a lawyer the other evening who told me how rich families do that." It was a lie, of course. In reality, she'd read about it in a business magazine and then bought a book by the same author, but she couldn't tell Vitale that. He might get paranoid and jump off the balcony into the canal. No, with her husband she had to manage the truth.

Massimo and Ulisse were eighteen and sixteen. They weren't any more interested in the business at this stage than their father was. They knew what their future held, but that was the future; this was now. They were more interested in getting good grades with the least amount of work and having fun. They would soon be going to university and from there would go straight into the business, GAB PLC, named after their grandfather: Grana, Aldo Bruno. Massimo was learning Spanish so he could join one of the GAB businesses in South America, which sounded like fun. Ulisse was learning English because he couldn't make up his mind where he wanted to go. There was almost too much choice. For Venetians, GAB stood for *Grana a Barche,* money by the boatload; there was almost too much money.

Vitale only half listened to his sons' plans for their future. He was sinking deeper and deeper into a project to restore the abandoned botanical enclosures and greenhouses in the public gardens. He didn't need to worry about his sons' ambitions just yet. By his calculation he still had a decade of leisure to visit botanical gardens around the world when he went on his annual inspections of his holdings and to sit with architects designing state-of-the-art greenhouses for the botanists he would bring to the university with endowed chairs. He had never been so happy in his life.

His financial advisers were happy too: Vitale was finally giving them the chance to advise. One day after meeting with these advisers, Vitale came home and announced apropos of nothing that he agreed with her idea of taking up residence in Lugano. His commercial lawyer, Dottor Bergamo, had told him that she wouldn't have to spend much time there; nobody bothered to check. Vitale thought it would be nice to have a villa on the lake with boats for the boys, and Dottor Bergamo had even suggested a villa for them to buy. Vitale went with her to see it the following day and they bought it at once. It sat up on the hillside and had open space for gardens running down to the lake. The climate was excellent for plants; much milder than the rest of Switzerland. He was beginning to feel guilty that he was always so distracted by his plants. This meant that in Lugano he could be distracted in the midst of his family.

One evening the Bergamos invited the Granas to dinner. It turned out to be a small dinner for ten. Alvise Bergamo had some new clients who were the owners of the biggest nurseries in northern Italy. He had invited them for dinner so they could meet Vitale who was making a new garden in Lugano. Bergamo put Bella on his right. He told her about Lugano, about its banks and its institutions. His big news was that he had arranged with Vitale for her to have an investment allowance in Switzerland over which she would have complete control but which she shouldn't worry about. His friend would act as her adviser; all she would have to do would be to give an occasional signature. And then he said, "The move to Switzerland was a step forward, but I worry about the company sometimes." Bella wondered what he meant about the move to Switzerland. She and the boys were resident in Lugano, not Vitale. "Vitale doesn't want to run it," continued Alvise, "but he doesn't want anyone else to run it either. He's not even looking forward to his sons taking it over. I would have thought he'd be thrilled at the prospect and hurry them in as quickly as possible. I keep telling him it's a miracle no one has tried buying up shares to take it over. It's ripe. His father left him holding a twenty-five percent stake. I wish he had fifty-one."

"He does," said Bella. "He is fifty-one."

Signora Bergamo stood up. Vitale came over to join Bella and Dottor Bergamo. "Did you enjoy talking to my Bella-bellissima?"

"I've never had a more enchanting companion," smiled Alvise, wondering how long it would be before his guests went home so he could share this gemlike illustration of Bella's total opacity with his clever wife, of whom he was so proud.

The Granas had planned to pick up a few friends at the Campana Gallery opening and take them to dinner at the Gritti afterwards, but after a quick sweep through the rooms Vitale came over to Bella, took her aside, and said he wanted to cancel the reservation at the Gritti and go home. Bella was surprised and agreed at once. She rang the hotel and rang home to ask the cook to get together a little supper of pasta and salad.

Bella could see that something was wrong. Vitale had no appetite. Was he in love? She watched him twirl his spaghetti then put his fork down with the spaghetti still on it. He sighed. Bella was alarmed. Her eyes darted around the room like a general surveying the field to identify which forces to send to the charge. He put his napkin on the table.

"I'm not hungry," he said.

"Don't you feel well?"

"I'm fine. I'm thinking about something."

"Are the gardeners giving you trouble?"

"No, that's going very well." His expression brightened, then clouded over again. "I think I'll go out on the balcony. Fresh air might do me some good."

"Go," said Bella. "I'll bring some grappa and join you in a minute." She ran to the bedroom to brush her hair and check her lipstick.

They stood together on the balcony sipping their grappa and watching the gondola serenade. Actually only Bella was watching the *serenata*; Vitale was staring into the water. Eventually the moving water took effect. He became confessional.

"Things are going badly in Chile."

"How do you know?"

"Our banker in Chile rang to say that he'd got wind of a plan by the family of our own CEO's wife to buy the land next door to two of our older shopping malls." Vitale was spilling his thoughts onto Bella the way men tended to do at the dinner table. "South Americans are as bad as Italians for zeroing in on a weakness."

"Do you trust this banker?" asked Bella.

"Who, David? He has the prettiest garden in South America, the most interesting too. Full of . . . he collects . . . well, that's another story. Yes. I trust him completely. He's one of my oldest friends."

"Oh, I'm so glad to know about him," said Bella. "Massimo is looking for a way to go to South America before he finishes his degree."

"He is?"

"He announced it this morning."

"Can you deal with that?"

"Of course, darling. Could I get in touch with your banker friend?"

"I'll have Marina send his phone number over to you tomorrow. You see, David has been trying to get me to buy that land for months, but I couldn't see my way clear to do it. Our shares are going down because our properties are getting old. They don't keep themselves going. Property is a bad investment. It has no capacity for self-renewal. If you could somehow introduce photosynthesis. . . . Business is the same; in business it's all image and faith and mirrors."

"Mirrors," murmured Bella. "I understand." She was good at easing a conversation along. "Did he have any suggestions about what to do?"

"He's thinking about it. I have to wait and see what he comes up with. It's such a worry, because, you see, it's a problem we could be having in every country. We need to spend money. And the shares are down."

"What makes shares go up?"

"Brokers and banks telling people to buy the shares."

"Well, at least David is a banker and a friend. That's already something." As she put her arms around him and gave him a squeeze, she glanced up and thanked her stars for focusing her husband's interests in the realm of bees instead of birds.

"Well, there's nothing I can do about it tonight." He sighed, giving her a quick kiss. "Let's turn in."

"Darling, I just remembered that I'm supposed to go to Lugano tomorrow morning. I think I've booked at the hairdresser's. Do you mind if I leave when you've got all these worries?"

"Of course not, darling. What can you do about it? It's my problem."

"You'll get through it, dear. Could you have the Chileman's telephone number left with the maid in Lugano so I can ask him about Massimo?"

When Bella got to Lugano, she did three things. First, she rang David the banker in Chile and got something going for Massimo. Then she went to the library and found the basic biology book she had bought for precisely these occasions: she had to remind herself about photosynthesis; she wasn't sure she'd grasped what Vitale meant by the problem with business. When she opened the book, *cross pollination*

"What makes shares go up?"

"Brokers and banks telling people to buy the shares."

"Well, at least David is a banker and a friend. That's already something." As she put her arms around him and gave him a squeeze, she glanced up and thanked her stars for focusing her husband's interests in the realm of bees instead of birds.

"Well, there's nothing I can do about it tonight." He sighed, giving her a quick kiss. "Let's turn in."

"Darling, I just remembered that I'm supposed to go to Lugano tomorrow morning. I think I've booked at the hairdresser's. Do you mind if I leave when you've got all these worries?"

"Of course not, darling. What can you do about it? It's my problem."

"You'll get through it, dear. Could you have the Chileman's telephone number left with the maid in Lugano so I can ask him about Massimo?"

When Bella got to Lugano, she did three things. First, she rang David the banker in Chile and got something going for Massimo. Then she went to the library and found the basic biology book she had bought for precisely these occasions: she had to remind herself about photosynthesis; she wasn't sure she'd grasped what Vitale meant by the problem with business. When she opened the book, *cross pollination* caught her eye, so she read that first. Certain words jumped from the page: "broadening, productive." She could see what Vitale liked about plants as opposed to business. For one thing the rules were mostly the same all around the world, whether you were planting in Italy or Chile.

The third thing she had to do was somewhat complicated, so she stopped at the hairdresser on the way. She hadn't made an appointment. She only wanted a quick comb-out. She hoped she could have the girl she had last time.

The girl was flattered that Signora Grana had asked for her. "*Buon giorno!* What can I do for you?"

"Just the quickest little comb-out," said Bella, pulling the cape around her shoulders. "I was so interested by what you were saying the other day."

"Remind me," said the girl.

"About the bank that was so secretive, where your boyfriend worked and got fired."

"Banca Bernardo. He was sorry to leave. His problem was he'd been a concierge and he'd been taught to learn as much as he could about the people who came to the hotel. He's gone back to working in the hotel. He's doing very well. It's all a matter of disposition, isn't it."

"That looks perfect," said Bella. She stood up and dropped a tip in the girl's pocket as she left. On her way down the stairs, she rang the lawyer who had helped them buy the villa and asked him to line up someone to meet with her at Banca Bernardo. She would be there in fifteen minutes.

By the time she left the bank, GAB PLC shares were on the move. She had put a series of call options for all she could afford for the next three months.

Bella was at the airport seeing Massimo off to Chile. "Now remember, darling, the name of the company CEO is Sancho Villa and his wife is called Olivia. They have a daughter your age called Viola, who is said to be very beautiful. I gather she's one of those typical South American flowers, interested in fun and staying out late. She's probably rather sexy and fast. I'm just telling you this before you meet her so you're forewarned. You certainly won't want to have anything to do with her."

"I get it," said Massimo, bending down to give her a kiss. "I'll ring when I get there."

"David's driver will meet you at the Santiago airport. He'll hold up a sign." She blew her eldest son a kiss. She wasn't worried about Massimo. David was a good sort. He'd even agreed to play the bumblebee. Mergers can be helpful, even if they're not necessary.

Vitale had arrived that morning from Venice. He hadn't been expected until evening, so Bella was happily surprised. Ulisse had gone to do an English course in London. At last, the two of them could enjoy some time together in Lugano. Vitale was sitting in his garden looking out over the lake.

"Hello, darling." Bella came and sat on the bench beside him. "What would you like to do for lunch? Would you like to go somewhere in the boat?"

"I can't do that. I have to go to a meeting at a bank, Bella." He turned and looked at her; he was clearly in a state. "Bella, I've come up here because it looks like GAB's been taken over. The accountants think it may be the Zeccas." His lips were trembling. "It's all because of my botany. I didn't do my job."

Bella's heart was pounding. She squeezed his hand. "Let's do something. What can we do?"

"I don't know. That's what I have to find out."

"How do you know they're doing this? I thought anybody who bought more than five percent of a public company had to identify himself. I thought predators weren't allowed to sneak up like that."

"Who told you that?"

"Can't remember. Somebody at dinner somewhere maybe."

"Well, the bank has declared itself. It says it bought the shares for commercial purposes to cover call options and won't name the client who placed the order. Everything was going so well. There were even buyers in South America. The share price was going up. There was all this buzz. So I agreed to buy that land with David. Then suddenly everybody in Venice started talking about GAB being bought out by the Zeccas. Now it's all lost."

"Which bank is it?" asked Bella.

"Banca Bernardo," said Vitale sadly. "It's the Zeccas' bank. Alvise managed to find out."

"Oh dear," said Bella. "I'd forgotten it was the Zeccas' bank. I've been buying those call options there too."

"You have? But why?"

"To help the company and keep things in the family."

"You've been manipulating the share price?"

"Sure. Why not?"

"But Bella! You own the company."

"You mean I bought it? It wasn't very expensive, considering how big it is. And the Zeccas are trying to get it away from me?"

"No, Bella. The lawyers moved the company to Switzerland when you moved here, and put it in your name. The alternative was bearer shares, which I didn't want. Remember when you signed those papers?"

"You mean the papers Alvise said were my life insurance?"

"That's right. It was his little joke."

SERVICE

Severino Boscolo was a young man who shared his mother's opinion of him. At the moment the adorable rascal was in high favor at the office for his recent contribution to the quality of life—he had endured a good hour of overtime one evening, adapting the outer knob on the office door so it could be removed by the first person to arrive at work. That way, supplicants who got desperate with waiting in a stalled queue could no longer open the door to see what the hell was taking so long and discover three public servants sprawled on their chairs smoking, chatting, and generally passing the time among themselves. This office carried out the initial vetting of every private building project in Venice and had the power either to pass the project on for the consideration of the Conservation Commission, or to block it.

Severino had come in on time this morning because he wanted to make a couple of long-distance calls on the boss's phone. The office had been open for only an hour and Severino was still alone, but he could hear the murmur of people waiting outside the door. His boss, Architetto Giuseppe Dimenzato, and his coworker, Mirco Busato—like himself, a would-be architect who hadn't yet passed his exams—were still having their morning coffee at Bar Torino in Campo San Luca. Severino was leaning on the window ledge of the municipal office building looking down the calle towards the Grand Canal, smoking a cigarette and daydreaming about the fun he'd had the night before with his friends tormenting three French girls at the disco on the Lido. They were sitting at Severino's favorite table. The girls had finally called a taxi and fled.

Severino watched a boy pushing a rack of suits up from the Riva where he had unloaded them from a delivery barge. The boy parked the rack directly under Severino's window and went into a shop. His olive skin declared him non-Venetian. No sense of responsibility, observed Severino. He emptied his ashtray over the suits to teach him a lesson but the ashes blew away. Severino's eyes fell on a bottle of Tipex. He grabbed it, opened it, and, leaning out, shook the contents over the suits. He closed the empty bottle and put it back on his boss's desk. Three knocks sounded at the closed door. He went and opened the door to his colleagues. A cry rang out in the street below. Severino and his two colleagues rushed over to the window. The delivery boy was brushing at white spots on the suits on the rack. The boy looked up and saw Severino, who pointed at the pigeons jostling on the eaves above and shook his head.

"They should be exterminated," he called down to the boy. "I could do it with my own hands."

"What happened?" asked the boss.

"The pigeons," said Severino with a shrug. "They shat on the boy's deliveries."

Rocco Zennaro was late. He liked to get here when the office opened so he could be at the head of the line, where he could see if anything was happening. But this morning, Architetto Fallon had asked him at the last minute if he would mind checking on the Palazzo Patristi permission, because the intern who usually stood in this line for the Fallon & Fierazzo Architecture Studio had been unexpectedly scheduled for an exam this morning. By the time Rocco got there the Project Surveillance Office of the Private Buildings Authority had been open for an hour and the line already snaked around the counter of the reception area, through the door into the stairwell and past the elevator. When Rocco stepped out of the elevator he had to walk away from the office to join the end of it.

"This is the line for Project Surveillance, right?" Rocco asked the man in front of him.

"*Sì, sì.*"

"Is anything happening?"

"We've moved up a couple of spaces since I came, but it could be that people up near the door gave up and went away."

A man joined the line behind Rocco. "Yesterday I waited for three hours for the privilege of watching them go downstairs to lunch."

Rocco realized that he was going to waste the whole morning and probably achieve nothing. The Project Surveillance Office was closed in the afternoons. In theory the staff needed the afternoon to catch up on the work they couldn't do in the mornings because of receiving the line of people checking on their applications. Rocco could see the incentive to give up on getting permission and risk carrying out minor, or interior, works illegally. The choice had to be made before filing the application because the application outlined the actual state of the property and detailed how the project would change it. This meant that after filing the request one could never take the position that the actual state was wrong on the official plans in the archive. That assertion of course had no validity as a defense, but it could mitigate the situation enough to make it safe for the *vigili* to work out a little settlement on the side so they wouldn't have to denounce the infraction to the authorities. Going ahead without permission could be a very expensive way to carry out a building project. On the other hand, if time was money, it was six of one and a half dozen of the other. Rocco was already beginning to think about giving up and coming back early the next morning when he saw one of the men from the office, Mirco Busato, start down the stairs. Rocco followed him.

"Ciao, Mirco. I was waiting to see you, but the line's too long; I'll have to come back early tomorrow."

Mirco looked sheepish. "Ciao, Rocco. I have to dash over to the Buildings Registry for a minute. They run us off our feet."

They were going out the door into the calle.

"Look here, Rocco, since the application is already filed, why don't you ring me this afternoon." He took out a card and scribbled a cell phone number on it. "I'll set up a site visit for you so you don't have to come back. Severino is handling the Patristi file."

"*Grazie mille,* Mirco, a thousand thanks," said Rocco, taking the card. "I'll ring around three o'clock."

"Make it four," said Mirco raising his hand in salute and turning to walk up the calle in the opposite direction from the Buildings Registry.

Severino Boscolo and Giuseppe Dimenzato observed the etiquette of city officials and arrived an hour late for their appointment with Architetto Fallon at the main door of Palazzo Patristi. They saw him waiting outside and accorded him a nod of recognition as they strolled across the campo. There had been no rain or wind to make his wait uncomfortable, but Boscolo and Dimenzato were in good spirits anyhow. The project in question, the restoration of the hideously brutalized Gothic arch over the great portal, was one that Fallon was especially eager to realize, and for this reason was ardently soliciting the necessary permissions to pursue that objective, first from the city and then from the Ministry of the Belle Arti. Architetto Fallon was proceeding with caution and taking nothing for granted. He had been careful to leave the main door free of scaffolding to avoid giving the impression that he might be assuming that permission to carry out the works on the arch would be forthcoming. This site visit by Dimenzato's office was only an early step in the process, but it was the *sine qua non.* The earnestness of Fallon's desire to return the arch to its original beauty—coupled with his arguments that the window that cut through the arch had been placed there by accident and the family had always, from the very day it happened, intended to correct the error; that every chunk and chip of the original stone had been preserved for almost a century with that precise purpose in view, and that he had the perfect craftsmen to consolidate the stone and restore it to its original appearance—was of no account whatever. The rule of thumb which would block the project was that the mistake was now a part of history and as such could not be altered. "You can't," as Dimenzato enjoyed reminding these aesthetes, "turn back the clock." True, everyone who saw the arch winced and shook his head with regret, but that reaction was valid for any mishap of history. No. The prospects for Architetto Fallon's project were not promising—unless he found a way to convince the authorities or, rather, unless they themselves found a way that they could be convinced.

Architetto Dimenzato shook hands with Architetto Fallon then stepped back to survey the arch. He shook his head. "What a piece of barbarity. I've often looked at it and wondered who on earth could have done such a thing."

Fallon nodded agreement and started to tell the story of how it happened.

"Oh, I know the story," said Dimenzato, "about the grandmother and her handyman. And she said I want a little window right here, and he made a mark. It cut through the arch but he put it there anyway. Things are different today. And you only need to look at *that* mess to see what a good thing it is that they are."

Severino Boscolo was down on one knee digging a camera out of his briefcase. He stepped back and photographed the arch from several angles.

Dimenzato watched him. "Be sure to get the coat of arms on the lintel." He turned to Vittorio. "People used to hack those off. We don't let that happen nowadays. If a family sold to their social inferiors they would chisel it off before moving out; if they sold to their betters the new owners hacked it off when they came in. Of course, those feelings don't exist anymore; except in a few rare cases."

They went inside to look over the plans and examine the pieces.

Dimenzato tapped the table with his fingers as Vittorio laid out the diagram. They were standing in Vittorio's makeshift site office on the mezzanine beside the window in question. The diagram showed an actual-size detail of the damaged section. The smallest chips of the stone were taped to the paper. Vittorio took the larger pieces from a box and positioned them where they belonged.

"I have to warn you," said Dimenzato, "that we really don't have the latitude to grant such permissions, as much as we would like to do it." He moved the stones around as though he were studying the technical viability of the project.

"Yes, but," chimed in Boscolo, a little too quick on the cue, "there is one factor which could help the case."

"What's that?" asked Dimenzato, assuming a blank expression.

"If he used the company Cantiere Italia," offered Boscolo, nodding eagerly to convince him.

"Ah," nodded Dimenzato as though weighing the suggestion. "It's true, they have the goodwill of the commission that makes the final decision. Who's the man over there who deals with these difficult cases?" He looked at Boscolo, frowning and trying to remember.

"Wait a minute." Boscolo rubbed his forehead. "It's . . . um . . . Danilo . . . no, *Daniele* . . . um . . . I can't remember his surname, but everybody knows him there. I was talking to him this morning. Wait a minute." He pulled a scrap of paper from his pocket. "Here's his cell phone number." He gave the paper to Vittorio.

"I'll talk to him," said Vittorio, "but I have some of the best stonemasons in the business working for me."

"Oh, you'll never get anywhere with your own people," said Boscolo, looking at Dimenzato for confirmation. Dimenzato tipped his head to one side and let him speak. "The commission will turn you down flat."

"I understand," said Vittorio, putting the scrap of paper in his pocket. "I'll look into the finances and see how much we can set aside for this."

Severino was almost skipping when he and Giuseppe Dimenzato set out across the campo on their way back to the office. "I tried out an Aprilia motorbike last weekend," he said, stopping in the street to talk as soon as they were out of sight. Giuseppe paused and listened. "I made it roar. I was charging down the Lungomare like a mad bull, *vrrrrooooom;*" he twisted the throttle on imaginary handlebars and pawed the ground with his foot. "I never thought I'd be able to afford it!"

"Calm down," said Dimenzato, continuing to walk

along the calle. "Fallon's no fool. But you'd better ring Daniele all the same."

Severino at twenty-nine was still a young man, but he was practically a broken man already. Today he could see no point in going to work and barely any reason to stay alive as he dragged himself towards the vaporetto station at Santa Elisabetta with a sick feeling in his stomach and a heart of lead. When he came level with the motorcycle shop, he could hardly bring himself to look at the window that had dealt him such a cruel blow the night before. On his way home from work he had sprinted around the cars parked in the shop's forecourt to approach the window of his beloved: the red Aprilia motorcycle that flaunted under two spotlights its gorgeous curves and power to thrill, like a tart in a window in Amsterdam. SEX MACHINE! touted the banner draped across the handlebars. He had taken her out for a test run the week before, and after that encounter he knew he had to have her. But she was gone, nowhere to be seen, even when he cupped his hands over his eyes and peered into the showroom. The shop was dark and closed for the day.

Severino was still young enough to embrace excess as the true way. Last night it was cheap wine; this morning it was misery. He decided to go straight for the motorcycle shop, steeling himself for the glorious devastation he was about to withstand through his own temerity. He planted himself, chin up and chest out, where he could see the empty window and renew his pain. But the motorcycle was there. She was back. How had this happened? The shop wasn't even open yet. Someone must have taken her out for a turn and come back late. He could hardly believe his eyes: Look at that overblown floozy! He had to put his foot down; this time he must not let her get away. He looked at his watch. The shop would be open in an hour. He had time to get to the office and telephone before anyone could get in and buy it ahead of him. He set off for the vaporetto at a brisk trot, singing like Renato Carosone, *Tu vuò fa l'americano, Mmericano! You want to be an American, Merican!* He got to Santa Elisabetta just in time to jump through the gate onto the big *motonave* that plied back and forth between the Lido and San Marco. He ran up the steps to the top deck and ordered a *caffé corretto* at the bar. *Tu vuò fa l'americano! Mmericano!* He sang under his breath as he watched the Public Gardens slide by. The barman regarded his elation as excessive for the present hour, but being a barman philosopher of the old school he only raised his eyebrows and charged a little excess on the grappa.

Severino was the last to arrive at the office. Architetto Dimenzato and Mirco Busato were already at their desks talking on the telephone. For a minute Severino thought they were working; then he noticed that they were only doodling on their note pads. His boss was drawing his usual busty nudes made out of circles within circles while Mirco was creating a meaningless paisley based on the letters of his name. Severino got straight on the telephone himself.

"Hi there, this is Severino. I want to reserve the red sex machine. . . . Right, right. . . . You said you could finance it one hundred percent? . . . *Bene, bene.* . . . When can I have it? . . . How long will that take? . . . Okay. I'll come by at about six this evening." Severino jumped up, executed a little tap dance beside his chair and sat down again.

His colleagues ended their telephone conversations and turned to him.

"What's with you?" asked Mirco.

"I just bought my motorcycle."

"How can you afford that?" asked his boss.

"You know how."

"You are mad, Severino. I told you to look on these windfalls as what they are—lucky strikes. You can't bank on them."

"You told me yourself yesterday that Daniele is working his way through the commissioners one by one and it's looking okay."

"But it's not his only project. What if he gets something more pressing, more lucrative? He could use up his goodwill on something else. Then he would have to put it on a back burner for a while. I'm telling you, you can't bank on these things."

"I can stop paying for my meals at home. My father can cover my room and board for a while."

"Get up and open the door, Severino. We've got to do some work today."

"Only let in two people," said Mirco. "I have to look at a couple of folders before I start seeing people."

Severino's mother had stopped clearing away the dinner. She was sitting at the kitchen table crying and wiping her eyes with her apron. "I don't want you to have one of those terrible motorcycles. They're too dangerous."

Severino's father was pacing up and down in front of her. Severino was leaning on the counter.

"I'm with your mother on that," said his father, "and you can't afford it."

"Well, I *will* be able to," said Severino. "I've been promised a commission for some work I sent to a contractor, but it's taking a long time."

"You should have waited to get it before you spent it."

"You think," said his mother, "that young people get killed only on the mainland, but it can happen right here on the Lido. My first boyfriend got killed down by the

Grand Hotel des Bains. Remember, Rino?" She turned to her husband. "Sandro was only seventeen when his mother bought that Vespa for him. She never forgave herself."

"Nothing's going to happen to me," said Severino.

"Sandro's motorcycle wasn't anything like as powerful as the one you've got," said his mother.

"It's going to make the neighbors furious," said his father. "It makes more noise than a jumbo jet. I nearly had a heart attack when you came in last night."

"*Uffa,* Papà. Okay, okay. I won't rev it up when I'm near the house." But the memory of the racket he'd sent echoing like an explosion up and down the street made him grin even as he said it.

"And for how much longer am I going to have to go without your contribution towards the household expenses?"

"Not long, Papà. Maybe for a couple of months. Anyhow, if I needed to sell that machine, I know twenty people who would buy it tomorrow."

"And you still haven't passed your exams," said his father. "Do you have any plans to finish your degree?"

"You drink too much," said his mother. "That's what worries *me.* I don't want to be in the *Gazzettino* like Contessa Panfili and Baronessa Patristi—whatever she's called now; she's got a different name—because *my* son has got himself killed on the road."

"Patristi?" asked Severino. "What Patristi?"

"It was the young boy. He was seventeen. He was with the Panfili boy, who was about your age. They turned a car over and burned up."

"That's the mainland, Mamma. It's different on the Lido. I wonder," said Severino thoughtfully, "whether that's slowing things down. It's a job at Palazzo Patristi that's supposed to be getting me this commission. How long ago was this?"

"I can't remember," said his mother. "You know these things happen on the mainland all the time. It could have been a month or two."

"Nobody's even mentioned it. It must not be important," said Severino, tossing his keys in the air. "I'll ask about it tomorrow. Well, I'm off. Don't wait up for me."

"You stay out too late," said his father. "You should show some consideration for your mother."

"I *did* tell you, Severino." Architetto Dimenzato still had his hand on the telephone he'd just put back on its cradle. "I told you the minute I put down the telephone from Daniele, just like I'm doing right now. You were standing with your head out the window smoking a cigarette. I told you what Daniele told me—that the works at Palazzo Patristi were going to be shut down and the palazzo put up for sale because of the death of the Patristi boy. You know it's all complicated by the fact that the restoration is being financed by the ex-Baronessa Patristi, the mother of the boy who died, who's now married to Architetto Fallon, who's directing the project. She told Fallon she wants the palazzo sold because the son she was restoring it for is dead."

"I can't hear when my head's out the window," said Severino. "There's all sorts of noise out there."

"You're going deaf from that bike," said Dimenzato. "Now I'm trying to tell you what Daniele called to tell me this time: The Padoanos, the ones with the big clothing business out in the Veneto, are set to buy Palazzo Patristi and want to keep the project going. Daniele is going to pick an architect for them. So it's looking good, Severino, except that it will take a little more time."

"Working with these people could try the patience of a saint," said Severino, getting up from his desk to smoke a cigarette at the window.

"That's what the people outside the door are saying about us," said Mirco, laughing. He drained his paper cup and dropped it in the wastebasket under his desk. He bent over to look. "Those filthy maids haven't bothered to empty the wastebaskets again! How lazy can you get?"

"You're right, Mirco. Go open the door and let in three people," said Dimenzato. "We want to get through at least half of these folders before the Conservation Commission meets next week. We'd better turn down most of them; the agenda's almost full."

*

Vittorio Fallon was packing up the site office in the old lace room over the front door of Palazzo Patristi. He stopped sorting invoices and looked through the infamous window in the broken arch out towards the campo. It was a melancholy business closing down the restoration before it was finished. The death of his stepson, Matteo, had changed everything. And yet Vittorio was aware that he had never been so happy as he was now. His baby son, Secondo, was one month old. Vittorio wanted to mourn for Matteo, but happiness for Secondo kept breaking in. He turned back to the table, swept the rest of the papers into a folder, and stuffed them into his briefcase. His stonemason, Rocco, was coming to take care of one last piece of work in this room today. Resting on the table was a tall slender marble box that Rocco had made to store the chips and fragments they had been hoping for over a year to use in repairing the broken arch. Rocco was going to consign them into safe storage that afternoon. Vittorio had invited Barone Patristi to come over at the end of the workday.

Rocco came in. "Ciao, Architetto. Here's the lid for the box." He put it on the table. Vittorio read the words engraved in the marble:

Matteo Patristi
In Memoriam

Rocco put his toolbag on the floor. "I've got something for you." He reached in his jacket pocket and pulled out a small pair of scissors in a leather case. He held them up. "They're from my wife as well. It's an old superstition. They protect baby boys. You have to hide them away where no one can get at them. As long as they remain closed, Secondo will be safe."

Vittorio held them in his hand, thinking. "That's wonderful, Rocco. Where can we put them?"

"I was thinking we could put them inside the box here with the pieces of the arch. I'm going to seal it up now."

"That's a wonderful idea, Rocco—like his big brother is somehow looking after him after all."

When Vittorio came back that afternoon, he found Edmondo Patristi in the site office looking at the inscription on the box.

"That came out well." nodded Edmondo. Rocco smiled with pleasure. He was standing with his chisel and mallet in front of a square hole slightly larger than the box, positioned below the window and to the right.

"That's a thick wall, isn't it," said Edmondo, bending down to peer into the cavity.

"Do you want a hand with the box, Rocco?" Vittorio started to push the box across the table but couldn't get it to move.

"People forget how heavy marble can be," said Rocco, heaving the box from the table and swinging it into the cavity in one move. "Marble makes a good wall. You find chunks of marble like this in walls all over Venice, pieces retrieved from old buildings. Waste not, want not." He wedged the box in place with bricks and cement, and then started the final layer of bricks. When he finished, the wall gave no indication that a box was hidden within. Rocco stood up and looked at his handiwork. There was something almost religious in the moment.

"*Questi fûro gli estremi onor renduti / Al domatore di cavalla Ettorre,*" murmured Edmondo, struggling a little to rise to the strange occasion. "Thus they honored Hector breaker of horses."

"*Sì?*" said Rocco.

Vittorio wasn't listening; he was thinking about the little scissors safely hidden under that cursed arch.

"Are we sure," said Edmondo, "that those Padoanos won't get permission to restore that arch?"

"Yes," said Vittorio. "It would be terrible if they did."

"I thought they were determined. I thought they were going to throw some of their money at it."

"I'm sure they won't succeed."

"I see," said Edmondo, with a shrug. "I wish I could have your confidence. With their kind of money . . ." He looked at his watch. "I have to go. Luisa's expecting me for drinks."

*

On Fridays Severino tended to go home at lunchtime to get a head start on the weekend, but the Friday after his mother made the scene about his motorcycle he suffered a black, black day. Severino didn't even take his lunch hour.

When Architetto Dimenzato came back from lunch he found Severino sitting at his desk going through folders.

"Did you read the *Gazzettino*?"

"No."

"It's all over," said Dimenzato. "That Cinzio Calabron drawing of the Patristi broken arch that everyone saw in the *Gazzettino* last month—thanks to that delinquent journalist del Banco—has done just what the Cantiere Italia was afraid it would do. I'm going to find a chance to mention that journalist to the Mayor. He's got a lot to answer for—I'm going to remind Grandi that the Padoanos could have sponsored cultural projects for him."

Severino was nodding. "Yeah, yeah." But Dimenzato was too irritated to notice that Severino didn't seem very interested in what he was saying.

"It's still in the window of that Campana Space II with a red dot on it. Did you hear who bought it? It was the architect's wife. She arranged for Calabron to donate it to the Accademia with the proviso that they have to show it for at least three months each year because she wants to make a memorial to the son who died in a car crash. Anyhow, you know what it all means."

"Yeah, yeah," said Severino. "The Patristi arch is now a landmark. Daniele rang me this morning; he said he knew from the beginning that Calabron's drawing could cause problems, but he couldn't do anything about it. The Padoanos are furious. The Cantiere Italia has lost the chance to finish the Patristi restoration for the Padoanos because they didn't manage to buy the drawing. Giving it to the Accademia was diabolical."

"Or stupid. She probably had no idea that her little memorial would cause such problems." Dimenzato took one of Severino's cigarettes and went over to the window. "What are you doing with those folders? Aren't those the rejected projects?"

"Yeah, they are. I'm just checking to see if we turned down anyone by mistake. Here's one, for example: it's that antiques dealer who lives on the Grand Canal. He must be rich."

VOCATION

The American Consulate in Milan was at pains to show the world that it did not wish to be reconnoitered by Franc Emil or any other extraneous person. That was why it had security guards packing sidearms roaming up and down in front and hanging around the doors. Franc Emil had sized up the hostility when he first looked the place over, but he kept coming back anyhow. This time he decided to try walking down the opposite side of the street with the air of someone with someplace to go. When he got level with the police cars he dropped down on one knee to tie his shoe and peer between the cars. *Cazzo!* A security guard in front of the consulate was bent over with his hands on his knees watching him. As Franc stood up he saw the guard crossing the street towards him with his hand on his pistol. A jolt of adrenaline charged him up for the chase, but he didn't run. Franc was right off his game. He walked towards the guard.

"Why are you hanging around here, kid?"

"I'm supposed to meet somebody."

"This is no place to meet somebody."

"I don't have a choice."

"You're telling me. If you don't beat it you're going to meet the *carabinieri* and take a ride out of here. Kid, we've got you on film, so scram before you get in trouble. We've been watching you around here for two days already."

"Look, it's about a girl. She's coming here. Her name is Beatrice Carey. She's from Ohio."

"Tell her to meet you someplace else. Go! Get out of here! *Vattene! Via!* Or you're taking a ride."

"I . . ." Franc gave up; it wasn't worth the fingerprints, mug shots, DNA, Interpol. Just the idea of explaining to the police how he came to be there made him want to run for his life. *"Beh!"* He shrugged and walked away. But it was a only a tactical retreat. After two days on the job he had no intention of giving up. *"Beh!"* He nodded to himself as he sauntered away, proud in defeat with his thumbs in his belt. *Ah sì, sì;* oh, yes: he should tell the police all about his daredevil train trips from Venice to Trieste, where a simple screwup like dropping off to sleep could land him in the tank. Why, *why*—he could never figure out—did that one train route hit him like a cosh on the head? He'd actually been wondering lately whether he might be constitutionally unfit for his profession. Vlado and Jana, the Albanians who adopted him before he could even remember, always said that you can't get anywhere as a thief unless you feel good about yourself. If you know you have as much right as anybody to everything in life, the opportunities just open up. But his problem was specific: The minute he sat down on that train to Trieste he felt like a drowning man sinking into oblivion. It was like there was something inside him working against him that refused to help. He thought it must have something to do with the terrible stakes. If he missed the station in Trieste he missed his assignation and his payment, but that was nothing in comparison to riding the train over the frontier where he would get caught without a passport to his name. In Venice he didn't really need one. The *vigili* and the *carabinieri* knew him the way the police know all the drifters. As long as they couldn't pin anything on him, they couldn't do anything to him, and they didn't really want to. He was a problem for them. They knew they couldn't deport him because he had no country. The anomaly was that on this journey he tended to have at least ten passports. This time he had twelve really choice ones—two from Germany, two from England, five from the United States, one from Canada, one from Austria, and one from Australia, each one worth 150 euros in readies to his contact in Trieste. But once over the border, they'd be worth a nice stretch in the slammer. On every trip he weighed the tactic of lodging the bag with the passports down beside the seat in case something unforeseen happened, but he never did it. He didn't like to let go of them. The chance of a catastrophe like someone making a grab for them or their spilling out onto the floor was too real. That thought alone should have been enough to keep him awake. This lot represented more than a month's work, and he needed the money. For another thing, his contact, Mo, was getting impatient. But hey, so was Franc. Mo'd been promising him a passport for a year. Franc wanted a Canadian one, but now he was afraid Mo's guys would trip him up with a bad one. Mo had a heavy call just now for western passports, and Franc Emil had started out as his best supplier. "What's with you?" Mo kept asking him. "Why aren't you coming up with the goods? Have you lost your touch or something?" Franc didn't know the answer.

The train had just passed through Portogruaro; the trip got longer every time. He ate his Mars Bar and drank a Red Bull. He saved the Coca-Cola and his *Paperino,* his Donald Duck comic book, for later. After all that chocolate and caffeine he should have felt like running up and down the corridor doing backflips, but not on this ride. He was just leaning over to rest his head against the window when he caught himself. He pulled out the *Paperino* he'd bought the day before, hoping for a story so gripping that he would forget about sleep, but instead he got a surprise that woke him up like a gun in the face. The book fell open like a pair of hands, offering him a passport he was sure he'd never seen

before. It made his heart pound. Was it a plant? He looked
up to see if anyone in the corridor was watching him. Could
he have lifted it from someone's pocket without even thinking when he was sitting on the vaporetto? He groaned out
loud. "Thirteen!" No, maybe not. Maybe he'd forgotten to
put this one in with the others. He was still alone in the
compartment, but he kept the passports hidden in the bag
just to be on the safe side and counted through them with
his fingers. Twelve. So this really was extra. He would have
to keep it until next time. It was one of the new American
ones. He looked at the photograph and laughed. There was
something about the girl's expression. She looked like she'd
just made a joke. Franc wished he'd seen her, but he was too
careful to look at the people he robbed. That was the first
rule in the book: No eye contact if you want to stay invisible. *Beatrice Carey,* he read. *Issued in Columbus, Ohio.*
Well, it was a cinch he couldn't give Mo thirteen passports.
Mo would kill him, and anyhow they'd already agreed the
money. He would have to hold on to it until the next time.
Beatrice Carey. She was cute.

Mo never came to the station; he sent a different person
every time. In fact, Franc had never seen him. Someone
had given him the cell phone number when he was passing
through Slovenia. A few days before Franc was set up to
make a consignment, Mo would ring Franc to tell him
how to recognize the messenger. Typically the guy would
hold a passport in his left hand and something else, which

was different every time, in his right. When Franc walked into the main hall of the Trieste station, a guy sauntered towards him with a passport in his left hand, calling attention to it by tapping it against his thigh as he walked. Franc took a quick look around and saw another man with a passport in his left hand and a newspaper—there it was: the *Corriere della Sera*—in his right. Franc too had a *Corriere della Sera* in his right hand. So the first guy was a cop who was looking for him but probably didn't know him by sight. Franc walked out the door and kept walking until he got to the bookstore. He stood with his back to the window until his contact appeared on the other side of the table. Franc walked behind a bookshelf. He left his bag on the shelf. The agent came and picked it up and left an envelope. Franc picked it up. He bought another *Paperino* comic book and left.

Franc never had the slightest problem staying awake on the journey back to Venice. He would read and look out the window. When he was new at the game, he used to buy a first-class ticket and work the train, but he was getting too lazy for that: If you made a hit, you really had to get off and get on a later train. There was plenty of work in Venice if he concentrated on it. The train going back was brilliantly fast. It pulled into Portogruaro in no time.

Franc looked across the platform. A train from Venice was pulling in on the other side. *Porca miseria!* he was so happy not to be on it, it made him happy just to look at it.

He stroked his upper lip with his finger, but his mustache was gone. It was strange to be without it. Jana had made him wear a false mustache when he was thirteen to make him look older and to disguise him. He hated it and started shaving to make his mustache come in sooner so he didn't have to wear the false one. Then this morning, while he was getting ready for this horrible trip he'd suddenly for no clear reason just shaved it off. The doors of the Venice train opened and Franc watched a fat woman with thin legs and tiny feet making a big story of getting a grip on the handrail and organizing herself to get off. As she climbed down, she bent over to confirm each step before placing her foot on it. Under her arm a rust-colored toy poodle looked up and down the platform with popping black eyes, showing the same frantic impatience as the people behind her looking over her shoulder. Safely landed, she continued to block them by bending down to place the poodle on the platform. Then she turned, straightened her jacket, and taking exaggeratedly dainty steps set off for the stairs to the underpass. But the poodle didn't follow her. It sat down like it was going on strike . . . no, it was hunching over. It was taking a crap: one, two, three. What a heap for a little dog! It must have been waiting all the way from Milan. No wonder it looked desperate. Finished, it gave a few perfunctory scratches at the pavement with its hind legs then trotted after its mistress, bouncing like it had springs in its feet, pleased with itself, feeling good. Franc thought it was cute for a poodle. From the opposite direction a conductor came swinging along the platform; he too had a spring in his step, he too was feeling good. And so was Franc. It was strange how the world reflected your own condition. He hardly ever looked at people except from a safe distance like this. As the conductor walked along, he was looking back, gesticulating and laughing over his shoulder with someone out of Franc's range of vision. Franc sat up. The conductor was walking straight for the pile. Franc wanted to shout, Look out! Stay out of the shit! but the guy had already stepped in it. At the first sense of sliding, he jumped, like the turds had exploded; his knees shot up and he bellowed a stream of imprecations that Franc couldn't make out. He seemed to hang for an instant in midair, held up by his shout, then he landed clear, his face distorted by the violence of his oaths. It was a lesson: Stay out of the shit! Franc laughed. He opened the passport. She was laughing. That was the second time today. What was happening?

Franc didn't know where he came from. He knew where he'd been since he was about five and he had a couple of mental pictures, from earlier, without captions: he could remember big marble steps, a railing, a big person beside him; and sometimes when the air was a certain way, a vision of a lawn came up with a sense of someone nearby

296

that he couldn't see. Nothing more. That was all he was ever likely to know of his true history. His adoptive parents lived like gypsies but said they were not gypsies. They claimed to be Albanian. They never said where they found him but always said he was not one of them. He wasn't sure how old he was; he thought he was about eighteen. He had gray-blue eyes with the even teeth and smooth skin of a gentleman, but he had the great nose of an adventurer and the black curly hair of a gypsy. He could have been any-thing. He stole his name off the sign on a boarded-up shop in Slovenia as he passed through. It could have been his real name. He had heard his Albanians talking about their years in Slovenia. They might have taken him from there. About three years back he decided he had been with them long enough and left them in Germany. He never expected to see them again. He walked over borders until he found his way to Venice. He knew all the gypsies and Albani-ans—he spoke the languages a bit—but he wasn't a part of any group. He was different.

Now it was coming home to him: He didn't feel good about himself anymore. That must be why he was getting so lazy. Was he losing his nerve? That passport showing up from nowhere bothered him. He could see it would be a good idea to hand it in, just in case it was a plant. But he couldn't do it in Venice; that could be playing into their hands. He decided to take the passport to Milan and turn it in at the consulate. Or he could just drop it down beside the seat here and let someone else find it. No. If the girl was real, he owed her a laugh. He'd take it to where she would find it. He checked the stamp. She'd only been in Italy for a day. He would continue on to Milan. He might do a bit of work there since no one knew him.

He would need a new shirt and some underwear now that he had some money. In Mestre, he got off the train and went to the Coin department store. He picked up a couple of shirts, pulled a pack of underpants and some socks off the rack, and took them to the cash desk. There was a line. The cashier was slow, chatting to each person as she packaged the goods and rang up the sale. This was going to take ages. He'd probably missed three Milan trains already. He looked around. *Porca Madonna,* he thought; why didn't I just take the stuff and go? As he was weighing the situation, the floorwalker came up and looked at him. By accident Franc caught his eye. *Cazzo!* Too late now. The floorwalker acted like he recognized him; maybe it was only by type. But he'd still have to pay. Franc couldn't believe how stupid he was getting.

As he walked away from the consulate guard, Franc was thinking that he was wearing the last of the clean shirts he'd bought—actually paid for—he shook his head in disbelief—and the hostel had no place to wash anything.

"Excuse me." A girl stopped him. "Do you speak English?"

Franc turned. Was this a trap?

"Is this the right way to the American Consulate?" She pointed the way Franc had just come. "My taxi said he couldn't come down here."

Franc looked where she was pointing. The security guard was still watching him. Franc threw him a complicit grin. The guard turned his back and pretended he didn't see it.

"Hello, Beatrice," said Franc, and even though it sounded like *Allo Bayatreechay*, it took her by surprise.

"That's my name in Italian. How did you know it?"

"I found your passport and brought it here."

"Have you got it?" She leaned towards him eagerly.

"No, I turned it in to the consulate."

"You mean they have my passport? I came to try to get a new one. This is so great! *Thank you!*"

"Go and get it," said Franc. "I'll wait here and take you for a coffee."

"I should take *you* for a coffee!" Her eyebrows went up and she gave him exactly the gleeful smile of the passport photograph.

Franc leaned against the building and watched her walk towards the guard, who stopped her and exchanged some words with her. He indicated Franc with his head. Then pointed at the entrance. As soon as she was out of sight the guard came towards Franc. He started talking while he was still twenty feet away.

"How'd you happen to get hold of her passport, you stinking gypsy?"

"I found it on a vaporetto, and if I really was a gypsy you know you wouldn't call me stinking."

"Yeah. Okay. Are you waiting for her?"

"Yeah."

"Go down there by that pole so you're out of the cameras. The guys on the monitors have seen enough of you."

"I can't tell you how happy my mother was," said Beatrice, laughing. She threw her hands in the air and rolled her eyes heavenwards to show her mother's relief. "Mom was going to come over and rescue me if I had problems at the consulate. She actually made me promise that I would take that nice young man to dinner!" Franc and Beatrice were sitting in the Osteria Assassini, recommended in one of her guidebooks for its rustic charm and interesting name. Franc couldn't give her any advice about it. He and his ilk generally avoided places with names like "assassin's alley" out of superstition, so he was completely unknown there. The waiters were treating him like any normal person.

Franc Emil and Beatrice Carey had come back to Venice on the train together, which meant that he didn't work that train either. She had regaled him with stories about beautiful Ohio and the Land of Opportunity. She wanted him to go to America. She wanted everyone to discover America. It was the Only Place, and Ohio was the Best Place. She told him about sailing on Lake Erie. He was interested and wondered if a person could sail all the way over to Canada. She told him about concerts where people took picnics and sat in the grass. He thought about people who specialized in that sort of crowd, posing as peddlers of amusing animated toys. One would distract the family while the other one put his bag, with its bottom open, on top of the thing he wanted to steal and then rummaged in the bag like he was looking for another interesting trinket while he lifted the handbag or wallet into the under sack and drew the string that closed the bottom. Franc used to watch Jana's old mother sewing those bags in the evening. She could sell them for a good price among the gypsies because hers worked the best. The top and bottom bags were separated so you could show the top bag to be empty when the bottom bag had something in it. Land of opportunity indeed. Venice was another but he couldn't tell her that.

"My father," said Beatrice, "says a man's character is the only important thing. He keeps telling me he is more concerned that I should marry a good honest man than a rich one or a snob or even an intellectual. I hope you'll get to meet each other."

Franc was mesmerized by this girl. He could hardly

believe she was real. On the other hand, he knew she was because he'd seen her passport. She told him about how her father had an assignment in London for two years starting in September. She had arranged with her university to let her do her last year on their study-abroad program at Oxford. Her girlfriend was coming back tonight from visiting Italian relatives, and in the morning they were on their way to Florence, Rome, and Naples before going to London. She intended to come back to Venice because her visit had been ruined by the worry about her passport.

Franc was seated on the bench that ran along the wall the full length of the room. Beatrice was opposite on a chair. The woman to his right had put her handbag on the bench beside him. He could see her wallet.

"Do you mind if I slip out to the restroom for a minute?" he asked Beatrice, sliding to his right along the bench towards the handbag. He pushed against it and excused himself profusely, pushing the bag away as if to apologize for bumping against it. The woman apologized and moved the bag to her other side, but he had already slid away to the left and got up. Once in the men's room, he locked himself in the cubicle and looked through the wallet—credit cards, lots of banknotes—wow—sterling, euros: a good haul. What if the woman noticed? It would be all over with Beatrice. Was it worth it? Here he was, being treated like he was the same as she—a conclusion she'd jumped to without any lies from him. All he said was that he had come to Venice to look for a job in something related to tourism and that he might study when he got some money together. It wasn't really a lie. He put everything back in the wallet and returned to the table. He got there just in time to see the woman pick up her handbag and leave. She and her husband nodded to him and to Beatrice. *"Buona sera."*

Franc nodded and smiled. "Wait!" he called, sliding from the bench and reaching under their table. "Is this yours?" He held up a wallet.

"No." She shook her head, then glanced in her handbag. "Yes! How on earth did it get there? Thank you. It has all my cards and everything. Thank you so much. I can't imagine how it fell out."

Beatrice looked at him like she wanted to kiss him. "You are so wonderful—always coming to the rescue."

"You know what?" said Franc. "One day I'm going to buy you a safe handbag. My mother once showed me which kind is worst—I mean *best*—worst for thieves and accidents and things." Even as he spoke, Franc wondered how Jana had shoved herself into this conversation; he thought he'd put her out of his mind forever. He couldn't have been reminded of her by Beatrice. Jana would never in a million years have praised him for the two botched jobs that were winning him the affection of this girl from another world. A kick in the shins would have been more Jana's style.

He walked Beatrice back to her hotel, but he didn't go in for fear of attracting attention.

"Franc, I'm coming back to Venice to see you again. I'll never forget how you rescued my passport and went to so much trouble to get it back to me. I can't write to you or anything because you don't have an address yet and neither do we, but I'll come sooner or later, maybe alone, maybe with my parents, maybe in a few weeks, maybe in a few months, maybe after I finish college. But I promise I'll come and I'll look for you in that campo with the statue of the man that always has a pigeon on his head—San Stefano. I'll meet you there on a Friday evening at seven on the steps of the statue. Promise you'll go there every Friday at seven?" Franc nodded. "And every Friday at seven I'll think about how we met." She gave him a peck on the cheek and went inside. She waved from inside the door, laughing. "Friday at seven," she mouthed through the glass, tapping her wristwatch with her finger.

Franc walked away wondering what had happened to him. He might have been considerably richer at this point, but instead he had a steady date with nobody, to do nothing every Friday at seven. Was there something to be gained by letting this girl run him around?

The next morning he awoke happy in the knowledge that he had some money for a change. He felt like trying something new. He joined the queue of men waiting in the barbershop near the Accademia. There was only one empty seat, the one farthest from the barber, up against the wall, separated from the others by a table piled with magazines. He sat down and found an old *Paperino* in the heap, but he didn't start reading it immediately. He had never been in a barbershop before, and he was interested in what the barber was doing. When he was little, Jana used to cut his hair, and after he got big he cut his own. That was why he wore it long—so he didn't have to cut it so often. He wondered if all barbers were as slow as this one. This guy snipped and snipped, then stepped back to get a better perspective, then snipped a little more; sometimes he snipped air like he was getting up speed for the next little snip, then he would step back again. Franc could hardly stand to watch him. Time obviously meant nothing to this barber. He opened the *Paperino* and started to read. When Franc finished the *Paperino* and looked up again, he realized that everyone who had been waiting when he came in had gone, and their chairs were now filled by others. The barber was sweeping up the hair around the chair. When he finished, he leaned the broom against the wall and signaled to one of the newcomers that it was his turn. Franc stood up.

"Look, I've been waiting for longer than anyone else here. I need a haircut."

The barber looked at Franc with the face of a man being told he could buy the Rialto Bridge for fifty dollars.

"I've been traveling. . . ." But Franc could see that this excuse for his gypsy hair wasn't cutting any ice so he added, "And now that I'm not a student anymore . . ."

The barber's face broke into a knowing smile. This was a conversion he was more than willing to facilitate. He snapped his fingers and pointed to the chair. "We'll soon take care of that." His waiting customers beamed their approval and sat back to witness the voluntary transformation from intransigent student to decent citizen.

And what a transformation it was. Franc, as he watched in the mirror, couldn't believe how different he looked with less hair and no mustache. When the barber finished shaping and trimming and clipping—he was really putting everything he had into the makeover—Franc was a new man and a clean-cut good-looking one at that. The only problem was a pallid ring all around his hairline. The barber stood behind the chair surveying his handiwork in the mirror and enjoying the approval of his audience, but he was troubled by the white ring.

"Wait a minute," he said, hurrying away to the back room. He returned with a bottle. He shook some cream onto his fingers and rubbed it over the pale areas all around the hairline. "I got this from my wife's beauty shop next door. In a few minutes it will turn a little bit suntanned. If you go to the Lido this afternoon, you'll get rid of the ring forever—unless you let your hair go like that again." There was almost a threat in his voice.

Franc walked over the Accademia Bridge feeling like he was invisible. He passed two *vigili* whose eyes skipped over him like they'd never seen him before. Fantastic! Why had he never thought of this? Habit drew him towards the Rialto. He was used to starting work there because it was always crowded. He went into one of the big snack bars on the waterfront and stood at the counter.

"Un espresso," he said, to the owner behind the bar.

"Get a receipt," said the owner, nodding towards the cash register.

"Sure," said Franc, amazed that the man didn't recognize him as a local; he obviously took him for a tourist. He stepped over to the cash register. There was a sign taped to the back of it: FULLTIME BARMAN WANTED. He paid, took the receipt, and moved back down the counter to the coffee bar. He handed the slip to the owner. "Give me an espresso, please. I wanted to inquire about the job. I just came to town, but unfortunately I don't have any papers. Would you be willing to try me out on an informal basis?"

"I can't really pay you like that," said the owner, "not without any papers." He thought for a minute. "I could let you work for tips and maybe give you a kind of bonus at the end of the week if you do a good job. But I couldn't guarantee you a wage or anything."

"We could try it out. When would you want me to start?"

The owner walked down to the snack counter, where a

middle-aged woman was taking a sandwich from the grill. She put it on a plate. He murmured a few words to her. She turned to look at Franc and shrugged her shoulders. The man took the plate and walked back to where Franc was drinking his coffee.

"Take this to Table Three outside," he said, handing him the plate. "Each table has a plastic number on it. See if they want anything else. I'm Italo. That's my wife over there: Edda. What's your name?"

Waiting tables was a whole new racket for Franc. It took him weeks to get a grip on it. For one thing, making tips depended on engaging with the target—making eye contact and trying to make himself memorable—just the opposite of picking pockets. But the income, considering that he tended to be lazy about his freelance vocation, was much the same, with the advantage of less built-in excitement. He caught on to the routine of smiles and banter, even though in his personal life he maintained the thief's reserve. He even established a following of people who kept coming back to the bar because they liked him. The approval made him feel good about himself. And that, he reasoned, was the explanation for the opportunities that assailed him everywhere he turned. If he bent down to retrieve a dropped napkin, his eyes would lock on an open handbag beside a chair with a wallet ready to jump into his hand. Once when walking home he passed the great doors of an imposing palace with someone's keys hanging forgotten in the lock. Without even thinking he looked over his shoulder to see if anyone was coming before he decided that those keys were not for him. One rainy morning crushed in a crowd waiting for the vaporetto he could feel a wallet in a hip pocket pressing against his wrist. Afterward, he wondered if he would have been able to resist falling against the man to distract him as the boat bumped against the *pontile* so he could snatch it—had not fate— just as he was orchestrating the theft in his mind—placed a hand on his own back pocket, which he slapped away without turning around. Surveying the crowd on the vaporetto he recognized the gypsy called Alim wearing that blank, elsewhere expression of a thief at work; he had a jacket hanging from one shoulder—the oldest trick in the book, practically the badge of a pickpocket—to hide his quarrying hand. Franc watched him as the boat docked at San Stae. The gypsy stared impassively as the last person disembarked; then suddenly, as if prompted by an impulse, he skipped through the half-closed gate onto the *pontile* and hurried up the ramp while the vaporetto pulled away.

"Ahhh!" cried a woman looking in her handbag. "That man that just got off has my wallet! And my passport! He was pressed right up against me. I could hardly breathe!"

That same morning Mo had telephoned Franc before he was even awake.

"I need merchandise. How long before you can start moving again? And listen, Franc, the next time you make a delivery, bring a set of photographs. I've got something in the works for you. It's a good one."

"I'll get back to you," said Franc. He hated the idea of resuming those train trips. "Things are still difficult here. I may have to take a holiday. I'm thinking of Germany. I'll let you know." So Mo was finally going to let him have a passport. Was this his big chance? He would have to give him probably fifty passports in exchange. He wasn't sure he still had the touch.

Franc was different from most people and he knew it, but he had something in common with the police: He noticed things that an ordinary person wouldn't see. For one thing, he could pick out criminals, not just because he knew them but sometimes by their looks alone, and he could see weapons in bulges and guess which people would keep knives in their boots. For another thing, he saw opportunities though the eyes of experience and noticed when they were being exploited—sometimes by people he recognized, sometimes by people he would recognize thereafter. The same day he was tempted on the vaporetto, he saw an Albanian called Rafi surveying the neighborhood around the bar. Franc decided to stay outside clearing tables until he went away; he didn't want him working his customers. Franc kept his back to Rafi on the off chance that he might recognize him even though he looked so different.

His altered appearance, like so many aspects of his life, had fallen to the management of happenstance. When Franc left the transients' rooming house in Cannaregio and moved into an efficiency apartment in Dorsoduro, he found himself in the same street as the barbershop. The barber kept an eye on him and hauled him in when he needed a trim. Haircuts and Friday evening appointments in Campo San Stefano were the control points in his new life. So far the haircuts had made more difference than the Friday appointments. All he had achieved so far on Friday evenings sitting at Bar Paolin in Campo San Stefano was to garner a few ideas about waiting tables.

As Franc picked up the loaded tray and turned around to look, he saw Rafi walk into the bar, order something from Italo, then head for the men's room. Franc went back outside and busied himself at the tables until he saw Rafi walking towards the Rialto Bridge. Franc went inside; he had a hunch. He went to the men's room and dug through the paper towels in the wastepaper basket. Sure enough there was an empty wallet and underneath it the useless bank cards and a Carta Venezia photo ID for the vaporettos. It belonged to Evamaria Palon, a nice-looking girl with dark hair and a serious expression. He'd seen her around. He went outside and looked up and down the *fondamenta*.

There she was, holding out her handbag and complaining to the busboy from the self-serve restaurant on the corner. She was close to tears. Franc walked over.

"I found these in our men's room," he said handing her the wallet and cards. "Why don't you come over, and I'll give you a cup of coffee."

Franc stood by the table and chatted with her. She told him she worked at the Hotel Bauer. She was the director's secretary, she added. She said she would send customers his way to thank him for finding her wallet and cards.

Looking back several weeks later, Franc thought the whole day had been marked by strange occurrences. All afternoon the orders kept coming out wrong and he nearly had a fight with Edda, and then with Italo, who defended her by suggesting that he wasn't making his orders clear. At ten, when he was stacking up the tables and chairs for the night and wondering whether he was suited to this kind of work, Italo came out to see whether he was finished.

"Franc, I need to talk to you before you leave."

Franc found him sitting at a table with two glasses of wine.

"Sit down, Franc," said Italo. "Have a glass of wine. Cheers. This has been a hard day for Edda and me."

Franc nodded and readied himself for a quick exit when

Italo finally came out with the regretful conclusion that Franc wasn't going to work out as a waiter after all.

"I'm going to have to take you off the tables," he said sadly. "You're good. You're very good, but I'm going to have to put you behind the bar. Edda's not going to be able to manage on her own." He sighed and rubbed his forehead. "I have to go into the hospital, and I don't know when I'll be back. To tell you the truth, apart from Edda you're the only person I trust."

Franc thought he must be a little bit sick himself; his throat hurt. He drank some wine and said, "Sure, but I can't live without the tips."

"I know," said Italo. "I thought tomorrow we could go around the corner to the *Municipio* and get you an ID card. You know Luigi the security guard over there; he checked it out for me. He says I should be able to vouch for you. If you can get papers, I can put you on the payroll and give you a regular income. I'll match your tips, but I'll have to leave it to you to get a waiter for the tables. I'm not a good judge of people. You're the first good person I've hired in all the years we've been here. When I bought this place in 1966—right after the big flood when you could buy ground-floor properties ten for a penny—Edda and I thought we'd set up a family business. By now our kids should have been running the place, but we never got any family."

"Well, sure," said Franc. "I'll look after the place until you get well."

As Franc was walking home, he realized he couldn't risk putting up a sign like they had done. *Porca miseria!* He might get someone like himself. He needed help to find someone good. Walking through Campo San Stefano he had an idea.

He turned his steps towards the Hotel Bauer. He went to the bar.

Franc climbed onto a stool and started chatting with the barman.

"This is a nice bar. Have you worked here long?"

"About five years."

"You must know everyone who works here."

"Pretty much."

"I met Evamaria Palon today."

"Does she work here?"

"She says she works in the director's office."

The barman shook his head. He picked up the phone. "Toni, on your telephone list do you have an Evamaria Palon? . . . Mmm. . . . Can you look on the sub lists? Do you have an extension? . . . Okay, thanks. . . . No, someone was looking for her." He turned to Franc. "She works in housekeeping. She's a maid. She doesn't have an extension, but you can leave a message at the front desk."

The next day Evamaria Palon came by for lunch. "I got your message. Did they tell you where I work?"

"Never mind; you can help me anyway. The boss is sick. He's going into the hospital and may not be back for a long time. I have to look after the bar and find someone to take my place. I was going to ask you to suggest someone, but maybe you'd like to work here yourself—unless you like making beds and cleaning bathrooms."

"I really want to be a secretary," she said, "but I suppose being a waitress might be okay for a while. I'm only temporary at the hotel anyhow."

Evamaria's performance in her first days as a waitress filled Franc with wonder. Did she seriously imagine that she could be a secretary? She couldn't even add up a column of figures. He was impatient and annoyed with himself for hiring her on an impulse, but Edda thought she showed some promise; she was considerate to the regulars and even to the tourists, which meant that people didn't get mad when she made mistakes. Furthermore, Edda was happy to have the companionship of another woman since Italo wasn't there. Edda told Franc to be patient. And what could he say since it fell to Edda to double-check every chit that Evamaria wrote and count out the right change for her? It wasn't that Franc didn't sympathize with Evamaria; he had grown up surrounded by people who could hardly write their names. He might have been like that himself had Vlado and Jana not been so unlucky as to arrive with him in Rome at a time when the authorities were clamping down on itinerants and making them send their children to school. Franc had liked school and got all the way through long division and joined-up writing before Vlado and Jana cut for Germany. His education—which encompassed even some Italian history—had given him the status of an intellectual and made him even more of a stranger to his lot than he already was. But that was all in another world.

Several nights a week after closing time Franc found himself sitting at a table with Evamaria, picking prices from the menu and giving her practice in adding them up. She knew she needed to get into Franc's good books, so she tried her best to learn quickly. Franc began to enjoy the role of teacher. They moved on to multiplication. Her progress was providential because she hadn't been there a month before her new skills were put to the test.

Italo Bacchi's recovery was slow and beginning to seem precarious. The doctors sent him home. Edda wanted to stay home with him and decided that Evamaria should take her place as cashier. "Practice makes perfect," Franc kept murmuring, as much to reassure himself as to encourage her while he prompted her on the eccentricities of the new electronic cash register. He was tense with dread when he saw her counting out money with the offhand authority of a bank teller. But by some miracle she seemed to have grown into the job, and more: Evamaria had been transformed into a career girl. Learning to add and mastering the electronic till was only the beginning. She now defined her job to include the role of secretary-receptionist to Mr. Emil. She hired her younger sister to take her place waiting tables and took it upon herself to keep the sandwich maker, the cleaners, and the dishwashers in line. She also made sure that every Friday evening Franc was free by six-forty-five to do his weekly duty at San Stefano. In truth, he was so focused on the bar and it was such an awkward commitment, occurring as it did during one of the busiest hours of the week for the bar, that he might have given it up, had he not overheard Evamaria telling her sister that she absolutely had to be there from 6:30 to 8 P.M. on Fridays to help her cover while Franc went to Mass. He almost laughed out loud. Evamaria had taken his "I have to go to San Stefano now, but I won't be long" to mean the *Church* of San Stefano instead of the *Campo* of San Stefano. But she was right in a way—the whole San Stefano business was so irrational it might as well have been a Mass.

The devil behind the scenes was Mo, who wouldn't go away. While Franc struggled to keep his past a secret, Mo was keeping up the pressure. He wanted passports and wouldn't leave him alone. Franc had been putting him off by saying that the police were watching him, but Mo didn't want to be put off.

"Why don't you go over to the beach at Jésolo for a while, or down to Rimini?"

"Those guys have their own territory," said Franc. "I'll have to lie low; I may have to leave town." The more Franc edged away from the underworld, the more he feared the police would close in and show him up. Now that he had an ID card, he had something they could take away. He wished he'd used a different name, but Italo wouldn't have understood. Then there was the job; the people who gave him the job were depending on him. Somehow he had to find a way to cut himself free from Mo. Leaving town was beginning to look like the only sure way, but he had one more idea that he could try before giving up. He bought a new SIM card with a new number for his cell phone then telephoned Mo from a public telephone.

"Mo! My cell phone's disappeared! I think the police have it. I'm getting out of here." Mo hung up without saying a word, and Franc knew no one would ever reach Mo on that number again.

During the winter Franc closed the bar on Sundays. It was difficult to get staff, and the only customers on Sunday mornings were the few old regulars who liked to play cards at the back tables. Instead, Franc spent Sunday mornings with Italo and Edda going over the accounts and reporting on the equipment, the suppliers, and the staff. He could see that Italo and Edda missed their old life at the bar, so he kept a few notes of funny things they might like to hear.

Around midday, Evamaria would join the meeting and help Edda make a big Sunday lunch for the four of them. As the weeks rolled on and on, they melded into a seamless routine with Sunday mornings and Friday evenings coming up again and again like marks on a wheel. Sometimes the weeks went by so fast that the marks blurred into a ring and he seemed always to be looking for Beatrice while at the same time sharing the week's headway with Italo and Edda in the company of Evamaria.

One Friday evening Franc was sitting in Campo San Stefano at Paolin's drinking his usual Aperol spritz and musing about the summer season coming up and the need to replace the old tables outside Italo's bar. The round tables like the one in front of him were fine for a bar where lots of people might want to crowd around a single small surface, but for him the square ones were better because sometimes tour groups asked him to make long tables. For Franc this respite became the Sunday sermon or the afternoon concert of his betters, a chance to ponder things he didn't have time to think about when he was working and was too tired to think about when he got home. It was here on a Friday evening that he had figured out how to get rid of Mo.

It occurred to him now that nine months had passed since he promised Beatrice Carey that he would wait for her here at this time until someday she returned. He could hardly believe that in all those months he hadn't missed a single Friday. His fidelity was largely thanks to Evamaria who not only covered for him while he was out, but reminded him to go and made sure he did. He had overheard her telling Edda in the kitchen one Sunday that Franc had this secret religious side to him and went to Mass at the Church of San Stefano every Friday evening at seven no matter what. Edda could see that Franc was a good man, but she couldn't see why he went all the way to San Stefano. Evamaria thought he might have some Polish ancestry. Franc could hardly believe the way his character flowered in the female imagination; first Beatrice attributed an ill-deserved sense of decency and now Evamaria made him devout and assigned him an ancestry. For Franc it revealed more about a woman's appetite for romance than it said about himself. Nevertheless, Franc didn't want Evamaria to know the reason he came to San Stefano. He shook his head. It was preposterous anyhow.

He looked over at the statue. Two children were running up the steps and sliding down the stone slopes that separated the steps on each of the four faces. They were practically clambering over a woman who was sitting on the steps reading a book. As he watched she stood up and brushed the seat of her jeans. Even from so far away he could see that the jeans had creases. Someone had lovingly—or more likely, dutifully—put those creases in her trousers. Judging from her clothes and manner, he didn't think she did much ironing herself. She kept her eyes on her guidebook while the children played around her and people hurried by in all directions. Franc had considered the possibility that Beatrice Carey might not recognize him but it had never occurred to him until now that she too might have changed and he might not recognize her either. The woman with the guidebook had hair the same color as Beatrice Carey's. Franc held up his cell phone and zoomed in on her face. He closed his eyes and took a deep breath. Could he remember anything apart from that captivating smile? He looked again. Too refined to search for him, was she sitting there waiting with her book, eyes downcast like a picture from a church? He realized now that he had never exerted himself to look for her because he trusted that the strange fate which brought them together in the first place would bring them together again. He had been trusting in providence, working and saving his money for the journey ahead. He wondered if she might have come before and couldn't recognize him—because even though in character he had traveled a long way towards her idea of him, in looks he was an equally long way from the boy she'd met.

The week before he had struck out on his own from Germany, an old gypsy woman told him that he was going to embark on a long journey home. That was why he headed for Slovenia: to see what would happen. What hap-

pened was that he hooked up with Mo and Mo told him
he might be able to get him a Mexican or Canadian passport. But nothing occurred to make him settle there. The
fortune-teller's words—even though he knew they were lit-
erally impossible—were what had prompted him to get
moving. Now, all at once he was gripped by certainty. He
wasn't drifting anymore; he knew where he was going. It
was as clear as if he himself had looked into the crystal ball
and seen with his own eyes where he would find his place
and his people.

He was in a hurry. He got up and went inside to pay at
the cash register. The waiter followed him. Franc apologized for not waiting for the bill; he had an appointment.
He left by the side door and hurried back to the Rialto
through the narrow minor streets. Evamaria would be up
to her ears with work, struggling to manage alone. He
would have to get more help. He couldn't expect her to go
on working like this forever. He tried to weigh how much
of her good opinion of him depended on the conviction
that he went to church on Fridays, and he wondered
whether she would hold him to it for the rest of his life.

FINISH

Barone Edmondo Patristi looked down from his balcony at the moon struggling to hold its image on the dark waves of the Grand Canal. He was lost in a rare moment of antipathy to romance and never even thought to raise his eyes to the friendly silence of the tranquil moon above. He was pondering deeper matters: *Felix qui potuit rerum cognoscere causas*—Happy the man who understands why things turn out the way they do. It was curious, for example, that the balcony under his feet was not really his own but the balcony of a rented apartment from which, to be sure, he could see his own balcony—three of them in fact—or could have done were the building not shrouded in scaffolding. What he could see were the red lights marking the scaffold's extremities, which too were reflected in the water below like red stars in the margin of a disputed contract. *Felix qui potuit rerum cognoscere causas.* Virgil was right. And what about me? *Sono come l'orso, "che dal mel non sì tosto si distolga*—" I'm like a bear, "there's no distracting me from the honey once I've had a sniff of it." And everything probably comes down to that.

Everyone had heard of Edmondo Patristi, scion of a legendary first family of Venice, and those who counted also knew that he was perfectly placed by his good looks, his erudition, and his splendid name to marry the one important thing he didn't have—a fortune. So it wasn't by chance that at the age of twenty-four he found himself placed at dinner on the right side of Dame Fortune herself: Loredana Fierazzo, the wonderful widow of one of the leading industrialists of the day; nor was it happenstance that at barely twenty-five he married her enchanting twenty-year-old daughter, Sofi.

This was one of those rarefied matches made practically in heaven on two of the highest pinnacles of society. For Edmondo the prospects were dizzying. Looking back over the ruins, Edmondo could no longer say exactly from where—or, for that matter, to where—he'd been transported by his beautiful, bountiful bride; everything was now lost in fog and legal terms. What he could remember was how much he missed the insulating comforts of his married life. He thought maybe he missed them more than he missed his estranged wife or even his children.

*

One of Edmondo's most distinguishing attributes was a remarkable mind which he had furnished with classical literature in an abundance verging on clutter; even his casual thoughts stumbled onto bookish instances, and his ordinary utterances picked up precious ornaments like burrs in a thicket. There among the library comforts of overstuffed similes and familiar phrases, propinquity and rapport lost their way and perished.

But Edmondo remained the ideal romantic character. He was engaging yet remote, like a figure in a book, with his inner self concealed beneath a patina as smooth and seamless as a polished stone: so near and yet so far. It was this remoteness that gave him the aura of mystery, of unplumbed depths and romance that attracted women and made them want to know him better. Time and time again it led him into temptation. Time and time again Edmondo extinguished the temptation by the only infallible means he knew: He yielded to it.

When he was twenty-seven and Sofi was expecting their first child, Matteo, Edmondo learned that the old saying about Venice—you can get lost there, but you can't hide— was equally true of the Venetian hinterland. Edmondo

Patristi and Velina Ferrari were a good thirty miles from Venice, settling in nicely for a romantic interlude at the resort hotel El Toulá near Treviso. They were sitting in the bar watching the waiter make a great to-do of opening a bottle of Prosecco and filling two flutes; he concluded the performance with a flourish and a bow in the manner of a magician who has just sawn his helper in two and stuck her back together like new. Edmondo nodded to him and raised his glass to Velina, but as the waiter moved away, Edmondo was distracted by something in the distance.

"Alea jacta est," he mouthed, almost silently, still holding his glass in the air. *The die is cast.*

"Sì." She nodded, raising her glass to his. *"Ale . . . ale . . . alleluia!"*

But Edmondo wasn't looking at her. He put down his glass and stood up. He had spotted Dora and Enrico Benvenuto standing at the door with their mouths open like a pair of carolers. He strolled towards them beaming with bonhomie. He brought them to his table and invited them to join him for a drink. He presented his companion as an interviewee for the post of secretary to help him when he was in the country, but he could tell from the way they fell to interviewing her themselves that he wasn't fooling anyone.

"Are you working now?" asked Dora with an innocent air.

"Sì," said Velina.

326

"Where?" asked Dora, smiling.

"*Ah, sì, sì,*" said the girl. "I work for my father. At home."

Enrico joined in. "You're lucky to get an interview in such nice surroundings."

"*Sì,*" said the girl. "It's very nice."

"I'd take the job," teased Enrico, "if he's going to treat you this well."

"*Sì,*" nodded the girl.

It was Edmondo he was teasing. Edmondo smiled.

"We hadn't got that far."

"*Sì,*" said Velina smiling at Edmondo.

He wished that someone had taught her to say something other than *sì* before he'd come across her handing out glasses of wine from a tray at the Verona Wine Fair. But it was too late now. He could imagine the scene being recounted with hilarity at dinner parties. Edmondo looked at his watch. "We have to be on our way. It's nearly time for your train, Velina. We'll finish our conversation in the car."

As Edmondo was paying the bill for the room, explaining that he had been called back to Venice and they wouldn't be able to stay after all, Velina was upstairs ruefully putting everything back in the suitcases. As Enrico and Dora crossed the lobby to the restaurant, they smiled and waved.

"See you in Venice, Edmondo."

He beat a hasty retreat back to Sofi, spiked the Benvenutos' guns with an elegant *mea maxima culpa*—my dear, I am completely at fault—and received for his pains a poignant affirmation of his wife's rather middle-class idea of marriage. He promised to do better and was the picture of discretion for several years until he happened to hit on a real secretary, a scheming, ambitious one called Marda, who drew him into compromising situations and then let the cat out of the bag on purpose. He managed to send her away but not to banish her ambitions.

When Edmondo was thirty-six Sofi presented him with a lovely daughter, Esmeralda, a baby sister for his son and heir, Matteo. Having a daughter pleased him, but he was all for ensuring the Patristi line with multiple heirs now that the family could afford it. He had been denied siblings in the name of economy but now he wanted to provide himself in the traditional way with at least an heir and a spare in the male line. He was just sidling up to the issue, or rather the agent thereof, when Marda, all honey and spice, came back for the kill. Edmondo Patristi succumbed. His marriage followed suit. But in one of the last acts of their union Edmondo and Sofi combined forces to send the aspirant baronessa away for good. Even in their quasi-estranged state, they agreed on one thing: There is the *established* middle class and then there is the *rising* middle class—*not,* in this case at least, to be encouraged.

Before the shadow of divorce overtook them, Edmondo and Sofi had been well along the road to a massive restoration of the Patristi Palace. In fact, it was Sofi who was driving the project because she wanted Matteo to inherit a modern and stable residence instead of what they presently lived in, which she regarded as a rickety heap. Esmeralda's inheritance was in good order. They had in the first years of their marriage bought back into the family the old Patristi Villa near Padua. Indeed, they had intended to remove themselves to the villa while the Venice palazzo was under restoration. Now everything was changed. While the divorce was being finalized, their architect, Vittorio Fallon, who had been working with them for over a year—a nice enough chap, in Edmondo's view, whom he thought he almost remembered from school or somewhere—was following the paperwork to obtain permission to start the work. The agreed terms of the divorce were that Sofi would continue to pay for the restoration and afterward live in the palace with the children, but the title to the property would be put in trust for Matteo. Similarly, the villa would be transferred to Esmeralda, with Edmondo having the usufruct for life. Sofi, who had the money, had everything under control.

Shortly after Edmondo went to live in the country and Sofi moved with the children into a Fierazzo palace that belonged to her Milanese mother but which she rarely used, the work at Palazzo Patristi started in earnest. As Sofi was in Venice and was the one paying the bills, as well as being the one who would be living in Palazzo Patristi with the children, she was the one caught up in the day-to-day consultations. A little over a year later, she let Edmondo be the first to know—after the children, of course—that she was going to marry the architect. It would have been more seemly in Edmondo's view to have a fling and leave it at that, but Sofi had her own views in these matters.

Edmondo decided he was glad to be sitting in the country contemplating the Euganean Hills where his earliest Venetian ancestors first arrived from Troy. He deemed it the perfect situation for sharing their chagrin at being dispossessed for a whimsical indiscretion with a woman. But for him it was worse: Marda was a long way from being the most beautiful woman in the world and even farther from being the valued daughter of an esteemed prince. Verily, his was not an escapade that men would sing about hereafter.

While Edmondo bided among the ur-lands of the ur-Patristis, back in Venice in the *salone* of Palazzo Patristi reposed a table that shared the qualities that made him so special. Its surface was famously handsome with a seamless patina of a dark and gleaming opacity that no one could fathom. Not even the most astute expert would commit himself to say what kind of wood, or maybe even stone, it was. Its darkness had a mesmerizing depth. Like an unlit room, it seemed to invite the observer to stare until his eyes could see through the deep shadows, not into the material of which it was composed, but into its storied past. It was legendary and priceless. The State had long since listed it as a National Treasure and decreed that it could never be moved without specific permission from the Belle Arti, the ministry that deals with the protection of historic artifacts in Italy. For Edmondo, the Patristi table was the chief symbol of the family's heritage, said to have been brought to Venice by their earliest ancestor in the Lagoon, Antiphonus, a lesser son of Priam, who fled from Troy with Antenor as part of the Saving Remnant, carting whatever he could rescue from his father's palace. The authorities identified the wooden trestle underneath as Roman and not the proper mate to the top that lay upon it, such infidelity—as Edmondo once and only once had joked while he was still married to Sofi—being practically the norm in the happy world of tables. The tabletop, however, was much older and so precious that the Belle Arti forbade invasive tests to resolve the mystery of its composition. In any case, the family knew what they knew and that was enough.

But now the Patristi story seemed to be coming to an end. Edmondo's parents had died within a year of each other when he was thirty-two, and two years ago Matteo, his only son, had been killed in a car crash. After that, Sofi didn't want to go back to Palazzo Patristi with Esmeralda. And since Edmondo couldn't afford to repay her expenditure for the restoration, he had to do what she said. He suggested a compromise in which he sold a part of the house to pay the bills, but he couldn't convince her. He reasoned with her that it was not his fault that Matteo had been killed. Finally, he cornered her by asking who in her right mind would ever have sent her child out in a car with that Panfili boy? Everyone knew how immature and unreliable he was. Sofi and Edmondo had never got on so badly, not even during the divorce.

At this point Edmondo wanted to avoid carrying out any more works on Palazzo Patristi than were absolutely necessary, because he would need some money from the sale to buy a pied à terre in Venice and to support himself. He decided to move back to Venice to manage the final works and supervise the sale. It occurred to him, too late, that Sofi and her husband had been running the whole show for long enough. When he told Sofi his intention, he was surprised. She agreed it was a good idea and suggested he ring Luisa Nolesworthy about renting something in her palace.

Like almost everyone else so gloriously encumbered, Lady Nolesworthy was looking for ways to realize on her palazzo. She had turned to the new rental agent that everyone was calling on, Irene del Banco, the multilingual wife of an earnest and not very rich journalist, but no agent could get the word out like the Venetian jungle telegraph.

"Luisa?"

"*Sì?*" Luisa thought she recognized the voice on the telephone but couldn't place it.

"Ciao, Luisa. It's me, Edmondo Patristi. I was talking

to Sofi yesterday about the works over at my house, and
she told me that you're thinking of converting your top
floor to tourist apartments."

"It's true. I don't need the space, and I could use the
income."

"Everyone's doing it. I would have done it myself, if
they'd let me keep my place."

"I've got Irene del Banco coming to look at it tomorrow," said Luisa. "I may make over the mezzanine as well."

"I was wondering whether you might let your top floor
to me for a year or so. I've got to get that restoration finished and sort out the building and the furnishings that are
still there, and I can't manage it from the country."

"Would you like to come and see it?"

"Yes. If I took the whole floor, you could divide it later
and maybe do the mezzanine first. If that would suit you."

"Let's talk about it. Come and look at it the next time
you're in town."

Edmondo moved in the following weekend. He was
pleased to be back in Venice, and he enjoyed having someone around that hadn't known him all his life to say hello
to every now and then. When he was coming and going,
he sometimes stopped in the garden to walk around and
maybe have coffee and read the newspaper with Luisa, if
she was there. She had an eccentric habit that he supposed

must be English of having her breakfast and morning coffee down in the garden on the terrace next to the kitchen door, encroaching on the servants' territory in what seemed to him the most invasive way. He was amazed they didn't object. On the other hand, he thought he'd heard the staff calling her by her first name.

Edmondo had paid an early visit to Palazzo Patristi to look at the works before the builders started making dust. He stopped on his way back upstairs to join Luisa in the garden for coffee. She handed him the newspaper.

"Look at that," she said, pointing to an article on the front page. "By enforcing the speed limits they've cut the number of accidents in the Veneto by half, but now they're complaining that they're not getting enough organs for transplants. Horrid, isn't it."

Edmondo took the paper. "They turned down Matteo's organs. You know why? Because he was dead. I said to the nurse: Do you think I'd offer them otherwise? And you know what she said? She said they can only use the organs if they take them out while the body is still completely alive. Grisly, isn't it."

"I suppose there's comfort in the fact that their not taking the organs means that it wasn't humanly possible to save him."

"Oh, look at this," said Edmondo. "Finmob, that's the

furniture company Sofi has a big interest in. Maybe they're going bankrupt. They've acquired a soft-furnishings retailer in Venice—oh, *no!*—they've acquired Morello & Figli, that draper's shop that Fallon inherited. They've paid him in shares and put him on the board. I suppose he thinks he's a gentleman now. *Madonna!* That's the rising middle class for you: First they rise, and then they rise some more. That reminds me: I'd better go up and look at the papers Fallon gave me about the proposed terms for the sale; I'm seeing the lawyer tomorrow. This afternoon I have to go back over there to show around some people that Vittorio found who seem ready to pay top dollar for it. They're called Padoano. They've built a whole garment industry from a T-shirt business."

"I've heard of them," said Luisa. "They rent a palace that used to be used for corporate headquarters. They give big, big parties and invite all sorts of people they've never met."

"So how about that," murmured Barone Patristi half to himself, as he got up to leave. "Fallon is on the board of Finmob." He nodded to Luisa. "See you later."

Edmondo looked out on the Grand Canal from his own balcony for the first time in almost two years. The scaffolding had finally been taken down and the façade was once again as white and dignified in its classic gravity as a mausoleum. Byzantine in its origins, the building had been face-lifted in the eighteenth century, when it was a trend among Venetian families to make their palaces monuments to sober equilibrium as life within cascaded into fatuity and dalliance. It was the time of masks and flirtations, of idleness and Casanova.

Looking from the balcony that would soon no longer be his, Edmondo felt the funereal quality of the moment. The last surviving male of the Patristi line, he had strayed, had been trapped, and was now about to be punished. The people Edmondo was waiting to show around his palace, a modest Signor and Signora Padoano, would be the instruments by which his heritage would be finally cut off. He could identify their motorboat even in the distance, the flashiest private boat in Venice—all brass and glossy wood scintillating in the sun, surging through the wine-dark waves, pressing towards his palace walls. He was Priam on the ramparts watching Achilles coming to kill the last hope of Troy. How did it go? *Lo vide . . . correre pel campo e da lungi folgorar . . . l'astro che cane d'Orion s'appella . . . scintillante . . . di cocenti morbid ai miseri mortali apportatore*—he saw him sweeping across the plain, gleaming and radiant as the Dog Star that shines brightest bringing evil onto men.

Here the aceldama was the Veneto roads, where the young die and their inheritance—like the riches of Eurydamas, who lost his sons to Diomedes—goes to others far from the family. Edmondo marveled that any blame for this disaster could be laid at his door. Was it his fault that the girl asked Bobino to invite Matteo? And was the girl interested in Matteo Patristi only because her older sister had been rejected by Matteo's father? For that matter, was Paris the cause of the fall of Troy? Or does the story go back farther? Priam had many sons by many women. It suddenly dawned on Edmondo that his own father had made a mistake to limit himself to one son. He had made the mistake of prudence, because he wanted to husband his wealth. He should have husbanded his wife—many wives. Sofi already had another son by her new husband. Happy the man, thought Edmondo as he turned back into the empty palace, where echoing voices bounced from room to room like so many tumbling puppies turned out of a box. The new masters came up the stairs behind the architect, laughing and joking. Happy the man.

Edmondo was not a happy man as Architetto Fallon introduced him to Signor and Signora Padoano in their twin Armani suits. The Padoanos had insisted on being shown around by the Barone himself because acquiring the house from him directly was part of the cachet. They were even thrilled by Edmondo's grave demeanor; they had heard much about his elegance and charm. They made a mental note to preside over Palazzo Patristi in years to come with the same patrician gravity.

After they had walked through all the rooms, admired the ceilings, the plasterwork, the marble doorways, the terrazzo floors, and examined the views from various windows, Carina Padoano turned a coy look on Edmondo. "Barone, would it be asking too much to see the Patristi table? We've always heard so much about it."

"*Sì!*" concurred Giuseppe Padoano. "*Molto importante.* Very important."

Edmondo noticed that Vittorio looked uncomfortable, even apologetic, but Edmondo was accustomed to requests to see the famous table. "Of course," he agreed, with the solemn grace he had donned for the occasion. The four of them went back down to the *salone,* where Edmondo and Vittorio lifted the quilt from the table. The four stood back to admire the storied artifact.

"For me," said Carina Padoano, "that is the most important part of the house."

Giuseppe nodded.

Edmondo looked at Vittorio. The architect winced and turned to Signora Padoano. "I think I told you that I did not believe the table would be included in the sale."

"We have assumed all along," said Signor Padoano, "that the reason for the very high asking price is the inclusion of the table." He turned to the Barone. "You'll be happy to know that we are going to restore the palazzo to the purpose for which it was intended. We plan to use the palace partly as a showroom in the oldest Venetian tradition. The table will be an attraction for clients and, in due course, it will become our company's trademark."

Edmondo threw Vittorio a look of cold disbelief, the gist of which—you charlatan, you rogue: first my wife, now my table—hit its mark.

Vittorio, visibly wounded, nevertheless rallied. "Look here. This is a specific issue that has to be agreed in a separate negotiation. We can't decide it like this."

Carina Padoano pulled a camera from her handbag and started to photograph the table. "I don't believe that the Belle Arti will let this table leave this palace," she said from behind the camera. She continued to take shots from different angles.

Edmondo was aghast at the effrontery and looked from one to the other in disbelief.

"Let me see your camera," said Vittorio. He took it and turned it over. "Let's go down to the mezzanine. We can look at these on my computer and I can print some for Edmondo as well. Tomorrow I'll pass by the Belle Arti and see what they have to say. I have to see them anyway to ask permission to move the table while they work on the floors."

Edmondo went home determined that no one should have his table. Patristi it was; Patristi it would remain. He rang Sofi.

"I met those *arrivisti* that Vittorio has lined up to buy Palazzo Patristi, and they are insisting on having the Patristi table; they say they will invoke the Ministry of the Belle Arti to say it can't be moved. I'm surprised it has come to this: I thought Vittorio knew I don't intend to part with my table."

"Edmondo"—sighed Sofi—"no one intends to part with Esmeralda's table. This must be a new development. I'll have to ask Vittorio when he comes back. As far as I'm concerned, there's no question about it."

"I'm glad to hear it. But they seemed to know all about the table and to want it almost more than they want the palazzo. Someone has wound them up about it."

"Okay. I'll ring you when I've spoken to Vittorio. *A presto.* Ciao."

"Ciao."

Edmondo put down the telephone. He was restless. Seeing the Padoanos in Palazzo Patristi had unsettled him. Without thinking he went to the lift. Where was he going? He would go take a turn in the garden. He found Luisa in her usual place sitting on the terrace reading *The Times,* which arrived at lunchtime. She was drinking tea. She looked up.

"Ciao, Edmondo. Lovely afternoon, isn't it. Would you like a cup of tea?"

He took the three steps up to the terrace in one bound. Above all Edmondo wanted someone to talk to, someone who could understand the bitterness of everything associated with divorce, with the shock of discovering that the

person you imagined loved you has these monstrous attributes, fangs that bite and claws that catch, all in the
service of an ugly appetite for revenge. He had never talked
to Luisa about his personal life, but in a way she was the
perfect person to understand about marriages made in
heaven ending in divorces made in hell.

Her ex-husband, Lord Nolesworthy, was another who
had turned out to be a cad. Or possibly not—opinion in
Venice was divided on everything, even on something as
obvious as this—and it didn't behoove Edmondo to press
his own point of view. For one thing, when Nolesworthy
decided to replace his wife in Venice with his new business
partner in London, a Bohemian glass heiress, he eclipsed
Edmondo Patristi as the rotten husband of the day, so the
Venetians were actually a little grateful to him, Edmondo
first among them. Anyhow, most Venetians believed in
their hearts that such titles generally suited foreigners better. The important thing was that they awarded their affection to Lady Nolesworthy and embraced her, with her little
daughter Flora, as their own. For one thing, Lady
Nolesworthy no longer had infinite cash reserves to draw
on. This in itself was companionable.

Rocco Zennaro came up these grand Venetian staircases
with a little less zip than he used to and was a little short of

breath when he passed through the great portal into the *salone* of Palazzo Patristi. He looked around. The room's lofty dignity had finally succumbed to the gloom of an idle building site. He was looking for the architect, but he couldn't see him because Vittorio Fallon was down on his knees behind the Patristi table.

"Hallooo?" Rocco's voice echoed through the open spaces like a chorus of wandering spirits.

"Rocco! You're back!" The architect's voice answered from both ends of the room. Rocco looked around and saw the architect's face appear over the far edge of the table. Vittorio got to his feet. "Any success?"

Rocco had taken his two apprentice stonemasons out to the cemetery island of San Michele, down around the back where they throw the old tombstones when they empty the graves for the new tenants. "I found a big slab of Greek marble out there, Architetto."

Vittorio stopped measuring the Patristi table and looked at him. "That could be interesting. Did you take the measurements?"

"Yeah. It's good. A little bit too long, but we can fix that. Too bad it's broken; it's actually in three pieces."

"Oh, you can figure out something. Go get it before someone else does and take it back to the workshop." Vittorio stood up and looked at his watch. "You should go right now if you can."

"No panic. I had them take it back to the workshop

342

straightaway. Those things disappear so fast, and I figured you can always use a good piece of Greek marble. It's old; the inscription's completely worn away. I can't see how it stayed at San Michele for all that time. Usually things turn around in twenty or thirty years. For my money it's been around longer than the cemetery. Somebody must have dumped it there. Anyhow, we've got it now."

"Rocco, what would I do without you? Every time I get in a jam, you dig me out. They don't make masons like you anymore."

"Oh, they do. Those boys are good, you know. They saw it first. They'll be able to work that marble. I'll watch over them, but I don't think they'll need much help from me."

"What about the woodwork?"

"Jacopo's already carved half of it. I took those old timbers from the church and all the photographs over to his shop two days ago. He started that same evening. He's like me, he likes a challenge."

Vittorio completed his sketch of the table and wrote in the measurements. "I forgot to ask you to leave the measurements for me, so I had to do it all over again." He put the paper in his pocket and handed one end of an old quilt to Rocco. Together they spread it over the antique table.

"I'm ordering two sets of crates," said Vittorio. "The table's not safe here now. We'd have to move it anyhow when they come in to restore the terrazzo.

"It's annoying about that arch," Vittorio went on, as

they walked down the stairs together. "You could have put it back exactly the way it was meant to be."

"So could the boys. They'd studied all the pieces and had it all figured out. Venetian masons work the same way today as the man who made it. But not for long. Nobody's going to bother with this kind of work anymore, and the craft that's been handed down will be gone with the wind. Poof. Forgotten."

"They missed the last chance."

"But you can't blame the Barone for not wanting to pay the price they were asking to let him do it."

"No. He and Sofi agree on that, at least," said Vittorio. "You know, Rocco, this has turned out to be a sad job. I was enjoying it, and now I can't wait to be done with it."

Esmeralda was staying in Venice with her father because she had to go to school. Her mother had gone to the country with the new baby to be near her sister, Natasha, and *her* new baby, and she had taken the nanny with her. It fell to Edmondo to go and wait outside the school to see his little daughter safely home. But once he got home with her, he managed to shed some of his obligations because, lucky for him, Luisa's little girl Flora adored Esmeralda and begged her to stay downstairs and play with her. Furthermore, Flora's nanny was happy for the help with her charge, and Esmeralda was happy to oblige; Flora was the best doll she'd ever had. This arrangement with the Nolesworthy household, at first a casual convenience, became a critical necessity when trouble blew up with the Belle Arti and Edmondo had to perform his proprietary duties at Palazzo Patristi during the investigation.

The Patristi table had disappeared. The Padoanos' accountant had discovered it to be missing when he was conducting an inventory of the finished upper stories of the palazzo. The ground floor was still impassable, and the construction company forbade anyone not involved in the works from coming onto the site, but the Padoanos were not much interested in the ground floor: their real objective in making the inventory was to document the presence of the table. So when the accountant didn't find it where it was supposed to be, he didn't stop to ask any questions. He was half expecting Patristi to try to pull a fast one, so he marched straight over to the superintendent's office and denounced the missing artifact to the Belle Arti, who sent the crime squad. It was an ugly moment. The police came armed with search warrants and a journalist. They summoned the owner and the architect. They sequestered Vittorio's office on the mezzanine and put armed guards at the entrances so no one could leave. Then they made Vittorio and Edmondo stand outside the office door until they called them in, one at a time, for questioning. Edmondo got off quite lightly; he was rarely there, claimed ignorance, and told them he himself was an injured party and would be consulting his lawyer about filing a de-nouncement of his loss. Vittorio, as director of the build-ing project, took the brunt. After an hour of hard questioning, during which he was able to give them no sat-isfaction, he was finally granted permission to call some of his workmen who might know something. They called for Rocco Zennaro. As he came in, the police told Vittorio to get out and wait outside. After a few minutes, they called for Rocco's assistants. A few minutes later, they called for two hod carriers from the ground floor work. Vittorio was wishing he could hear what was going on inside his office and was considering putting his ear to the door when it opened and two policemen, followed by Rocco, his two apprentices, and the two hod carriers, set off toward the stairs. Two more policemen followed. One of them indi-cated with his head that Vittorio should fall in behind his workmen. Rocco led the way to the ground floor. He stopped in front of a door.

"Who has the key?" he called out. One of the hod carri-ers stepped forward and handed him a key on a tagged ring.

"You should have handed this back in," said Rocco.

"I forgot," said the hod carrier, "and we had some more stuff to put in there." Rocco opened the door and let the police and the workmen file in; Vittorio was the last to squeeze inside. They were in a storeroom filled with used materials discarded in the restoration. There were panels leaning against the wall, window frames stacked on top of a pile of rubble, shutters piled in a corner. On the floor in the middle of the room was a slab of stone broken into three pieces. The surface was stained like wood and buffed to a gleaming patina, but white stone was visible in the breaks—though the stain had even penetrated into the breaks, so they obviously weren't new. From underneath, the legs of the carved trestle, now in pieces beneath it, protruded at crazy angles.

"Well?" said Rocco to the hod carriers.

"The boss told us to move it so the men could repair the floor. We didn't know it was so fragile," said the one who'd handed him the key.

The other one added, "He told us to put it in here where we could lock it up. But when we went to put it down, the planks we had underneath slipped out of my hands so the whole top fell down and smashed the wood. I had to jump out of the way. It caught my leg a bit. Do you want to see?"

The policemen shook their heads.

"That's when it went into three pieces," said the first one.

"So it was an accident," said Rocco.

"You'll have to leave everything like it is," said the police. "Give us the key. We're going to seal this room until the Belle Arti come to deal with it."

*

When the Belle Arti came they had their restorers with them ready to take the table away. They threatened that they might well consign the Patristi table to the national collections for safekeeping, but they modified their tone when Vittorio Fallon provided them with a custom-made crate to put it in; they hadn't given any thought to the matter of transporting the artifact. Nevertheless, the Padoanos, who had already given the architect permission for Edmondo Patristi to have a copy made for sentimental reasons, were obliged either to pay for the restoration or to let the Belle Arti keep it in custody. They paid, but they complained bitterly that the cracks, which had never before been visible, were now glaringly apparent as documentation of the damage it had suffered, even though tests indicated that the breaks were old and the seepage of the dyes into the cracks gave visible evidence of the same hypothesis. That was the theory put forward by the Belle Arti when they completed their investigation and finally were able to attach analytical documentation to the Patristi table. They concluded that the Greek marble had at some point, possibly even in antiquity, been stained with some organic substance—there was evidence of a mollusk extract, as in Tyrian purple; there were traces of berry juice and possibly even saffron; and there was evidence of exposure to great heat on the surface—but the analysis had been compromised by the application of modern dyes and waxes, for which failure to protect a national treasure the Patristis would have to pay a fine. For the careless treatment that opened the old breaks, Architetto Fallon also had to pay a fine.

By this time, Edmondo had regained his equilibrium and returned to his normal philosophical nature. He instructed his lawyer to pay the fine immediately without appeal, and he congratulated the Padoanos on the alertness of their accountant, who in the course of his inventory had sounded the alarm that the table was missing and in doing so had made possible a satisfactory resolution to the whole sensitive issue, including the authorization of an approximate copy. The words with which Carina Padoano gave closure to the matter put the affair in its proper context: "In the end, the Barone showed his class."

Edmondo had his own closure the day he drove out to the villa to receive the furnishings that had been cleared out of the palazzo. There was so much that had been accumulated by the family over so many centuries that he could barely find space for it in the villa. Some he put in the stables to sort through at a later date. Likewise for the most important crate which he had carried into the great cedar closet off the master bedroom, there to wait until the time was right for unpacking. As he stood on the steps watching the empty van retreating down the avenue of cypresses, Edmondo felt unexpectedly optimistic and supposed that there was something reassuring about so much of the Patristi history coming back to the family origins in the Euganean Hills. In fact, there was an apposite phrase drawing itself together in his memory. Was it Virgil? *Durate, et vosnet rebus servate secundis*—Endure, and keep yourself for better days. No, no, it was his grandmother's voice telling the story of what she told old Antonio when she discovered the broken arch. "Go back to the beginning and start again."

Edmondo was sitting in the garden with Luisa watching their daughters playing together. He had just come back from the country and was feeling more like himself than he had for several years.

Little Flora continued to be devoted to Esmeralda and wanted to be with her all the time. Esmeralda was equally charmed by the toddler—as well as by the fact that her father had completely forgotten that schoolchildren have to do homework, so she was practically on vacation. Her teacher understood perfectly that fathers are hopeless and resolved to wait and report the lapse to Esmeralda's mother when maternal discipline resumed.

"Girls are born to be mothers," said Edmondo, observing with equanimity the difference between the sexes as his nine-year-old daughter helped the two-year-old put her doll to bed.

"Little girls are lovely," said Luisa. "I can't imagine what a boy would have been like. I thought I wanted a son."

"I had a son and lost him."

"I guess everyone wants to have both," said Luisa.

"Do you still want a son?"

"I haven't given it much thought since the divorce. I guess I would really, but it's not very likely."

"I wanted to have more. In families like mine it's normal prudence to have at least two sons. Priam had fifty. But then he had concubines."

Luisa looked at him and raised her eyebrows: "Oh, it's DNA every time," she said, laughing.

Edmondo gave her a wry smile and one of those "I can't help myself" shrugs of a lovable rascal.

The maid came to take away the post and the tea tray. "Luisa—I mean, Lady Nolesworthy—Daria wants to know if you would like to have your dinner here in the garden, and how many will you be?"

Luisa blinked.

Edmondo jumped to his feet. "My dear, I must be going. I should probably show my face at the club tonight. They've been complaining that I don't help to keep it going, and now that I'm not in the country I have no excuse."

Luisa stood up. "Edmondo. Please stay for dinner. I was thinking about the girls. Do you think Esmeralda would mind eating early with Flora? Why not ring your maid and tell her that Esmeralda will eat down here."

"The maid goes home at six," said Edmondo. "She's going to leave something for us."

"Then it's decided. The girls can eat together at six and we'll have dinner afterwards here on the terrace."

When Edmondo came back downstairs at seven-thirty, Esmeralda ran up to him.

"Papà. Flora doesn't want to go to bed. Can she come upstairs with me and sleep in my extra bed? Her nanny says she can put her to bed upstairs but that she's going out and won't be able to fetch her back downstairs until quite late."

"Don't worry, Nanny," said Luisa. "I can pop up after dinner and bring her down to her own bed if both of them promise to go to sleep properly. Esmeralda has to go to school in the morning. Is that all right with you, Edmondo?"

"*Sì, sì.*" Edmondo wasn't paying any attention to the women working out their domestic arrangements. He was walking along the path savoring the pleasures of a garden in Venice. He was beginning to see that Palazzo Patristi wasn't such a wonderful house. Since he'd been living here, whenever he had a minute to spare he always took a turn in the garden, both coming in and going out. That was how he had happened to strike up a friendship with Luisa. When they were in the garden together she started offering him things: a cup of tea, the newspaper, fruit. He stopped in front of a bank of roses, wondering if they liked being fumbled by bees: hairy little lovers. This germination of

352

plants was a slow, tedious process, as far as he could see. He wondered what was in it for the bees. Then he remembered: of course, they went in for the honey. Basically, all species are alike.

"Edmondo," Luisa called across the garden. "Would you like a glass of Prosecco before dinner?"

"Yes!" He strode towards her. He felt like celebrating.

Luisa and Edmondo sat in the garden after Daria had cleared the table, chatting about food and wine and the shortcomings of Mayor Grandi, smoking to keep the mosquitoes away.

At ten o'clock Luisa put her napkin on the table. "Edmondo, I'd better go up and get Flora before it gets too late, in case I wake up Esmeralda."

Edmondo stood up. He looked at his watch. "I say, we can have a cup of tea. The maid sets it up in an automatic machine with a timer. It's just turning on now."

When Luisa came out of the elevator she was surprised. "You've moved everything around. It's nice this way."

Edmondo brought a tray with a glass teapot, two teacups, a milk jug, and a sugar bowl from the kitchen. He put it on the sideboard and poured out two cups. "Help yourself to sugar."

He went over to close the window. "Look how clear the sky is. It will be hot tomorrow."

"Do you take sugar?" asked Luisa.

"No, thank you."

"Neither do I." She brought his cup to the window. "Oh, look. It is a clear night. I didn't notice it in the garden." She stepped out onto the balcony.

Edmondo followed her. "*È quindi uscimmo a riveder le stelle*—and so we issued forth to see again the stars."

"What a beautiful night," said Luisa. "Is that Dante?"

"It's the end of the *Inferno*."

"Oh look," she said, leaning out over the balcony as if to see better. "Isn't that the Bear?"

"The Bear?"

"Ursa Major."

"*Orsa Maggiore, sì,*" he said stepping forward to look. "It is the Bear," and added, almost under his breath, "it's always the bear." He was standing so close to her he could smell the strange, honeyed perfume of her hair.

ALSO BY JANE TURNER RYLANDS

*"Engaging. . . . Rylands writes with playful elegance
and a crisp layer of understated wit."*
—Los Angeles Times

VENETIAN STORIES

In these brilliantly realized, linked tales, the real Venice is
revealed—not the iconic tourist destination the city has
become, but the mysterious society that resides behind its
elegant doors and shuttered windows. With a sly and affec-
tionate delicacy, Jane Turner Rylands, an American expa-
triate who has lived in Venice for thirty years, portrays a
dozen Venetians—a construction foreman, a countess, a
gondolier, a postman, an architect, a Baronessa, an English
lord—as they pursue their respective interests. And in turn,
through the perspective of those who live and work in this
most alluring of cities, *Venetian Stories* illuminates canals
and palazzos, churches and gondolas, large concerns and
small rituals, with an uncommon intimacy.

Fiction/Short Stories/1-4000-3262-8